THIS GIRL

Rowena Summers titles available from Severn House Large Print

The Caldwell girls
Daisy's War
Dreams of Peace
Taking Heart

THIS GIRL

Rowena Summers

Severn House Large Print
London & New York

This first large print edition published in Great Britain 2005 by
SEVERN HOUSE LARGE PRINT BOOKS LTD of
9-15 High Street, Sutton, Surrey, SM1 1DF.
First world regular print edition published 2004 by
Severn House Publishers, London and New York.
This first large print edition published in the USA 2005 by
SEVERN HOUSE PUBLISHERS INC., of
595 Madison Avenue, New York, NY 10022.

British Library Cataloguing in Publication Data

Summers, Rowena, 1932 -
    This girl. - Large print ed.
1. English - France - Fiction
2. World War, 1939 – 1945 - France - Fiction
3. Love stories
4. Large type books
    I.   Title
    823.9'14 [F]

ISBN 0-7278-7436-5

Printed and bound in Great Britain by
MPG Books Ltd, Bodmin, Cornwall.

For my family, as always

One

May 1926

Jess Newman hated being called in to the headmaster's office on account of her daughter. Lisa was in trouble again – and her grandmother constantly warned that 'she's old beyond her years, and there'll be trouble from that young madam, or my name's not Cissie Newman.' At least she didn't have an eye for the boys yet, despite being a little beauty at not yet eleven years old.

In the headmaster's room in the small junior school in mid-Somerset, Jess fiddled nervously with her gloves as she prepared to be interrogated. Even if it was no longer the sins of the parents that caused the problems, they still bore the brunt of it.

'Now then, Mrs Newman,' the headmaster began in his usual pompous manner.

Jess interrupted without thinking. 'Our Lisa's not a bad girl, Mr Davidson. She's got a generous nature, and whatever she's done I'm sure she didn't mean it.'

7

She was an unsophisticated woman, rabbiting on as always when she was nervous. Making things worse, as Ron was forever telling her. Never knowing when to pause for breath and let somebody else do the talking. Not that Ron could be bothered to come with her, she thought bitterly. He was always too busy with his blessed union meetings, saying that the children were her business – except when it suited him to boast about his daughter getting a good mark in English or sums. He'd have preferred her to make her mark in a street football game, like her young brother, Wally. And now there was this general strike starting tomorrow, and Ron would be in the thick of the rallies, leaving her to deal with family problems.

The headmaster held up his hand, and, like his pupils, Jess was silenced. Her handbag slid off her lap, and she bent to pick it up with clammy hands. Her face was beetroot red when she straightened up. By now her hat was askew, and trickles of sweat ran down her back.

'For God's sake, woman, it's not you the fellow's going to give a ticking-off to,' Ron had bellowed. 'If our Lisa's done summat wrong, she's got to be punished, and I'll take my belt to her to finish the job.'

He would, too – and enjoy it.

'What makes you think Lisa's done something wrong, Mrs Newman?' the headmaster said. 'And would you like a cup of tea while we talk?' he added.

She shook her head, even though her mouth was as dry as dust, but although she was dying for a cuppa she was sure she wouldn't be able to hold it still, and she'd disgrace herself by spilling tea all over his good office lino.

'So let's get down to business,' Davidson went on briskly, sensing that she was in danger of going to pieces. She must have been pretty once, which probably accounted for the amazingly beautiful child she had produced. The bombastic husband had no doubt knocked all the stuffing out of her over the years before she gave birth to one late child and then another, but those children had certainly inherited the father's spirit, not the mother's.

He shuffled some papers inside a folder with the name Lisa Newman on the cover. It contained all Lisa's school reports and various misdemeanours.

Without warning, Davidson jabbed his finger at the papers as if he was jabbing a person, and Jess flinched, instantly defensive of her daughter, no matter what she was about to hear.

'*This girl*, Mrs Newman,' Davidson spoke deliberately, his eyes never wavering from Jess's face. '*This girl* has the potential to do great things with her life. She will come through the scholarship examination with flying colours, which is why I am urging you – no, I am begging you – to send her to the grammar school when the time comes—'

'Oh no! It's out of the question! My husband—'

'I'm well aware of your husband's strong political objections to any kind of preferential schooling. I suspect the whole town knows them,' he added dryly. 'But Lisa is a special case, and I must impress on you that *this girl* is streets ahead of anyone else in her class. You and your husband would be doing her a grave disservice if you didn't allow her to take this chance.'

'Well why can't she do that at the big school?'

Davidson sighed. 'They don't have the facilities for further education that the grammar school does. They can't give her the same learning opportunities to make full use of her phenomenal memory.'

Jess didn't know what phenomenal meant, but a heartbeat later they were both surprised at her nervous laughter now that she felt she was on safer ground. It was her daughter they were talking about, and she knew her better than most.

'I'll grant you, Lisa remembers things quickly, but I'm sure it's no secret that she does as little learning as possible!'

'That is entirely my point. Sometimes she

seems hardly to give a lesson any attention at all, and yet she always comes out with top marks in all her classes.'

'You aren't trying to tell me my girl's a genius, are you?' Jess said. 'Because I tell you, Mr Davidson, my husband won't stand for any of that nonsense of setting her apart, and nor will I,' she added as an afterthought. 'We're just ordinary working folk and never had such things in our family.'

Davidson felt his earlier sympathy for her slipping fast.

'I'm not suggesting that Lisa's a genius, but she deserves more than we or the local senior school can give her. I hope your husband will not be too short-sighted to understand that the girl has a wonderfully photographic memory.'

Jess knew his words were for her as much as Ron, even though much of it was going over her head. She was a simple country-woman, married to a working-class man. She had a brief image of him, sprawled out in his favourite hand-me-down chair, his vest spattered with the evening meal, his braces stretched taut over his belly. The top button of his working trousers would be undone to let out the gas, as he called it, while he had his regular forty winks as the rest of the family tiptoed around him. The only time he came to life, barring the daily grind at the factory, was for union or Labour business, when he put on his suit and his bowler and went down to the Union Hall or to the Labour Club for a bevvy.

In Ron's mind you worked for eight hours a day, you played for eight and you slept for eight, though 'playing' for him meant dabbling in politics and things that were beyond Jess's ken, and probably his, too, she suspected. He had rigid ideas, and he expected his children to follow him into factory work, same as he was perfectly content to do. She could never see Ron agreeing to sending Lisa to the grammar school. It was against his principles, and pigs would fly first.

'This letter to you and your husband will explain what all the teachers here have to say about Lisa, and I hope it will help you to come to the right decision.'

She took it gingerly, knowing it would spark off a furious argument at home, and one that she couldn't win. She looked Davidson squarely in the eyes.

'First of all, our Lisa's got to pass this scholarship exam, hasn't she? And second of all, we ain't heard her side of it yet.'

Going home on the tram, she didn't know why she'd said it. Lisa wouldn't have a say in it once Ron had made up his mind, and that was already decided, as sure as God made little fishes. It was only Ron's opinion that

12

counted. Even his mother eventually kow-towed to him – after giving him a piece of her mind, but she always agreed with him in the end.

Six-year-old Wally was the apple of his eye, simply because he was a boy, and happily played football or shove ha'penny in the street with the other factory kids. It was only Lisa who defied him whenever she thought she could get away with it. Lisa, who had brains, and should be allowed to take her place at the grammar school if she was clever enough to pass her exams.

A spark that Jess thought had been quenched for ever began to simmer in her mind. Why shouldn't her girl be given the chance to get herself out of the rut that every family in the area was in? In her dreams the drudgery of factory work wasn't for Lisa. Instead, she was imagining a Lisa of the future, admired for her beauty as well as her brains, the darling of society and the busi-ness world...

In many peoples' eyes the fringe of the town was spoilt by the factory. It was the only industrial eyesore in an otherwise peaceful and beautiful rural setting that was mainly farming country with open fields and meandering rivers. On the other hand, the factory meant work, and the means of putting food on the table, and times were hard enough for all to be fully aware of that.

' 'Ere, missus, ain't this your stop?' the tram conductor yelled. 'If you're staying on, you'll have to give me another fare. We'll all be stopping soon to support the strike, so then you'll have to walk 'ome.'

Jess stepped out of the tram into the dull grey afternoon where the houses were all huddled together in narrow cobbled streets, so close you could hardly see the sky above, and where lines of washing were often stretched across the street from the houses of obliging neighbours.

'Showing your drawers for all to see,' complained Granny Newman, who didn't hold with such things, and refused to allow it in the Newman household.

Jess paused, holding her side from a stitch and realizing she had been periodically holding her breath ever since the interview with old Davidson and the unlikely dreams that had emerged from it.

As she neared the house she could see Lisa leaning perilously out of an upstairs window, calling to her friend across the street. Posh folk in the towns had telephones now, but they hardly needed them in Filbert Street, because you only had to shout and the neighbours would come running.

Was that what she wanted for her girl? To end up marrying an oaf like Ron, who had been all that Jess wanted when he was courting her, but had soon changed into the bully he was now. Jess had never been ambitious, and the years had stolen any thoughts of bettering herself, but why couldn't Lisa have it all?

'Mum, what do you think our Wally's done?' Lisa shrieked at her. 'Gran says our Dad's going to skin him when he gets home.'

Jess sighed. What with Ron already as tense as a flea on heat with all this general strike nonsense, and Lisa hollering out of the bedroom window loud enough to wake the dead, she was conscious of net curtains being twitched from windows as the gossips tried to catch what was going on, and she could no more see Lisa becoming a grammar schoolgirl than flying to the moon.

Lisa was still yelling. 'He's only gone and broken our Dad's saw, trying to cut down some tree branches to make a bow,' her daughter screamed excitedly.

Jess groaned. Wally would be in for a tanning, and the whole household would be subject to Ron's black moods. His shed where he kept his tools was his pride and joy and Wally was forbidden to go near it. As the front door opened, Ron's square-set mother stood there with arms folded over her flowered overall, which she wore day in and day out, except Sundays, when she wore her best black dress to church. These outfits were only replaced at night by her voluminous nightgown.

'You've heard then,' Cissie Newman greeted her. 'There'll be a right how-d'you-do tonight. Young Wally won't get away with no cow-eyed looks at his father this time.'

'The whole street's probably heard,' Jess snapped, pushing past her, and too tired after her ordeal at the school to mince words with this old harridan.

'So what's to do with that young miss?' Granny Newman wanted to know next. 'What's she been up to this time?'

'Nothing at all.'

Cissie sniffed. 'Makes a change then. What did the headmaster want to see you about if it weren't to make a complaint about her?'

Jess felt herself bridle. It was one thing for her to be expecting the worst, but that was a mother's right, and not Cissie's.

'He wanted to tell me he thought she'd do well in the scholarship exams.'

Cissie gave a mocking laugh. 'And much good they'll do her when she works down the factory.'

Lisa came clattering down the stairs, glaring. 'I'm not working in no factory! Mr Davidson says I can do a lot better than that.'

She whirled out of the house, banging the door behind her and leaving it rocking on its hinges. Cissie turned on Jess.

'See? She's already getting above herself

16

and she ain't even done these exams yet. She needs curbing right now.'

Through the window they could see Lisa rushing across the street to her best friend Renee's house, her long red hair flying out behind her like a blazing beacon. Renee's father had been killed in the last war and her mother worked at the factory all day so Lisa never wasted time in knocking. She flopped down in one of Renee's sagging armchairs and caught her breath.

'Guess what I just heard,' she announced, her green eyes as wide as saucers.

'Dunno,' Renee said. 'Your ma's lost a farthing and found a tanner? Or else old Davidson's going to expel you.'

'No, stupid. The old goat thinks I'm a brainbox. He told my mother that I'll do well in the scholarship.'

'Pull the other one, it's got bells on,' Renee said. 'You never do any lessons, so how can you be a brainbox?'

Lisa laughed, showing perfect teeth inside the rosebud mouth that Renee envied so darned much. Just like that Clara Bow at the pictures, she often moaned, while hers was more like a perishing letter box.

'It's because I can remember stuff,' Lisa said importantly. 'I can read fast and re-member it all, not like you, who needs to write things down dozens of times to get 'em inside your thick skull.'

17

Renee ignored the insult. 'So what you going to remember down the shirt factory then? How many buttons make five?'

'I told you I ain't working down no factory. *This* girl's going to *be* somebody, you wait and see.'

'A tanner says you'll end up at Dooley's factory, same as me,' Renee said.

'All right. A tanner says that in five years from now I won't be working at the factory, and in ten years' time everybody will know my name,' she added recklessly.

'Ten years from now you'll be twenty and old.'

'And you'll be married to some snot-nosed farmer just to get out of this dump, and have a couple of kids snivelling around your skirts,' Lisa told her. 'But I won't. I'll be doing something important.'

Renee laughed nervously. She wasn't sure she liked it when Lisa got that determined look on her face, as if she could see into the future. But she knew that her own future was probably just as Lisa said. Marry young and have kids, just like her mum.

'Where's your money then?' she asked, half angry at the prospect, half drawn to the romance of it all.

'Don't you know *any*thing?' Lisa said pityingly. 'You don't have to have the money now. It's a sort of a pledge. A promise. You shake hands on it, and you only pay up when things happen like you say they will.'

'You mean I've got to wait ten years before I get my tanner?'

'Or I get mine,' Lisa said confidently.

Ron Newman came home from work with his guts on fire, and in no mood to hear any domestic nonsense. He was more interested in hearing the militant speaker at the strike rally that evening. But his mother made sure he was going to hear it, despite the warning looks from Jess as she dished up their fish supper.

'Your Wally's been up to summat today, our Ron. I told him he's got to be a little man and tell you himself.'

'What's that then?' He gave a token grunt at his son, then looked suspiciously at his mother and knew that something was definitely up.

He sat back with his arms folded over his fiery guts. There was summat very wrong in there, but since he didn't hold with doctors he'd be damned if he was going to have them poking him about and cutting him up. He'd sooner put up with the squits and the pain and go to his grave in one piece, the way the good Lord made him, thanks all the same.

'Come on, boy. What have you done that's got your gran so riled up?'

For once, Wally couldn't speak. When his dad was in a good mood he could get away with murder, but he knew the signs. If Gran had let things wait until after supper he might have got away with it. Now he knew he never would.

'Well, have you all been struck dumb?' Ron roared, his face darkening and what little good humour he had disappearing like morning mist.

Lisa broke the silence. 'Wally's gone and broke your saw, trying to cut down a tree to make a bow,' she burst out.

Without waiting to hear any more, Ron scraped back his chair, yanked Wally out of his and marched him out to the back yard, with the boy hollering and struggling all the while. Shortly afterwards, in amongst his ranting and raving, they heard the whack of his belt on his son's backside, and Wally's accompanying screams.

'I hope you're satisfied, Mother,' Jess snapped. 'Couldn't it have waited until we'd eaten? And you too, miss,' she rounded on Lisa.

'Well, somebody had to say it,' Lisa said sullenly, only to be met with a cuff around the ear from her grandmother. She pushed her chair back, her eyes bright with unshed tears. 'I don't want any rotten supper and I hate you all.'

'Lisa, come back here,' Jess shouted, as she rushed for the stairs. But she was beyond listening, and she slammed the door of the room she shared with Wally. Minutes later he came sobbing into the room and flung himself on his bed.

'Does it hurt much?' Lisa said without much sympathy, having felt the belt herself enough times to know the answer.

'Shut up!' he shouted. 'You told on me and I hate you.'

'Gran would have told on you if I hadn't, and, anyway, I just told her and Mum that I hate them all as well.'

Wally lifted his head from the pillow and raised one watery eye to look at his sister, trying not to betray his admiration at such daring.

'Why?'

She didn't really know. She was ten years old, nearly eleven, and she didn't know what was wrong with her, except that Mr Davidson had said she was brainy and could do great things if she wanted to. And she *did* want to. She wanted it more than anything in her life before.

'Why d'you hate everybody?' Wally said, when she didn't answer.

She gave him a quick hug. 'Well, I don't hate you, so that's something, ain't it? Isn't it?' she corrected herself, as if only just realizing how sloppily she talked.

'Get off me,' Wally said, pushing her away. 'Girls smell all funny.'

The sounds of raised voices could be heard

21

even through the closed door, and Lisa shushed him quickly as she crept to the door and opened it a crack.

'Shush, Wally. I want to hear what they're saying.'

Ron was shouting as usual. 'I thought you were sorting things out with that head-master. There's no need to bring me into it and I don't need to read some poxy letter to know the girl's been making trouble.'

'You do need to read it, Ron,' Jess said shrilly. 'Mr Davidson was very pleased with our Lisa, and he's sure she'll pass those scholarship exams.'

'Well at least she'll know how to count her wages every Friday when the time comes. That is, providing we get enough wages to speak of – and if I don't get down to that strike rally soon I'll never know what the motions are, will I?'

'Read the letter, Ron. He wants us to send her to the grammar school if she passes the exams,' Jess said, cursing him and his posh-sounding *motions*.

'Are you mad, woman? Do you never listen to anything I say? The girl will *not* go to no grammar school. She'll leave as soon as she's fourteen and go to work. I didn't even get that much schooling, and it never did me no harm.'

'Will you *please* just read what the head-master has to say?'

22

Listening upstairs, Lisa caught her breath raggedly at the sound of paper tearing, knowing it was the letter being ripped to shreds without her father even looking at it.

'I ain't got time for all this nonsense, and I don't want no bloody supper nor no more tongue pie. But remember this. No girl of mine is going to no grammar school and putting on airs and graces as long as I've got any say in the matter.'

A few minutes later the front door banged behind him, making both children jump and scuttle back into the bedroom and over to the window to watch their father go swaggering down the street with his bowler crammed on top of his head, a jacket thrown carelessly over his working clothes.

'He must be really angry,' Lisa said. 'He never goes out dressed like that for something important.'

'Is he still angry with me?' Wally said, sniffling.

'I think he's angrier with me now, for being a clever clogs at school. That's plain daft, isn't it?'

She'd never called her father daft before. The Ten Commandments told you always to honour your father and mother, but with tears stinging her eyes she was past caring what she said. One thing she did know, though. Come hell or high water, she

23

thought recklessly, she was going to that grammar school.

The household had gradually settled into an uneasy peace by the time Jess came upstairs and brought them both a bit of bread and cheese instead of the supper they had missed. Much, much later, when the night was dark and chilly with frost, they were awoken from sleep by a commotion coming down the street, followed by a loud hammering on the front door.

'Is it me dad?' Wally whispered, as Lisa rushed to the window.

'I don't know,' Lisa said, puzzled. 'There's a huge group of men with torches, and they're all shouting at once. People are coming outside, so whatever it is everybody'll know by morning.'

She opened the window to lean out, and then their front door opened and her mother stood on the doorstep in her nightgown and shawl, the oil lamp in her hand throwing an eerie red glow over the proceedings.

'What can you see?' Wally said hoarsely, scrambling out of bed to rush to the window, but Lisa suddenly pushed him back inside, her heart pounding like a drumbeat in her chest.

'Get back to bed, Wally, it's nothing to do with us.'

'If it's me dad, I want to see him,' he

shouted, stamping his bare feet on the cold lino.

'You *can't*. He's not there. He's not – he's not –'

'Is that our mum crying?' he said suspiciously. 'What's she crying for, our Lisa? Where's me dad?'

She wouldn't answer, and tried to coax him back to bed. And then the bedroom door opened and their grandmother came into the room, her face ghostly white in the glow of her lamp.

'You children go back to sleep now. Do as you're told, and stay where you are,' she added sharply, her voice threatening to break.

Wally was whimpering now, and Lisa told him shakily he could get into bed with her. He climbed in and clung to her, not knowing what was wrong, but just knowing that something terrible must have happened.

But Lisa knew. She had seen the wooden box that was carried into the house as the group of men had parted to make way for it, just like the Bible story of the Red Sea opening up. She knew it was her dad inside the box, and that he was never going to be angry with her again.

Two

A long while later, Jess tiptoed into Lisa's room. By then a thousand thoughts had travelled around Lisa's imaginative brain, and Wally was asleep, tightly clutched to her chest. She moved gently away from his constricting arms.

'Is me dad dead?' she whispered numbly.

Her mother nodded and held out her hand. Lisa slid out of bed and followed her out of the room. Seeing how red and blotchy Jess's face looked, she knew she should be crying too, but she just felt horribly sick and scared. She had never seen a dead person, and she didn't want to see one now, especially not her dad, when they'd just had words and she was never going to be able to say she was sorry.

The thoughts were all jumbled up in her head, and her body was shaking as they went down to the front room that was hardly ever used except for dusting and polishing once a week, or when the vicar called, and where her gran was leaning over the thing in the wooden box now.

'Come and give your dad a goodbye kiss,

my love,' Cissie whispered, 'then you won't have nightmares about him.'

Lisa stared, her throat closing as she wondered why she would ever have nightmares about her dad. But as Cissie drew her forward she was truly terrified about what she would see, and her legs trembled so much they hardly held her up.

But her dad didn't look so very different from when he'd gone stamping away from the supper table – except for the gigantic bruise on his temple that looked as if it was filled with dark blood in his grey face. Then she realized that his eyes were open a fraction, glistening ghoulishly as her gran brought the lamp closer.

Lisa gave a horrified scream, trying to remember that this really was her dad and not some ogre who was going to hurt her. The dead couldn't hurt you. The vicar said so, so it had to be true.

'Give him a kiss, Lisa,' her gran said more sharply.

She couldn't bear the thought. They'd never been a family for kissing, and she couldn't see why she should do it now when her dad was dead, but as Cissie pushed her head towards the box she barely touched her lips to his cold cheek, well away from his mouth and that monstrous bruise.

'Can I go back to bed now?' she asked in a choked voice.

'Don't you want to know what happened?' her mother said, just as choked. 'Better if you hear it all from us, Lisa love, than from street gossip. Come into the parlour and we'll have a cup of cocoa.'

Lisa did as she was told, keeping well away from her dad's chair. Who would use it now? Who would want to, the moth-eaten old thing with bits of tape holding it together? Without warning, the tears suddenly poured out of her in a torrent.

'Let her be, Jess,' she heard her gran say sternly, as Jess made to comfort her. 'She'll be all the better for letting it out.'

No I won't, you stupid old bat! Me Dad's dead, and me and Wally probably killed him between us for being so wicked.

She wondered if she'd shrieked it aloud, but since nobody boxed her ears she knew that the words were all in her head.

'Lisa, you know about these union meetings and workers' rallies that your dad was so keen on,' Cissie said, stronger than all of them, despite being as old as the Mendip Hills. 'Well, because of the general strike that they were all arguing over, the fights were more violent than usual, and people got hurt. Your poor old dad got the worst of it when somebody bashed him over the head with an iron bar. His pals said he died straight away, so he didn't feel any pain.'

She spoke in an almost brutal way, as if not

feeling any pain made killing somebody any better, and Lisa was aware of someone sobbing. Her head jerked up to see Wally halfway down the stairs, his nightshirt soaking wet where he'd peed himself, his face contorted with terror at what he was hearing.

She pushed past her mother and grandmother and ran to gather him up in her arms, stinking as he was. All other thoughts were forgotten in her need to protect him. He was no longer the rough and tumble little street footballer his dad always wanted him to be. Right now he was Lisa's baby, the way he had been when she had first laid her awestruck eyes on him when she was four years old, so small and frail. He had clutched her hand with his tiny fingers, and gazed at her with his unfocused eyes, and from that moment he was hers to love.

'I'll take him upstairs and clean him up,' she said, still too choked to speak properly, 'and then we're going back to bed.'

She began to feel that if she didn't do something practical this night might never end. There were no trams or buses tomorrow, because of the stupid strike that she didn't understand, so there was no school. Anyway, she wouldn't have gone to school. You didn't, when your dad was lying dead in a wooden box in the front room, did you?

★ ★ ★

When morning came Lisa knew she must have slept, because Wally was lying warm and soft in her arms again, exhausted with crying. The streets were eerily silent: no milkman rattling his cans and calling out cheerily to his customers; no newspaper boy on his rounds today, because the trains hadn't delivered any newspapers. It was as quiet as death, as if all the streets in all the towns in all the world were sad because her dad was dead.

Lisa sucked in her breath as she heard an unexpected sound. Somebody was whistling, and there was a rumble of cartwheels on the cobblestones. She leapt out of bed and watched as Farmer Bray banged on the side of a milk churn and yelled out that anybody who wanted milk straight from the cow should bring out their jugs for a penny a pint. It sounded so daft that Lisa found herself giggling, and then remembered that she had to be sad.

She saw Renee waving to her from across the street, and she leant out of the window, shivering. It was early, and the sun wasn't up yet.

'Is it right your dad got killed last night?' Renee said excitedly.

Lisa nodded numbly, wondering what to say. You couldn't shout out the details across the width of a street. It wasn't decent.

'Can I come over?' Renee went on.

'I'll come over to you,' Lisa said, and shut the window firmly.

She wasn't old enough to know the procedures of death, but her mum wouldn't want the house full of Renee's chatter. During the night there had been ghostly comings and goings, the murmured voices of the doctor and vicar, and she had heard the clatter of a horse and cart stopping for a while and then moving away. But, since her head had been buried beneath the bedclothes for much of the night, she couldn't even be sure about that.

Before she left Wally on his own she wrote him a note in large letters that she had gone to see Renee, and left it on her pillow. Otherwise he'd probably scream the house down when he found she wasn't there, thinking she was dead, too.

She smothered a sob and raced out of the house to Renee's. The street was coming to life now, and people were crowding around Farmer Bray's cart for their jugs of milk. They glanced at Lisa, then turned away, muttering as if she had done something wrong, she thought in bewilderment.

'Why didn't anybody speak to me?' she burst out to Renee's mother before even saying hello.

'People get embarrassed when a neighbour dies, especially the way your dad did, Lisa. They don't know what to say for the best.

They'll all be sorry, though. He stood up for his principles, which is more than most of us can say.'

'What will they do to the people who killed him? Will they be hung?'

Renee's mother looked shocked. 'Why, I don't know what will happen to them, but in all that scuffle I doubt if anybody saw what happened. They'll probably call it an accident.'

'So they'll get away with it,' Lisa said bitterly. 'It won't bring my dad back, anyway.'

She didn't know why she was able to continue working things out logically as she always did, but if she was going to be faced with people who were too afraid to speak to her on account of her dad dying she felt defensively that she had to keep his name alive. She told Renee so in her friend's bedroom.

'Did you see him when he was dead?' Renee whispered. 'What was it like?'

It didn't seem like a crude question. Lisa had been curious, too, even though she'd been filled with dread. She was more detached from the memory now, but it was a minute before she answered.

'He was still my dad, but he was all cold and grey, and he had this great lump on his head that looked as if it was about to burst open and spurt blood all over me at any minute.'

Renee gave a little scream, her eyes filled with shock. 'Lisa, you're horrible! He didn't look like that, and you shouldn't say such awful things!'

'I was only telling the truth, and if you didn't want to know you shouldn't ask. You're such a cry baby, Renee. How are you ever going to manage in the big school without me holding your hand?'

'Stop showing off – and why won't you be there to hold my hand?'

'I'm going to the grammar, and now me dad's dead he can't stop me.'

Seeing Renee's face, Lisa knew it had come out all wrong. She didn't mean to sound boastful and selfish and uncaring. She *did* care about him, even when he shouted at her and Wally and frightened them half to death, and she didn't want him to be dead ... but he was, and there was nothing anybody could do about it ... and he couldn't stop her now.

'I think you're a hateful pig, Lisa Newman,' Renee snapped.

'Oh, Renee, don't let's quarrel,' she said, suddenly tearful. 'I've had poor Wally clinging to me all night, and I thought you were going to cheer me up. Anyway, if this strike thing goes on for ages we won't be going to school for months and months, and nobody will be taking exams then, will they?'

Renee's mother appeared with some toast and milk and spoke sharply.

'I doubt the strike will last more than days. Once the country grinds to a standstill the government will give in to the miners' demands for better wages, so make the most of it.'

'I thought you wanted to do the exams, to show how clever you are,' Renee said, after her mother had left them alone.

'P'raps I do. I just don't want to talk about them.'

'What shall we do then?'

'How about what we were talking about yesterday?' Lisa said, to keep her thoughts away from what might be happening at home. 'What we'll be doing in ten years' time, I mean. We'll write it down and put it in sealed envelopes addressed to each other, then on a certain day in the future we'll open the envelopes together and see if it all turned out like we thought.'

A long while later, the two pieces of paper had become smudged with butter and marmalade, but were ready to be put into the sealed envelopes. They had argued and giggled over them, especially at Lisa's assertion that she wasn't getting married until she was at least twenty-five, at which Renee hooted.

'I *won't*. Boys are all right, but I'm not getting married to one of them for years. *You* will, though, and you'll have lots of babies.'

'Don't you want babies? You always used to call Wally your baby.'

'I suppose I want them one day, but Mr Davidson thinks I'll do great things, so I'll have to have a career first.'

It sounded so grand it started Renee snorting and mocking and starting a pillow fight, nearly destroying the secret documents in the process.

'Anyway,' Renee complained next, 'I'll have forgotten what we said, but I bet you can close your eyes and remember everything I wrote. Go on, I dare you.'

Lisa obliged, but she didn't need to close her eyes to know that it was true. Renee's scrawl, with many spelling mistakes and crossed-out words, was as clear to her as if it were printed right in front of her. She could recall every word, every comma and full stop, every silly little drawing Renee had inserted. The teachers called it a gift, but she had been able to do it all her life, so there was nothing magical about it as far as she was concerned.

The sound of outdoor boots pounding up the stairs made them exchange their envelopes solemnly, with the instructions clearly marked on the outside that they were not to be opened until they were together, sometime in 1936.

Wally burst into the room, his hair wild, his eyes still red from crying.

'Our mum says you've got to come home now, our Lisa, cos there's things to do,' he shouted. When he was feeling upset, he never spoke like anybody else. He just shouted. His dad used to say proudly that he'd do for a soldier, even a blessed sergeant major, shouting like that.

'I'm coming,' Lisa said, swallowing at the memory, and stuffed the envelope into her pocket, to be put away with her secret things.

'Our dad's not in the front room no more,' Wally bellowed as they ran across the street. 'Gran says some men took him away in the night, and we're to have a burying next week.'

That was what all the comings and going were about during the night then, thought Lisa. She had been to a few country funerals. They were grand affairs, with the coffin placed on a scrubbed farm cart draped with a flag or blanket, or whatever the family chose, and drawn by two black horses decorated with black plumes. Family and friends, workmates and neighbours all walked behind it to the churchyard. Then, once the burying was done, they all crammed into the local public house, adults and children alike, for a bite to eat and drinks of scrumpy or lemonade according to age, while they told yarns about the dead person until all the crying was over and folk were laughing and spluttering into their pint pots over some of the antics he'd got up to in life. It was almost like a holiday. The strike had put paid to many folk working, but those that didn't have to stay home would do so anyway, to give an extra fine send-off to Ron Newman.

'Now then, Lisa,' her mum said briskly, when she went indoors, 'there's no school, so you can help me sort out your dad's clothes to give to the poor house.'

Jess turned away so that the girl wouldn't see the way her throat worked as she spoke. It was best to be firm and sensible, and it wouldn't do for them all to be wailing and keening. She had to set the example, even though she would miss the old bugger, for all his cantankerous ways.

'I will pass the exams, Mum,' Lisa said, 'and I will go to the grammar school, won't I?'

'I can't think about that now, love.'

But a week after her dad died, such thoughts helped to keep Lisa's mind off the slow, sad procession wending its way towards the churchyard, while she clutched her brother's damp little hand and tried not to hear his sobs. Her mum was on one side of them and her gran on the other, and behind them stretched a small army of followers. Some were men she didn't know, who seemed to think her dad had been a very fine fellow, and by the time the burying was all over and they had retired to the local public house all of them were saying he'd be proud to know the strike was going the workers' way and would be over almost before it had begun.

The know-alls said they'd never find anybody responsible for the attack. There were too many involved, the ringleaders had scattered and the police were too busy trying to keep law and order now. It would be pronounced as accidental death by persons unknown. Some whispered that Ron Newman had only got what he deserved, being the rowdiest of the lot, but the Workers' Benevolent Fund dibbed up for the funeral and saw the widow right, and the Co-op penny insurance did the rest, so his pals decided they had done right by their man.

Sure enough, eight days after the country had been brought to a virtual standstill it was all over. Trams and buses and trains ran again; lorries delivered goods to shops; newspapers appeared with graphic details of how the coal miners had triumphed in their quest for a decent wage; and Lisa Newman went back to school to prepare for the scholarship exams that she knew were going to send her to the grammar school.

But she had reckoned without her grandmother. Once the exams were over, there was the summer holiday, and she was still visualizing the hundred per cent of answers to the English exam she knew she had got right. She couldn't sleep for trying to imagine the grammar school and the bus ride every day to get there, and as she crept down the stairs to go to the outside lavvy she heard her mum and gran talking in the parlour.

'She'll get above herself, Jess,' Gran was saying tartly. 'It'll be going against Ron's wishes, but you never took much account of that, did you?'

'That's not fair,' Jess said angrily. 'I was loyal to Ron for as long as he lived, but our Lisa's got a good head on her shoulders and she's got to have her chance.'

'You'll probably be glad he got killed then, so as not to stand in her way.'

Lisa heard her mother gasp. 'You're a wicked old woman for saying such things! I cared for Ron, even though he made it hard for anybody to love him at times. But Lisa's my daughter and there's a lot of Ron's guts in her, and if her teachers think she'll do well at the grammar I won't stand in her way.'

'And who's going to pay for the fancy uniform?'

'I'll find the money, don't you worry about that.'

Without waiting to hear any more, Lisa scuttled silently out of the house and down to the lavvy, shivering in the night. She sat on the wooden seat with her nightie pulled up to her knees and her head bent while she thought about what was to be done to get her a grammar school uniform. It was unthinkable not to be dressed the same as everybody else.

School holidays didn't mean she could do nothing, nor go to the seaside like posh folk did; she and Wally had to do their share of chores. But next morning, once they were done, she went running across the fields to where haymaking was in full swing on the surrounding farms. By the time she went home again she'd got a job with Farmer Bray's missus, taking scrumpy out to the men in the fields and buttering mounds of bread for them to eat with their cheese and pickled onions when they came in starving for a midday bite.

The job only paid coppers, plus a few eggs and scraps of bacon for her mum, on account of what Mrs Bray called Lisa's initiative, but it was all going to go towards paying for the uniform she was going to wear at the grammar school.

'That's *if* you pass, and *if* your mother lets you go,' Renee the pessimist reminded her, guiltily wishing Lisa wasn't so keen to go and leave her starting in the big bad secondary school on her own.

'I will. You'll see,' Lisa said, brimful of confidence.

★ ★ ★

The day the letter came she could hardly wait for Jess to open it. She was so excited and nervous at the same time that she was almost in danger of peeing herself like Wally still did occasionally.

'What's it say?' she hollered, dancing from foot to foot in an ecstasy of anticipation.

Jess passed the slip of paper to her. The words jumped up and down in front of her eyes, and finally settled on that one, single, beautiful word. PASS.

'I've passed,' she gasped, tears stinging her eyes. 'Oh, Mum – Gran – I've passed. Oh, I wish me dad was here so I could tell him!'

The tears flooded her face then, and she tore out of the house, waving the precious piece of paper in her hand, and rushed over to Renee's.

'You've done it then,' Renee said. 'Knew you would. I s'pose you won't want to be friends with me now.'

'Why not?' Lisa said in genuine astonishment. 'You didn't pass, I s'pose? So what? We're still you and me, aren't we?'

Renee wasn't very bright, but her sad little smile made Lisa's heart stop for a second.

' 'Course it'll make a difference. You'll be going to the grammar and I'll be going to the other one. We won't be together any more, and I'll miss you something awful,' she added with a gulp.

'Stop it or you'll have me crying as well,'

41

Lisa said sharply, her throat starting to feel full. 'I came to tell you my good news, and we guessed what yours would be, didn't we, dummy?'

Renee nodded, grinned weakly and held out her hand. 'We'll always be friends, then, won't we?'

' 'Course we will,' Lisa said, shaking her hand furiously. 'We'll be friends until death – or something like that.'

Renee giggled and told Lisa that she wasn't as clever as she thought she was, saying that. Everybody knew there was nothing *like* death. You were either dead or you weren't, and once you were dead, you were dead for ever ... but not for years and years and years yet, she added quickly, just in case God was listening.

Three

July 1931

Lisa had been at the grammar school for five years, and now that it was over she realized it had gone in a flash. She had made some wonderful friends, and a few enemies, mostly girls who were jealous of her abilities. It was a great feather in her cap for a girl from the sleepy little mid-Somerset village of Mallory to end up as head girl, and that was something else some of the townies couldn't forgive.

But she always got glowing reports at the end of every term; she was top in her class in every subject and the mistresses called her a natural at French and German. She practised it on Wally, and although he didn't have her brain power he was picking up enough of the foreign phrases, so that between them they often teased Gran by talking in either of the languages.

'You shouldn't go on so,' Jess told them. 'She's getting frail and she doesn't understand your jokes.'

43

'She never did, Mum,' Lisa said dryly. 'She wouldn't know what a joke was if it came and hit her.'

Jess looked at her girl, who was such a stunning beauty now, her hair twisted into a thick plait of polished bronze, her clear, wide-set eyes as green as emeralds.

It still gave Jess a little shock to see how fast she was developing. And despite the teachers at the grammar school encouraging her to stay on and even try for college, Lisa was having none of it. A very determined girl was her daughter. Her French tutor had come to the house one day when Lisa was out, throwing Jess into a right old tizzy as he spoke to her in long words that she barely understood.

'She is an excellent linguist, Mrs Newman, and her memory is amazing, especially photographically. Such talents shouldn't be wasted. She could go far, and the whole world is open to her. If she could be persuaded to stay on at school for another year it would be more than beneficial to her.'

'But what use will another year be when she could be earning her keep like any good daughter should?'

'She's an exceptional young woman, Mrs Newman, and I urge you to think twice about letting her do some menial kind of work just to earn her keep.'

'She don't want menial work. I daresay she

wants to be a teacher.'

She had no idea if it was true, but she remembered how Lisa coaxed Wally into learning French and German so effortlessly. She only said it to be rid of this stiff-necked chap and let her get on with making supper.

'Well, if that's the case,' he said more keenly, 'further education would be a great asset to her, and I'll be in touch again in due course, Mrs Newman. Meanwhile, I have a written reference for her, which her tutors felt she should have for any future employers so that they can be aware of her full potential.'

He handed over the envelope, and Jess wondered why on earth she had said such a daft thing about teaching. Lisa wouldn't be pleased when she came back from the Bray farm, where she spent much of her time now, helping out. If she wasn't so nonchalant about boys, Jess would have suspected her of taking a fancy to young Eddie Bray, wicked-eyed rogue though he was, but she still spoke about her *career*, without the faintest idea of what it was going to be.

She was sixteen now and, according to Cissie, she should be bringing proper money into the house instead of bits and pieces from the farm. Even Wally had his paper round and handed over his dues every Friday night.

'She'll find her place in time, Mother,' Jess

told her, knowing the old woman was right, but not having the heart to insist on sending Lisa off to work in a factory or a corner shop when she was destined to do so much more.

Cissie continued to grumble. Frail though she was now, and more cantankerous by the day, she still had a voice in her son's household and never let any of them forget it.

'You take too much notice of what these teachers tell you. And all that nonsense with learning French and German – what's the good of it? Nobody speaks such tripe around here, and you ain't letting her go off to no foreign parts, I hope. We fought the Jerries in the last war, and your father would turn over in his grave if he thought his girl was hob-nobbing with 'em.'

'I'm sure she'll do no such thing, Mother,' Jess said, exasperated, and pausing in the middle of the weekly wash to straighten her back.

She plunged her hands into the soapy water, vigorously scrubbing Cissie's drawers on the washboard before rinsing and putting them through the mangle, and half wishing it was the old girl's neck she was wringing.

A few days later she was overcome with remorse when Cissie died in her sleep. Wally had gone fishing for tadpoles early that morning, and Lisa was at Renee's house, experimenting with hairstyles and face powder, and blotting their lips with beetroot juice.

Once Lisa and Wally had been told about their grandmother the news quickly rippled around Mallory. There were tears, but it didn't give any of them the shock that Ron's death had done five years before, because this was the natural order of things. Cissie was old and her time had come. And the day she was laid to rest in the village churchyard, close to her husband and her son, Lisa made her announcement.

'Mum, a few weeks ago I wrote to a family wanting someone to teach their children to speak good English. If they'll accept me, I want to take the job. I like being with children, and these people don't want an older teacher with all sorts of qualifications. They want someone young enough to play with their children and make learning fun.'

She started off confidently, but by the time she finished her voice was shaky, and Jess realized she was avoiding her eyes. She was also canny enough to realize how carefully her daughter had phrased the sentences. Wally's eyes were popping, too. He was eleven now, and he didn't want Lisa to go away from home, especially as she was always helping him with his school work.

'Where is this place, our Lisa?' Wally asked.

Lisa hedged. She had only confided in

Renee that morning, and Renee was full of warnings about white slavery and that kind of stuff. But she knew what Jess would say, and she had warded off this moment as long as possible.

'Mum, you always championed me about going to the grammar school, even when Dad was against it, and Gran thought I'd be putting on airs and graces.'

'What do you know about this family?' Jess said sharply. 'You're only sixteen, and it'll still be my say-so before you go chasing any wild schemes.'

But it won't be Gran's say-so as well – or Dad's, Lisa thought, guiltily glad that they couldn't object and spoil everything.

Her heart thudded as she handed over the letter, and Jess stared at it, frowning.

'What's all this?'

Wally peered over her shoulder and spoke excitedly.

'That's French! Crikey, it's French. Are you going to France, our Lisa?'

'She most certainly is not, and you can stop using that sort of language, Wally!' Jess snapped. 'I never heard anything so stupid. France is for French people, not for ordinary country folk like us. You'd best start at the beginning, my girl.'

Lisa had a serious bout of the jitters now. She knew she should have asked what her mother thought. But that was her – rushing in, sure that this was her destiny and that she mustn't waste a moment of her precious life, or the chance might be gone for ever.

The advertisement in the glossy magazine had looked so wonderful, so perfectly right, that it might had been created especially for her. It wasn't a magazine she normally read. It had been in the doctor's waiting room when she had gone to get her Gran's medication, open at a page of information about folk who wanted other folk to work for them.

The words had leapt up at her, inviting her, wanting her, drawing her in as if they were holding out accommodating arms to her, Lisa Newman, and to no other girl in all the world...

'Well, miss? I'm waiting,' she heard Jess say, in a harsh voice that could have been her dad's and her gran's all rolled up in one and gave no space for dreams.

Lisa gave a nervous swallow and then she was gabbling again, because if she didn't she might never say it at all.

'Mum, when I saw this job advertised I knew it was what I wanted to do, except that I never knew I wanted it until I saw it, so I wrote a letter and sent it off before I had time to think too hard about it, and now I've had this reply, see?'

'Speak sense, girl.'

'I *am*. I saw the advert and I answered it.' She was almost tearful now, except that she so rarely cried, and it would make her seem childish when she wasn't a child any more. She was a young woman with the opportunity of a lifetime.

'Well, since I'm not clever enough to understand this French, you'd better tell me what the letter says,' Jess said, sarcasm hiding her concern. The mere thought of going to France still had ghostly undertones in the minds of older folk. There were plenty who had gone there not so many years ago, wearing battledress and dying in the mud of Flanders, and Renee Yates's father had been one of them.

'You trust me to translate it properly, then?' Lisa said, just as sarcastic.

Jess finally recognized that the beautiful young woman staring at her so defiantly was no longer a child, but someone capable of making her own decisions.

'Of course,' she said stiffly. 'I don't think you've ever lied to me.'

'Well then,' Lisa said, finding it hard to fight back the tears all the same.

It was weird, but in the past few minutes she and her mother seemed to have entered into a different kind of relationship, and she didn't quite know how or why the relationship had shifted.

'I can read bits of it, too,' Wally said importantly. 'I'll see she don't tell you the wrong things, Mum.'

50

'Thank you, dumb-bell,' Lisa said, but her stomach was gradually settling down as she told her mother rapidly what M. Henri Dubois had written.

'There's two young children, and they live south of Paris,' she said, praying that Jess wouldn't think this was a descent into evil. 'The children are highly strung and are anxious about returning to school after being unwell for some time. When they're older they'll be going to boarding school, but the parents think that having someone to live in their house to care for them, and to teach them English and sums, will be the best for them for now.'

'But you'd be no more than a servant. They'd expect you to do all sorts of jobs as well as looking after these children.'

'No, I'll be a sort of governess, and I really want to do it, Mum.'

'You want to leave your home and family and live in a foreign place where you'll know nobody at all?'

'Yes, I do.' And nothing was going to make her change her mind.

'Well, I'm sorry, but I'm certainly not going to let you go off to Paris, of all places, to live with strangers.'

'You haven't let me finish telling you what's in the letter,' Lisa went on, her voice growing tighter by the minute. 'M. and Mme Dubois will be in Bristol shortly, and would

51

like to interview me to see if I'm suitable. I sent them my reference, so they know all about me, and they insist that you're present as well, to assure you of their good intentions.'

If anything was guaranteed to throw Jess into a panic, the formal wording was it. She had a countrywoman's suspicion of foreigners, even of folk outside the village. The fact that her daughter wanted to live among them was both foolhardy and courageous, but the thought of meeting them herself was nerve-racking ... and yet, seeing the steely look in Lisa's eyes, it had to be done. She would be failing in her duty if she did not agree.

'I haven't said that I approve of any of this yet, Lisa, but since it's gone this far I suppose we must meet these people and hear what they have to say,' she said finally. 'Not that I shall understand a word of it!'

Lisa threw her arms around her mother's neck in a rare gesture of affection. 'Yes you will, because they both speak English. I wrote to them in French to prove that I was fluent, and that's why M. Dubois answered in the same way. So I can write back and agree to the meeting?' she asked excitedly.

'All right,' Jess said reluctantly, wondering how an ordinary woman like her had produced such determined children with dreams beyond her imagination. Wally was talking about being a newspaper reporter, and it looked now as if she would be losing her daughter. First Ron, then Cissie and now Lisa ... Jess shuddered, as if a goose had walked over her grave, and told herself not to be silly. She didn't believe in superstitious nonsense, and those that believed everything went in threes, were just plain daft.

'You're not really going to France, are you?' Renee said, implying that it was like entering the gates of hell. They were lying on the grass in their favourite meadow, squinting up at the sun with their hands linked together behind their heads, their feet idly dangling in the cool river water where Wally so often fished for tadpoles. Even the whiff of cow manure wafting across from the nearby farm couldn't dispel the pleasure of just being here with nothing to do but breathe in the summer air.

'If I want this job, I'll have to,' Lisa said.
'Have these people got pots of money then?'
'Probably. I don't know.'
Renee didn't know how to react. Already, Lisa seemed to have gone streets away from her, and she hadn't even had the interview yet. Renee sensed the loss of something she had known all her life, which was fast slipping away from her.
'Is that what you want as well, Lisa?'

'What? To have pots of money? Of course not. That's not why I'm doing this.'

'So why are you doing it?'

Lisa sat up. 'For pity's sake, my teachers were for ever egging me on to go to college, which I'd hate, and Mum would probably have me working in a village shop. But I've got a brain, and I'm going to use it.'

'Teaching French kids how to speak English?' Renee scoffed. 'It's not my idea of using your brain.'

'No, your idea of using your brain is how to keep Eddie Bray's wandering hands away,' she said with a grin.

'I do no such thing,' Renee said indignantly, sitting up just as fast, and then grinned back. 'Well, no, I don't mean that, do I? Of course I'd keep his wandering hands off me, if he *had* wandering hands.'

'You mean he doesn't? What a disappointment!'

Renee didn't say anything for a minute, and then she laughed. 'Well, that's daring if you like! Does that mean you'd let a boy do things, and, well, touch you anywhere he shouldn't?'

Lisa tossed her hair. She had let it out of its confining plait today, and it shimmered down her back in the sunlight like the rich colours of autumn leaves.

'I might. It would depend on how much I liked him.'

'Even before you were married to him?'

Lisa burst out laughing. 'I told you I'm not getting married until I'm at least twenty-five. Or have you forgotten the things we wrote five years ago?'

'I know *you* haven't,' Renee said crossly, feeling so very less mature than this about-to-cross-the-English-Channel friend. Lisa had always been more confident and more beautiful than she was, and she eyed her friend's rounded bosoms and long, slim legs with a feeling of jealousy mixed with sheer misery that they were going to be parted after knowing one another all their lives.

'Oh, I'm going to miss you so much!' she burst out, and then they were hugging one another and vowing undying friendship, no matter what.

'It won't be for ever,' Lisa said, her own eyes brilliant with unshed tears. 'We can write letters to one another, and I'll want to come home to see Mum and Wally, especially for Christmas and stuff like that.'

But she gulped as she said it, and her stomach was doing those strange somersaults again, because if the French family expected her to stay away from her Mum and Wally and home for Christmas and stuff, they could just think again. She'd have to make sure this M. Henri Dubois understood that at the interview ... the thought of which was scary enough to make her throw up, if anybody wanted to know. But that was something nobody was going to know about.

Jess had been to Bristol once with Ron for one of his union meetings, before he decided she was more of a nuisance than an asset. She hadn't liked the city. She was comfortable among country folk, not among strangers in the midst of hot and noisy cities – even this one, with its snaking, silvery river and the high cliffs above it with Brunel's graceful suspension bridge crossing the Avon Gorge.

The hotel where they were to meet M. and Mme Dubois overlooked the gorge, and she was very nervous, while at just sixteen years old Lisa looked calm and in control of herself. Whatever her feelings, her daughter had always been able to hide them, Jess registered.

Now Jess's hands were as clammy as they had been all those years before, summoned to the junior school and told that her daughter had a phenomenal brain and a photographic memory. She still didn't fully understand it, but, obviously, other people did.

'Cheer up, Mum,' Lisa said, as the bus from the station took them to the hotel. 'Don't look too much like a mother hen, or M. Dubois will think I'm going to go running home every other week.'

'You know I don't like meeting strangers, and especially foreigners. And you haven't got this job yet,' she added.

Since Jess had never met any foreigners in her life, Lisa didn't know how she could be sure. But she kept up a flow of conversation about the ships they had seen on the river and how lovely this green part of Bristol looked away from the centre.

It was a relief when they reached the hotel, where Lisa asked the receptionist to inform M. and Mme Dubois that they were here. If her knees were knocking she was determined not to give it away, because it would never do for the French people to think she wasn't capable of being in charge of their children. She lifted her chin and tried to appear as if she entered elegant hotels every day of her life.

She was told that she was expected in the lounge overlooking the gorge. As soon as they entered, an affluent-looking gentleman rose from his chair, while his wife remained seated. She looked so chic and fashionable that Lisa knew Jess would panic, and her heart sank as she was greeted in rapid French.

'Forgive me, M. Dubois,' she replied, 'but as my mother doesn't understand French, could we please speak in English?'

'Of course, my dear. Then let us make the introductions,' he said easily.

57

He spoke with such perfect diction that she wondered why he didn't teach his children himself. But Lisa assumed he would be a businessman, and wouldn't have the time. There might even be a cachet in having an English girl to attend to such things.

She then discovered that the delicate and softly voiced Mme Dubois didn't have such a fine command of English, and, since she was at home with the children most of the time, this seemed to answer the question.

Jess began to relax, as if realizing that although they were poles apart in their way of life, they were both mothers. And after mentioning Lisa's reference, filled with such high praise for her abilities, it was obvious that the husband was as anxious for Jess's approval as for Lisa to tutor his children.

'They can be difficult,' Monique Dubois told Lisa apologetically. 'You will find them lively, and a little naughty at times, but I hope you will – how do you say it? – I hope you will be able to deal with them.'

'I have a younger brother,' Lisa said, 'so I have some experience of children.'

'And you will be happy to leave Lisa in our charge?' Monique said, turning to Jess. 'It is most important for the mothers to have respect for each other, is it not? She would be treated like one of our own, Mme Newman.'

'It sounds as if she is going to be a lucky

girl,' Jess murmured.

'I think it is we who are the lucky ones,' Monique said, with a slight nod at her husband, signifying that they had found the perfect angel for their little imps.

'Then if we can agree the terms of our arrangement, I will return in one month to fetch you, Miss Newman. Does that suit you both?'

He took care to include Jess in his offer, and the terms he mentioned were more than agreeable. They were staggering to Jess, and again she had to admire Lisa for not seeming completely overwhelmed by the thought of such riches, and of living in a rich man's house. But her daughter had one last question to ask.

'There will be holiday arrangements, M Dubois? I will want to visit my family from time to time, especially at Christmas. My mother will expect it.'

She stared at him more boldly than she felt, her heart hammering with all the excitement of the day, and was rewarded by a hearty laugh.

'Naturally you will have proper holidays, *ma chérie*. We would not dream of preventing you from seeing your family at regular intervals. So it is agreed?'

He put out his hand, and Lisa took it, sealing her fate.

Four

Two weeks later, Lisa was still feeling ecstatic. It was the chance of a lifetime that didn't often come to ordinary girls like her. She had always pooh-poohed the idea that her language abilities made her different, even though her teachers had frequently told her so. As far as she was concerned, it was normal.

She had certainly never been a swot, nor spent hours poring over her books. She just learnt the pages off by heart and recalled them when she needed to sit for an exam. It may be called a gift by some, but to Lisa it was the way things were.

'You're bloomin' clever, our Lisa,' Wally said, as he watched her sorting out clothes and magazines, while wondering how soon he could suggest moving into Lisa's bigger bedroom when she left for France. 'I wish I was clever.'

'Why? Do you fancy living in France?'

'Not likely. I wish you weren't going, neither,' he added, and then went red at admitting it. '*Renee* wishes you weren't going, I mean. Why couldn't you get a job

60

round here?'

Lisa could see the suppressed anger in his face, and knew it was due to the sense of approaching loss that he didn't know how to express. Nor did her mother, and her new job had caused an odd kind of restraint between them all. A thought flickered that if she ever had children she wouldn't hold back from showing that she loved them.

She turned away from Wally's scowling face and aggressively folded arms, afraid that she might burst into unaccustomed tears, and the feeling made her sharper than she intended.

'I don't know any families round here who speak French and want their kids to speak English, that's why, you dummy. But I'll be home for Christmas, so don't forget to buy me a present,' she added.

'I might. I'm asking Mum if I can have your bedroom, anyway, so you'll have to have mine when you come back,' Wally shouted, hopping off the bed with one angry movement and storming downstairs.

Lisa flopped on her bed for a moment, arms clasped behind her head, and stared up at the patches on the ceiling. She didn't want to fight with Wally, and she didn't blame him for wanting her bigger bedroom. If she was only going to come home for short periods of time in future it was only fair. She felt a tremor run through her body, because for all

61

her bravado it was an enormous step to take, like Christopher Columbus and Marco Polo and all those adventurous explorers of history. She was a pioneer, riding into the sunset, facing Indian braves and untold hardships, struggling against mountainous storms at sea...

'Lisa, stop dawdling up there. Come downstairs and help me get the tea,' her mother shouted, and the grand images faded, leaving her grinning at her own fantasies. What was a little boat trip across the English Channel to teach two small children compared with all those gallant heroes' adventures? Her dad would have said she was getting above herself, and so she was.

Renee obviously thought so, although much of Renee's resentment was because she was going to lose her best friend in a couple of weeks while she herself was starting work in a factory. Although looking after a couple of kids all day long didn't seem like much of a job to her, especially when they were foreign; to Renee it was as weird as looking after aliens from outer space. There was time enough for all that malarkey when you got married and had them bawling at your feet all day.

'Well, it's what I want to do,' Lisa told her crossly that evening when she had escaped to over there before she got any more tongue pie from her mother. 'You won't miss me, anyway, now you've taken up with your bloomin' farming chap.'

'He's not a bloomin' farming chap. You know very well his name's Eddie,' Renee said dreamily.

Her sudden change of tone made Lisa feel even crosser, as if her friend had somehow gone to a place where she couldn't follow. In a split second, it was as if there were secrets between them.

'You want to be careful, Renee. You know what they say about farming chaps. I would not want to go out with one of them, knowing what they do with animals, milking and calving and all that messy stuff. You never know where their hands have been.'

Renee began to laugh. 'You may be going to France to live with your posh friends and you may be able to talk French all day long, but you don't know the first thing about falling in love, do you?'

Her face went a deep shade of red as she finished, and Lisa shrieked.

'You aren't telling me you're falling in love with *Eddie Bray*, are you? He's covered in spots and he goes blotchy as soon as he looks at you, and his fingers are all podgy from milking those cows...'

She paused as Renee's expression got madder. 'Or perhaps that's what you like. Oh my Lord, Renee, you haven't let him – you know – touch you or anything? You were the one who got all shocked when I teased you about it once.'

'Don't be daft,' Renee said, not quite meeting her eyes.

They hadn't seen so much of each other since school ended, and Renee's excuse had been because she was now earning a bit of money at Bray's farm before she started her job at the factory. But Wally had come home from his fishing trips with tales of seeing Eddie Bray doing things with some girl, and Eddie Bray had paid him a few pennies to say nothing about it. Lisa had dismissed it as tittle-tattle from Wally's overactive imagination, and hadn't bothered to try and get it out of him, sure it had been some fast girl from the village.

But could it really have been her best friend, with whom she had shared all her secrets for all these years? Renee would have told her ... unless there was something too secret to tell anybody. Something she was ashamed about ... But wouldn't Wally have recognized Renee? She got off Renee's bed as speedily as Wally had got off hers.

'I'm off,' she announced, before Renee either started hedging or telling her things she didn't want to know.

'You've only just got here, so where's the bloomin' fire?'

'Sorry. I've got things to do.'

The feeling that things were never going to

be quite the same between them again was as sad as it was strange. They had taken it for granted that it was Lisa's new job in France that was going to separate them, but Lisa realized that secrets could separate people even more than distance.

But Renee and *Eddie Bray*? They had always thought him a bit of a likeable buffoon, but to fancy him as a – a *lover* – never!

As the daring word slid into her mind, Lisa shuddered. She wasn't averse to boys, but she had a vivid memory of the biology lessons where the teacher had delicately described how animals mated, and then said so briefly and casually, almost like an afterthought, that that was the way all animals, including humans, mated. And it had been enough to throw the whole class into a tizzy.

Anyone with an enquiring mind, like Lisa Newman, was far too curious to let it rest there. The biology mistress, always uneasy at Lisa's thirst for knowledge, was persuaded after class to give Lisa more specific and graphic details. Then Lisa jolly well wished she hadn't been so nosy, and she wished it even more now, when the thought of Eddie Bray and Renee *doing things* was enough to make her sick.

She marched up to Wally's bedroom where he was doing disgusting things with a box of maggots.

'If Mum catches you with those things up here she'll give you what for,' she told him, trying not to shudder.

'They're bait,' he said sullenly. 'Fishermen have to have bait to catch fish.'

'I know, but they shouldn't be in a bedroom.'

He looked at her suspiciously. 'You're not going to tell, are you?' he said, scooping the squirming things back into their box, ramming the lid on tightly and securing it with a rubber band, to Lisa's relief. Were all eleven-year-old boys this revolting, or only this particular one!

'That depends. First, you've got to tell me something.'

So it was true. The two people Wally had seen canoodling more than once among the trees were Renee and Eddie Bray. Not that he'd seen much, but it was definitely Renee, and he kept quiet because Eddie had paid him to do so, so Lisa had better not tell on him.

But no wonder Renee often had that soppy look on her face now – and if Eddie Bray could produce it, then there must be something about him, though Lisa couldn't think what. She never thought for one minute that they could really be *lovers*, though – not *all-the-way* lovers. Renee couldn't be that wicked.

It would be just a bit of kissing and larking about – and Lisa knew that for all her cleverness she had no idea how it felt to fall in love. Nobody could teach you about feelings, anyway. You had to experience them for yourself, and that was something that had already drawn Renee away from her. There were obviously more lessons to be learnt in life than ever came out of a schoolroom.

It was almost a relief now to leave Mallory. She didn't like secrets, except when she was the one sharing them. Then they could be spectacular and important. When they didn't actually involve her, yet she knew all about them anyway, it made her feel uncomfortable.

But she hugged Renee tightly when they said goodbye, promising to write, and told Renee to tell her *everything*, especially about her love-life, mind – while knowing perfectly well that she wouldn't.

'You tell me all about the handsome French chaps you meet, too,' Renee said, her eyes suspiciously damp. Unlike Lisa, she had always been able to turn the tears on and off like a water tap. It was a useful accomplishment sometimes, when she failed miserably at a school test.

'I'm not going to meet French chaps. I'm going to work.'

'You're bound to meet them, unless the whole country's full of women and children.

67

And I'm not sure I believe in immaculate conceptions,' she added.

Lisa was shocked at such blasphemy, and Renee laughed.

'Your face is a picture, Lisa Newman. I'm just reminding you to enjoy yourself and not spend all your time working.'

'You're daft,' Lisa said, 'and I never thought I'd say it, but I shall miss that daftness a lot.'

'Oh well, that's something in my favour, I suppose. I always heard the French didn't have a sense of humour,' Renee countered, and then they were hugging each other again, and swearing to be friends for ever, no matter what.

Neither Wally nor Jess could deal with emotions, and after Wally disappeared to go fishing Jess gave her daughter a perfunctory hug and a fierce instruction that she was to come home immediately if there was any sort of trouble. Though just what kind of trouble she meant was unclear, and the tension between them was too palpable for Lisa to enquire.

'I'll be all right, Mum. You've met M. and Mme Dubois and you know they're respectable people.'

'It's still a foreign country, and you're still a child,' Jess muttered, even though this so-sophisticated girl in her grown-up clothes and her glorious autumn hair bundled into a chignon for neatness contradicted her words.

'Well, you'll always be my mum, so nothing's going to change that,' Lisa said, perilously near to choking. 'And if you don't let me go I shall miss the train to Bristol, and I'll have blotted my copybook with M. Dubois before I start. I'll write the minute I get to France, and tell you all about the house and the children.'

Jess let her go, marvelling at her composure in going to Bristol where she would stay the night in the hotel with her new employer. From there they would take a train to Dover for the ferry to France. M. Dubois' chauffeur would meet them there and drive them to the family home south of Paris. It was a different world, Jess thought uneasily.

But Lisa wished Mme Dubois would be in Bristol too. She was sure she would run out of conversation long before she and her employer reached France. Then, out of nowhere, she seemed to hear one of her old tutors' voices in her head.

Always remember, Lisa, that you have the ability to go far, and you can be anything you want to be.

She stared out of the train window as it rattled towards Bristol on the first step to a new life. She had sought it, and she was going to make the most of it, otherwise it would all be wasted.

It was the first time she had stayed in an hotel, and it was grand enough to make her almost turn tail for home. Almost.

'This will all be new to you, Miss Newman,' M. Dubois said kindly when they had taken an early supper.

'Yes,' Lisa mumbled, hardly knowing where all her new-found savoir faire had gone, but gone it had, like a puff of smoke. Even the French words that slid so effortlessly into her thoughts didn't help

'If my wife and I didn't have every confidence in you, my dear, we would not have hired you. And may I call you Lisa? We would also like the children to address you informally, so that you can be comfortable with one another.'

'Yes, I would prefer that,' Lisa said, relieved. The thought of being called Mlle Newman had charmed her at first, and then made her feel like a schoolmarm. She was sixteen, and not ready for the spinster role yet, thank you very much!

'Why do you smile?' M. Dubois went on, seeing how her lips twitched.

'Oh, it's just a silly thought about something my best friend and I once said.'

'Yes?' he prompted.

Lisa felt her face go red, but as he waited

she had no choice but to go on.

'It was about my plan not to marry until I'm at least twenty-five,' she said, feeling more of an idiot with every word. 'I can't think why I thought about it at that moment, unless it's because Renee – my friend – is going out with a farm boy now, and I made a bet that she'd get married the minute she can. Not that I'm a gambling person,' she added hastily, in case he thought she might be about to corrupt his children into wicked ways.

He laughed. 'I never thought that you were. You have a delightful innocence about you, Miss Newman – Lisa – which, coupled with your extraordinary linguistic ability, I am sure will appeal to the children.'

'Thank you. I'm looking forward to meeting them very much.'

He told her about the family home where she would have a bedroom and sitting room, which to Lisa seemed like luxury. Until now, she had been unaware of the kind of house in which the Dubois family lived, but he produced photographs of the mansion set in rolling grounds that sloped down to a lake with a forest beyond. She was glad her mother hadn't seen these photos. Jess would be petrified at what her girl was getting into, and start echoing Ron's oft-repeated words that her girl would be 'getting above herself'.

Once she was in the unfamiliar bed that

night, she memorized the detailed descriptions Monique Dubois had sent her of the children. Pierre was six and Danielle, who was eight, was always known as Dani. There were photos, too; they were beautiful children with their mother's chic appearance, even at so early an age, and pert expressions that promised that they would be handfuls.

That was fine by Lisa. She didn't want to be teaching cabbages, and much preferred lively children. They were highly strung, according to Monique, which often led to tantrums, but Lisa was confident she could deal with those. She'd dealt with Wally often enough. At the thought, she was beset with a burst of homesickness she hadn't expected. She'd dealt with him chasing her around the garden with a worm on the end of a fishing line. She'd dealt with him threatening to tell on her and Renee for sneaking out of the house at night unless they paid pennies for his silence, the little blackmailer. She'd dealt with his sobs the night their father had been brought home stiff and dead. She'd helped him with his eagerness to learn French and prove himself as good as she was – which he wasn't.

She shivered in the cold sheets, and told herself this was no way to go on. She'd made her choice and she was glad of it. She was. She definitely was.

★ ★ ★

As they reached the Dubois mansion the following day, after the long drive in the family car with the chauffeur, whose autocratic presence had temporarily silenced Lisa, she told herself nothing could surprise her now. But even the photographs had done nothing to prepare her for the sight of the lovely old house, its mellow stones almost glowing in the late-afternoon sunlight, the turreted roof resembling every fairy tale she had ever been told.

'It's more beautiful than I ever imagined,' she gasped.

M. Dubois smiled at her reaction. 'The photos I showed you probably did not do it justice,' he agreed.

She turned to him indignantly, forgetting that she was speaking to her employer, and a very wealthy one at that. 'No, they didn't! You didn't show me any photos that made it look like a fairy-tale castle! I shall feel like Cinderella!'

'Nonsense, Lisa,' he said with a laugh. 'You will feel like a very valued member of my household, the way that Gerard here does.'

The uniformed chauffeur grunted his agreement, winking briefly at Lisa in the driving mirror, proving to her that he was human after all.

Minutes later Monique Dubois appeared at the door of the house with the two small children holding her hands. Lisa remembered that they had been unwell and were supposedly delicate, but they looked robust enough to her, if a little small for their ages.

'Come and be introduced, Lisa,' Henri Dubois was saying, leaving the chauffeur to bring the luggage out of the car and hand it to a black-clad housekeeper who had appeared from nowhere. Talk about how the other half lives, thought Lisa, committing every detail to memory to write home later to her mother and Wally and Renee. It would be enough to make their eyes pop with envy and disbelief. And with that thought all her nerves vanished.

'Welcome to your new home, Lisa,' Monique said in her careful English. 'The children have been impatient for your arrival, and have insisted that they are the ones to show you your private quarters.'

Lisa eyed them quickly, sensing the excitement beneath the shy smiles. She was well attuned to the devious ways of children, and knew how they tested newcomers. She doubted that it was any different in France from anywhere else. Would there be an apple-pie bed waiting for her? Or some unspeakable object beneath the bed covers destined to make her shriek in terror? Or was she doing them an injustice?

'That will be lovely,' she told them innocently, speaking in French. 'So which of you is Pierre and which one is Danielle?'

She got the expected howl of indignation at their gabbled and furious response, and laughed. 'Why don't you tell me in English so I can understand?'

She caught Monique's small smile of approval. It was perfectly obvious which child was which, but Lisa had immediately put them on the defensive and taken any wind out of their sails.

'I'm Pierre!' the boy shouted.

'Dani,' the girl shouted just as loudly.

'Good. So will you show me where I'm going to live?' she asked.

They looked at her blankly. She had spoken in English again, and she guessed at once that this non-response was their way of showing her that her task was not going to be that easy. She turned to their mother.

'Oh dear, it looks as if someone else will have to show me after all.'

Dani spoke quickly. '*Non*. I show you, mam'selle.'

'*Merci*, Dani. And my name is Lisa.'

She sat up late into the night, writing letters in the ornate bedroom with its heavy furniture and serious whiff of old money, as her Gran Cissie used to call it. She couldn't sleep yet. Her mind was too filled with this strange new life, the grandeur of the mansion and its grounds that seemed to go on for ever; the children who hadn't been

75

overwhelmed by her presence, but, apart from an initial resentment on their part, seemed fairly docile – so far; and the fact that she had done something none of her contemporaries had done. She was here, in France, living a life that promised to be anything but the humdrum factory work that Renee did.

'You wouldn't believe it, Renee,' she wrote to her.

The house is much bigger than I expected, and it's got those funny pointed turrets on the top, like a real castle. My room is as big as our whole house and yours put together, and that's just the bedroom. I also have a sitting room, and they call it my private quarters. It's a scream, isn't it? As soon as I can I'll get some photos. My mother will want some, too, and if I can't do it before I'll get them to bring home at Christmas. I'm to have a whole week off then, and even though it's only two months away I think I might bring home some real French presents. What do you fancy? And don't say a French chap, either. I haven't seen any yet, except the chauffeur, and he's forty if he's a day and lives with his wife in a cottage on the estate. She's the house-keeper. There's also a couple of maids and a cook. Madame Dubois doesn't seem to do anything much, except arrange flowers and do her embroidery and visit her friends a lot. I had a bit of a gossip with one of the maids, who told me all that. None of them speaks much English, so it's a good job I speak French. Well, if I didn't I wouldn't be here at all, would I?

She paused in her letter-writing, chewing the end of her pencil. It was true, and it could still catch her by surprise at times. Never in her wildest dreams had she imagined this day, when she would be sitting up in a four-poster bed in her cotton nightdress, writing about the wonderful new place where she was living, and all because she was good at French. Her dad would probably be turning in his grave if he knew what she was doing, and so would her gran, with her mistrust of all foreigners, no matter where they came from.

But they weren't here, and she was. She finished her letter to Renee and started one to her mum and Wally, being sure to describe the enormous kitchen with the huge range that would make her mum envious, and the lake at the bottom of the sloping gardens that was filled with fish, and the dark forest where the Dubois children had been quick to tell her nobody ever went after dark, as it was filled with demons and ghosts.

Little devils, Lisa thought with a grin. They probably imagined themselves as Hansel and Gretel, and were just trying to scare her. But she didn't scare that easily, and as soon as she was able, she thought, with a delicious shivery excitement, she was going to explore her surroundings and find out for herself.

Five

Lisa prided herself on being adaptable. She expected some suspicion from the servants, but once they found that she could speak their language fluently, and wasn't averse to a bit of below-stairs gossip, she was quickly accepted.

She awoke on her first morning to the sound of her alarm clock. She stretched leisurely, and then felt her heart leap in shock at the pair of green eyes staring down at her from her chest. No ... not green eyes ... but a scaly green body ... and a croak coming from the throat of the monster ... followed by barely suppressed giggles. She lifted her head to see the small bodies of her charges, still in their nightwear, awaiting her reaction. Thankfully, she just managed not to scream.

'What are you doing here?' she snapped. 'Don't you understand what the words "private quarters" mean? And get this thing off my bed at once.'

She spoke in French, not sure how much of an education they had had in English yet, and determined not to show any fear or disgust. Wally had presented her with worse things than a large green frog, and if they thought she was going to panic and forget how to speak in a language they could clearly understand, they could think again.

Pierre looked at her defiantly. 'He's my pet. He's called Georges.'

'Well, take Georges out of my bedroom and put him where he belongs, and we'll see what your parents have to say about this at breakfast.'

She didn't intend to say anything, but the fear that she might would be just as effective, and when nothing was said they would respect her more. It had worked with Wally and it would work with these two.

They scampered away with Pierre hugging Georges to his chest, and only when she was alone did Lisa give herself the luxury of a shudder, and run to bolt her bedroom door, which she must remember in future.

She took a bath in the bathroom attached to her quarters, which was exclusively hers, revelling in such luxury, even though she had only had a bath the night before in the Bristol hotel. It was a bit different from having one once a week in the old tin bath in front of the fire at home!

Perhaps she wouldn't tell her mother too much about such luxury – but she had assured her that the Dubois estate was miles away from Paris, which Jess had implied was a place of debauchery.

Since Lisa had no idea what debauchery her mother had been hinting at, she had let this pass without comment.

Breakfast was noisy, and the children were encouraged to chatter and to voice their opinions. Mealtimes were relaxed, Lisa discovered, but a daytime routine was to be strictly adhered to, and as soon as the meal was over she was to take Pierre and Dani to the schoolroom to begin their lessons.

'Are you a proper teacher?' Dani demanded. 'You don't look old, like the ones we had at school.'

'That's because your parents want me to be your friend as well as your teacher. But I speak French as well as you do, and I understand everything you say to me. So what we'll do today is write down in our exercise books some simple English words for everything we talk about. We will begin with the word friend.'

They stared at her impassively. Clearly, teachers were not meant to be friends, but Lisa ignored their blank faces and ordered them to open the exercise books and to copy the words she wrote on the blackboard.

'You are my *ami*, Pierre, and you, Dani, are my *amie*. *Mes amis*. But in English you are both my friends. There is just one spelling for the word friend, whether a boy or a girl.

This is something that makes English easier for you to learn than for people in my country to learn French.'

She had no formal training in teaching, but the way to get through to these two seemed to come by instinct, and by the end of the morning they had mastered some simple phrases as well as being given a short vocabulary list that she had prepared in advance.

'We will add to the list each day, and when your father comes home from his business in Paris at the end of the week you will surprise him by speaking in English, and show him how clever you have become, my friends.'

At the resentment in Dani's eyes she thought she had gone too far. But then the girl shrugged in a way that only the French could, even those as young as these two.

'If you think so.'

'And we will speak in English as much as possible, *non*?' Lisa persisted.

'*Oui*,' they said in unison, their faces cracking into wide grins.

'I think it's working now, Mum,' she wrote to her mother after a couple of weeks.

At first the children were naughty and I kept finding Georges in unexpected places. They didn't want to accept me, but because Mme Dubois insisted that

I take my meals with them all and become part of their family life they didn't have much choice. I speak French all the time except when I teach the children their lessons, so I'm getting plenty of practice! M. Dubois works at an office in Paris, and the chauffeur drives him there on Monday mornings and fetches him home again on Friday evenings. He stays in an apartment all the week. Gerard, the chauffeur, has offered to take me for a drive to show me around the countryside when I have some time off. It will be very grand to be driven in that big posh car. I like his wife, too, and the maids in the house are very friendly.

She made sure to mention them, in case Jess thought she was being taken advantage of by a chauffeur who had access to a big posh car.

She smiled. Being take advantage of was something she didn't have the faintest idea about, although it seemed from Renee's enthusiastic letters that she and Eddie Bray were becoming very cosy indeed, though there was no hint of Renee being taken advantage of, either, thank goodness.

Apparently, whatever Eddie did was all right with her, even though she never said exactly what that was. But every hint was having the effect of making Lisa feel more restless. She supposed it must be quite nice to have a boy of your own, even if the biology stuff did come into it. But that would only be after you were married, she thought hastily, and there was no lack of people getting married and doing it and having babies, so it couldn't be all that bad or too embarrassing.

M. and Mme Dubois certainly seemed happy to see each other on Friday evenings, and always went to bed early, but she veered away quickly from such thoughts, because she certainly didn't want to think of them doing it. It wasn't right to be thinking of her employers in such a way. But then there was Gerard and his housekeeper wife, who lived in the cottage on the estate, and she wouldn't mind betting some of the saucy maids had boyfriends too.

She went back to her letter-writing before her imagination took her to places that were still as alien as an unknown country, feeling unaccountably cross that all these people seemed to be aware of things that she didn't. And she was supposed to be the clever one with the enquiring mind.

'M. Dubois is getting the photos of the house and children for me to send to you soon,' she wrote to Jess. 'I persuaded Gerard to stand beside the car with his wife Mimi, as well, so you can see how smart he looks in his uniform.'

And it would prevent her mother from thinking there was any funny business going on between Lisa and the chauffeur. Just as if! When she fell in love, it would be with someone nearer her own age, not a middle-aged man with a paunch from drinking too much wine, the way they all did here.

But even if – and when – she did, she still had no intention of marrying anyone until she was at least twenty-five. She hadn't changed her mind about that.

'I know you want to go home to see your family at Christmas, Lisa,' Mme Dubois told her, 'but the children have decided they want you to share in our Christmas celebrations, so we will have a practise Christmas a week early, and then our proper one when the day arrives.'

'Oh, but that's so much trouble!'

'Nonsense. You're almost one of the family now, and my sister and her family will be coming to stay for Christmas and the New Year, so it will give you a chance to meet them. They have all heard about this para-gon we have found for the children.'

Lisa wasn't too sure about being inspected like a trophy, but there was nothing she could do about it – except ask the children during lessons about their relatives.

'We will write some new nouns in our exercise books,' she announced. 'These are aunt and uncle, nephew and niece. I will write the French and English words on the blackboard as usual, and you will copy them, and then we will think of some sentences about them all. So, first of all, tell me the names of the relatives who will be coming to stay here at Christmas.'

There would be Aunt Hortense, Uncle Jaime and two boys, Antoine and Alain. No girls. And the ages of the nephews?

'Antoine is old,' Pierre was dismissive of his cousin. 'Older than you, I bet.'

'He's eighteen,' Dani said importantly. 'I'm going to marry him when I grow up. Alain's fourteen and he never talks much.'

'I like him,' Pierre said. 'He tickles Georges and makes him croak.'

So there were two cousins, Antoine and Alain, and they would be arriving a couple of weeks before Christmas and staying for the New Year, so they would still be here when she got back from England. Lisa felt no compunction at pumping these two about their cousins, because she had every intention of making Renee green with envy about meeting a dashing young French chap called Antoine, and by the time she went home she would be able to describe him properly.

A shiver of excitement ran through her veins. There had been times when she had wondered vaguely if she was completely normal, because she didn't have the same sort of urges, as Renee brazenly called them, as her friend. But the thought of meeting this older cousin was changing all that, and she wasted no time in asking Pierre and Dani if they had any photos so she would know what they looked like.

'You musn't like Antoine too much, because he's going to marry me,' Dani said at once, with an instinctive suspicion of Lisa's motives.

'Good Lord, I only want to know what they look like, that's all. I'm not thinking of marrying anyone for years and years.'

'That's all right then.'

She glared at Lisa, and there was such a glint of jealousy in her eyes that Lisa was shocked. She was an eight-year-old child, but a woman's emotions were already brimming inside her. Lisa didn't believe Antoine was going to be such a charmer, anyway, even if he did seem so godlike to Dani Dubois. That evening she partially revised her opinion when Monique produced the family photograph albums.

'Hortense is my sister,' she was told, 'and the boys are her pride and joy. They live near Biarritz, so they always spend a long visit here at Christmas and New Year. Antoine is shortly to join my husband's firm in Paris, so we'll be seeing more of him. He'll enjoy some home comforts when he's away from his own family.'

Lisa stared at the photo of the handsome young man standing with his arm draped around his younger brother's shoulders, He was dark, with the swarthy looks of Continental people well used to the strong sunlight of southern France, and his eyes were like coals in his classically sculpted face. Lisa thought she had never seen anyone who resembled a film star more.

'Papa will bring him home especially to see me, won't he?' Dani said importantly, at which her mother laughed and ruffled her curly hair.

'Oh, you and everyone else, *ma chérie*. This young lady has got what you English call a crush on her cousin, Lisa,' Monique teased.

Lisa could hardly credit what happened next. Apart from a few spats between them, the children had shown none of the temper tantrums she had expected. Not until that moment, when Dani obviously couldn't bear to be teased on so sensitive a subject as young love.

One minute she was gazing rapturously at Antoine's photo, and the next her face was scarlet with rage as she pummelled her mother's chest, her fists clenched as Monique laughingly tried to ward off the blows. Then, to Lisa's horror, Pierre joined in by bellowing loudly, stamping his feet and finally wetting himself.

'*Oh la la, mon pauvre,*' Monique said in

distress. 'I thought we had finished with all that!'

She looked so helpless that Lisa decided to take charge. She had already realized that Monique Dubois was not comfortable with the messier side of children, and one of the maids had confided that she had vowed never to have any more. It was only for Henri's sake that she had succumbed a second time, to give him a son.

What would have happened, wondered Lisa, as she whisked a protesting and kicking Pierre away to the nursery to clean him up, if Monique had continued to have daughters? Would the dashing Monsieur Henri have insisted that she did her wifely bedroom duty until the son and heir came along? Was that what proud and virile men did?

She had never thought about it before, nor that men might put such store by having a son – unless they were disgustingly rich and had acres of property for a son to inherit. Leaving it all to a daughter would mean that when she married another man's son would share it, and any Frenchman – or Englishman, come to that – would have his masculine pride sorely tested. But since he would be dead by that time it wouldn't matter, Lisa thought cheerfully, pulling off Pierre's damp little knickers.

'I don't like you,' he scowled, his lower lip

jutting out.

'I don't like you right now. Do you know how to say that in English?'

'Don't want to! Don't care!' he shouted.

'I think your Papa will care if he knows how hard you kicked me. Look at the bruise on my leg. Did you ever see such a big one?'

His attention was diverted as she flexed her leg, where the ugly bruise on her shin was already turning purple.

'It's a beauty, isn't it?' she went on, as if it were a trophy. 'I think we should count how many days it takes to disappear, and you can be the clever one by doing the counting in English. Yes?'

He was silent while she continued cleaning him up and putting him into clean clothes. He stared at her unblinkingly, and she stared right back.

'I like you a *bit*,' he said finally.

The le Blanc family from Biarritz were due to arrive two weeks before Christmas, and Lisa would be going home a week later. By now the children were insisting that the Christmas trimmings were all put up before their cousins arrived, and, indulgent as always, the parents and servants brought down boxes of trimmings and baubles from the attic. Excitement rippled through the house, and the children were as controlled as they could be, considering.

How different it was all going to be here from her own modest Christmas at home. There was never much money to spare on frivolous things, and her dad had always called it wasteful to put up trimmings. It was Cissie who had insisted on them singing carols on Christmas Eve, then going to church on Christmas morning, and cooking a small chicken to celebrate Christ's birth.

Here the decorations were lavish, and late one afternoon an enormous fir tree was brought in from their own forest by Henri and Gerard, and placed in a huge earth-filled pot in one corner of the drawing room, ready to be adorned with silver cones and baubles and draped in tinsel. As daylight faded, massed candles were lit, throwing a soft rosy glow over it all and turning the room into a vibrant, living thing. Everyone shared in decorating the tree: the chauffeur and his wife, Monique's personal maid, the kitchen maids and the cook, and all were given a glass of mulled wine and hot fruit pies, even though it was nowhere near Christmas yet.

Lisa thought she had never seen anything so enchanting. If it hadn't been for the need to be with her own family, she would have been tempted to ask if she could stay. If this was a sample of what Christmas was really going to be like, with the addition of the relatives as well...

They arrived in a huge car driven by the man that Lisa was instructed to call Uncle Jaime, at which the large man with the bristly moustache seemed perfectly happy. His wife, Hortense, was just as large and jolly, and such a contrast to the more delicate Monique that it was hard to believe they were sisters.

Then there were the boys. Alain's ambition was to fly aeroplanes, which his parents found hilarious, considering he had a fear of heights. Antoine's favourite pastime was climbing in the Pyrenees, and he was undoubtedly what those with a less generous opinion would call a playboy; he was as beautiful in real life as in his photographs. He wasted no time in picking up a besotted Danielle and swinging her around until she screamed with delight.

'Leave the child alone, Antoine,' his mother said laughingly. 'You'll make her sick at this rate.'

'Perhaps the beautiful young English lady would like me to swing her around instead,' he said daringly, his eyes having roamed expertly over Lisa.

'I would not!' she said smartly.

'Lisa doesn't like boys,' Dani chanted. 'She's not going to get married for years and years and years.'

Lisa felt all eyes turn to her. When she had casually said as much to Dani, It hadn't been meant to be remembered, nor said in that faintly vicious little manner, nor brought out in company as if she was a freak. Especially as Antoine was grinning at her now as if he could be the one to change the fact that she supposedly didn't like boys. It wasn't true. She loved her brother, and she wasn't averse to any boys she had known – but she hadn't met one yet who could make her heart spin the way the storybooks told you it would when you met 'the One'. And Antoine wasn't doing that – only with annoyance.

Instead of the expected objection to bedtime that evening, Dani glanced at Lisa, then at her father.

'Of course, Papa,' she said, as sweet as sugar. 'As long as Lisa takes us up and tells us a bedtime story.'

She was so transparent. Normally she refused to let Lisa near the bedroom she and Pierre shared, but that was until she had the chance to keep the interloper away from her beloved Antoine. It made Lisa smile, but it also made her uneasy. Could a child of eight really know the sensations of falling in love? While she, at sixteen, obviously did not!

But she did as she was bidden and took both children upstairs when the time came, and read them their bedtime story, conscious all the while of Dani's small triumph, and of Pierre already snuffling noisily as he fell asleep.

'Goodnight then, Dani,' she said at last.

' 'Night,' the girl said, and turned her back on her.

She was on the landing at the top of the staircase when she heard her name mentioned. From this angle no one could see her, and Hortense was speaking firmly. Her accent was different from the others, but Lisa could follow it easily.

'The girl is young and pretty and she speaks excellent French, but is she suitable? She is hardly a qualified teacher, and the children will need more education than simply to learn English and do a few sums.'

Monique replied. 'You don't realize how ill the children have been, Hortense. There is time enough for more formal education.'

'But we should think about it, *cherie*,' her husband said slowly. 'They are thriving now, and we shouldn't protect them too much. Perhaps we should think of Lisa as more of an au pair as well as having her continue to teach them English, but also hire a qualified person to instruct the children until they go to boarding school.'

'It sounds like a good compromise, Henri,' his brother-in-law said. 'I'm sure you don't want to get rid of the girl since the children have taken to her so well.'

Lisa's heart was beating painfully fast. She had been here for several months now, and she had quickly fallen in love with the house

94

and the countryside, and the French way of life – and the children, too, when they gave her the chance to show affection. She didn't want to be dismissed, or to make people think she had failed ... but as the discussion went on in the same vein, she breathed a little more easily.

She didn't hear the quiet footsteps on the stairs until the faint cough alerted her to the fact that someone was aware of her presence. She stood up awkwardly from her crouching position, embarrassed and tongue-tied.

'Is it one of your quaint English sayings that eavesdroppers never hear good of themselves, mademoiselle?' Antoine whispered, in the tones of a conspirator.

'I'm sorry,' she said, scrambling to her feet, her face burning.

'Don't be embarrassed,' he said, smiling. 'Be happy that you will be invited to stay, and that we will get to know one another.'

So he had heard the discussion as well.

'How can that be when you live so far away?' she muttered.

'Ah, but when I join my uncle's firm in Paris in the spring, I shall come here for the weekends, except when my parents say they cannot possibly do without me, and insist that I go home to visit them.'

Charm oozed out of him and Lisa wasn't sure whether she liked it or not. He was so suave and smooth. He was unlike anyone she had ever met, and to stop her topsy-turvy feelings she made a mental note to relate this weird conversation at the top of the stairs to Renee in her next letter home.

'I think you're being called,' she said in a strangled voice, as his brother's voice came from somewhere below.

'And you, too, will be required. It's a family tradition that we play charades in the evening, so you and I must be on the same team, I think.'

He held out his hand, and, without thinking, Lisa took it, and was drawn a little closer to him. She felt a tingle run through her, like a small shock. It wasn't an unpleasant feeling, more of a little shock of pleasure at the warmth and pressure of his touch. It made her breathless, as if she had been running hard.

Six

They assured her that her salary would remain as before. But now that the children's health and confidence were restored it was felt that they should be prepared for boarding school and experience schoolroom discipline. So a new tutor would come to the house daily, but Lisa would become the children's au pair.

She had told Renee about Antoine le Blanc and Renee's replies had become all twittery, as if she was already dreaming of a double wedding.

'Don't be daft!' Lisa wrote back at once. 'Remember I'm not getting married until I'm at least twenty-five, and certainly not to a good-looking French chap who thinks he's God's gift to women!'

Although she'd had an unguarded moment of twitteriness herself when Antoine had grabbed her beneath the mistletoe, and she'd realized with another little shock that it was the first time she had been kissed by a male person, apart from her father and Wally, who didn't count.

Oh, there was a lot to tell Renee when she

got home – and a few things she wasn't about to tell anyone!

When it was time to leave, it was with mixed feelings. She longed to see Jess and Wally again, and she was taking them crystallized fruits and bon-bons and other sweetmeats. There was also a silk scarf from this generous family, which was sure to make Jess go red with embarrassment.

But as well as her eagerness to be home there was a real pang at leaving this warm and happy household for the long, cold journey back to England. She would be travelling alone, once Gerard had driven her to Calais for the ferry to Dover. As she left the house she saw Dani entwine herself around Antoine's legs as he scooped her up, and the girl waved triumphantly to the departing limousine, her other arm hugging her cousin's neck.

'Little minx,' Lisa murmured – but not quietly enough for Gerard to miss it.

He smiled. 'The little one, she is enamoured of her handsome cousin, *non*?'

'Definitely *oui*, Gerard,' she replied with a grin.

'And she plays with his affections, I think?'

Lisa laughed, knowing he was teasing in his good-natured way. She leant back in the car, breathing in the sensual smell of the luxurious leather upholstery, and began to feel more relaxed.

'Oh yes, as only a small determined French mam'selle can!'

'Ah yes. The French learn quickly of the ways of *l'amour*; more quickly than you English. I'm told it is because the cold, damp climate cools the affections.'

She was laughing freely now. 'What rot! Our Queen Victoria was so in love with her Prince Albert that she mourned him for fifty years after his death! And since they had nine children I hardly think there was any lack of *l'amour* between them!'

She hadn't meant to be so frank, but although they had no children of their own Gerard and Mimi were the sort of easy-going parental figures who invited confidences. He was the kind of father Lisa would have loved – if such a thought hadn't been disloyal to Ron, she thought hastily.

'Then I hope you too will find such a love, Lisa,' Gerard said softly.

As if to underline that she hadn't found it yet ... which she knew very well, even if she did find Antoine charming. But that wasn't love.

'There's plenty of time for all that,' she said easily. 'My best friend will walk down the aisle long before I do.'

'Then perhaps you are more discerning than she is.'

The car took them smoothly through the

wintry French landscape, which grew more bare as they neared Calais. Gerard avoided Paris, saying the city traffic would delay their arrival at the port, but Lisa vowed she would go there one day and partake of the fleshpots – even if she had no idea what they were! It just sounded so deliciously wicked, but if the respectable M. Dubois worked there, it couldn't be too bad.

After a seemingly endless journey, she finally arrived home. She almost fell inside the house, but the excitement of being there soon swept all the exhaustion away. There was a small welcoming committee waiting to greet her: her mother and Wally, and Renee, too.

'Oh, it's so good to see you all!' she said, when they had done their hugs and kisses. 'But if I don't get these shoes off soon I shall never be able to walk again.'

'What have you brought me, our Lisa?' Wally yelled predictably.

'What have you done to your hair? It makes you look far too old,' Jess said, looking disapprovingly at her sophisticated daughter as if she were some alien being.

'Marie did it for me. She's madame's personal maid. Don't you like it?'

Her lustrous hair had been twisted into a thick plait and then caught up at the back with a ribbon bow. Marie had assured her it was the last word in Parisienne chic.

'You don't look so much like our Lisa now,' Wally said with a scowl.

'And you'll not find any personal maids to do your hair here,' Jess said tartly. 'Stuff and nonsense, I call it, and vanity's the work of the devil.'

'Oh, Mum, it's only a hairstyle! But what's that lovely smell coming from the kitchen? I can't tell you how much I've missed your cooking.'

Jess looked mollified. 'I knew you'd want something warming after all that French muck you've been eating.'

Wally sidled nearer. 'Have you eaten frogs' legs yet, our Lisa?'

'No, and you wouldn't want me eating Georges, would you?'

While she was explaining again who and what Georges was, she felt an odd sense of detachment. She had fully expected this homecoming to be wonderful, but these first tense minutes had felt as prickly as a pincushion.

Even Renee seemed on edge, but that was probably because she was bursting to tell her about her latest antics with farmer Eddie. They didn't get the chance until later, when they were stuffed with rabbit stew and perched on the narrow bed in Wally's old bedroom, which was now for Lisa's visits.

'So how are things going with the great

romance?' Lisa asked.

Renee giggled. 'He's giving me a ring for Christmas.'

'What? Your mother will never agree to you getting engaged when you're only sixteen!'

Not even Renee's mother, who didn't always notice where her daughter was, or what she was doing, or whom she was doing it with...

'It's not an engagement ring. He won it at the funfair. The stone looks like a real diamond, mind, but I shall only wear it on my engagement finger when we're alone.'

She carried on gabbling about this ring that had been won at a funfair that didn't have a real diamond, and had probably been won for a tanner.

'You mean in case your finger turns green! You're potty, Renee.'

'No, I'm not. You're just jealous because me and Eddie are getting married in a few years' time, and you've only got a stupid French chap with a daft name.'

She was fuming now, her face an angry red, and Lisa stopped taking clothes out of her small suitcase and folded her arms instead.

'Well, if we're going to argue all the time I'm here, I shall wish I'd never come home at all. Antoine's name isn't daft at all, and he's not my chap either!'

They glared at one another, then burst out

laughing simultaneously.

'Everything's back to normal then,' Renee choked. 'But what's he really like? Do you have a big crush on him?'

'Not even a little one,' Lisa said with a grin. 'He's all right, and he kissed me once – no, twice, because that's the way they do it – a kiss on each cheek. Dani has the real crush on him.'

'What, the devil-child?'

'She's not a devil-child. They're both a handful at times, but I won't be in sole charge of them any more. They're to have a proper teacher and I'll be a sort of nanny, I suppose, but I'll still teach them English.'

'So why don't you come home and get a proper job?'

'It is a proper job. All rich French families have an au pair for their children. That's what it's called.'

'Your mother always said you were going to be nothing but a glorified maid.'

'My mother doesn't need to know then, does she?'

Neither of them took any notice of the creaks on the landing outside the bedroom door, and just put them down to the wind howling around the house.

Next morning Jess dumped the big brown teapot on the table with a bang, which heralded problems ahead. The way she doled out porridge for breakfast added to the sense of impending trouble. And this was Christmas...

'What's all this about you not being a proper teacher for those French kids?'

As Wally choked over his porridge, Lisa guessed that the creaks on the landing last night had been due to that little sneak and not the high winds that were still bending trees and rocking fences. She glared at him.

'I *am* a proper teacher, but the children need more education than I can give them, so I shall just be teaching them English and social skills.'

'And what are they when they're at home?' Jess snapped.

'Things our Wally could do with learning! Like not listening at keyholes to other people's conversations, and not putting your elbows on the table. And especially minding your own *business*!'

'I didn't mean nothing,' Wally muttered belligerently.

'Of course he didn't. You've got too big for your boots since you started working for those French people, Lisa, just as I thought you would.'

Lisa felt her stomach churn. She was only sixteen, and if her mother demanded that she come home she would have no option.

'Mum, this is a good job, and I'm living with a respectable family. The children are used to me now, and I would hate to give it all up. They also pay me well, and I was going to give you a surprise on Christmas Day, but I think I'll give it to you now.'

She scrambled away from the table and went flying upstairs. Minutes later she was back, handing Jess an envelope with shaking fingers. Inside was a Christmas card for Jess and Wally, and also what seemed like a huge amount of money.

As she looked at it, Jess's face went crimson, and Wally whistled through the gap in his teeth.

'Cripes, our Lisa, did you rob a bank?' Wally gasped.

'Language, Wally,' Jess said automatically, because she simply didn't know what else to say.

'It's for you both, Mum, and I'll be sending you more from time to time. For a start, why don't me and Wally go and get a tree from the Bray farm and then buy some trimmings to brighten up the house for Christmas?'

She would never say so, but the contrast between the sparseness here and the warm and inviting house she had left in France was startling and depressing. There was a complete lack of Christmas ornaments, since Ron had always disapproved of such wastefulness. But her dad was no longer here to object.

'Yes!' Wally shouted, full of excitement

now. 'Can we, Mum?'

With both of them clamouring, and the unexpected amount of money in her hand, Jess no longer had the heart to argue.

'And you got all this money from teaching French children to speak English?'

'That's right. All that grammar school learning wasn't wasted after all, was it?'

Jess knew when she was beaten, and by the end of the day the house was looking bright and cheerful with a small decorated tree in the living room and the coloured paper-chains she and Wally had painstakingly made all afternoon. It was nothing like the appearance of the Dubois house, but a lot more festive than when she had arrived, Lisa thought with satisfaction.

She was also determined that as well as the goose that Jess would roast alongside the parsnips and potatoes for their Christmas dinner, her mother would have a few extras, like a bowl of nuts, a box of dates and some Christmas oranges. Her parents had scrimped all their lives, and had little to show for it. As a final touch, Lisa bought a glowing red plant for the middle of the table, the kind that Ron had always thought such an extravagance.

'I don't think I ever had flowers bought for me before, except for my wedding bouquet,' Jess told her daughter.

Lisa gave her a quick hug. 'Then it's time

you did. Flowers shouldn't only be for weddings and funerals. They should also be to tell people you love them.'

Jess turned away, flustered at such a show of affection. It was what came from being among those demonstrative French folk, she thought darkly, but she was touched by the way Lisa was trying to please her, and she wouldn't deflate her by telling her so.

'It's been a good Christmas,' Lisa told Renee, the night before she was due to leave. 'I wish you could come and see how the other half lives, though.'

'I can't see me ever going to France. Not unless Eddie fancies taking me there sometime, and pigs would fly before he'd leave the farm.'

'Well, I'm quite glad to be going back now that Mum's started nagging again. She still thinks I'm going to be a glorified maid, even though I keep telling her it's nothing like that.'

'There's nothing new in that, is there? But maybe you really want to go back because you've fallen for this Antoine chap.'

Lisa shook her head vigorously. 'I told you I haven't. I shan't even see him very often from now on, so what would be the point?'

Her reasoning had always been that if something wasn't very likely to happen there was no use in fretting over it. You might as well forget it. Even falling in love.

But when she had reversed the chilly train journeys to reach Dover, and then the ferry trip across a choppy English Channel that had her stomach heaving, her heart gave a contradictory jolt to find Antoine waiting in the limousine with Gerard.

'I didn't expect a welcoming committee!' she said, flustered.

It was a bitterly cold evening and the streets were sparkling with frost, but inside the car it was warm and cosy, and it felt like heaven after the arduous hours before.

'We thought you would appreciate the company,' Antoine told her. 'If it hadn't been so late, Dani would have come, too, but her father put his foot down.'

'I'm not surprised!' Lisa said, knowing that it wouldn't be for her company Dani had wanted the ride. A tantrum was probably on the cards for tomorrow, then.

It was already dark, and seated in the back of the car alongside Antoine, Lisa felt a faint sense of alarm. She was properly chaperoned by the fatherly Gerard in the driving seat, but there was still a feeling of intimacy in the back that didn't make her feel altogether comfortable.

The French would call it her stuffy Englishness, she thought in annoyance. And Jess would call it taking sensible precautions ... but then Jess would probably be scandalized at the thought of her taking a long night-time drive in the company of a virile young man like Antoine. Which only had the effect of making her feel almost reckless. Almost.

Antoine said, 'We have so little time to get to know one another properly before my family departs next week, so I couldn't miss this opportunity, *chérie.*'

'There's nothing to know about me,' Lisa said with a nervous little laugh. 'I have a mother and a brother, same as you, and my father died some years ago. We live in a small village where everyone knows everyone else. I've got a best friend called Renee who lives in the house opposite mine, and that's it.'

Antoine laughed. 'You are a delightful person, Lisa. You dress so modestly and you speak my language so beautifully that one could easily mistake you for a French-woman, especially with that glorious hair.'

She almost snapped that she dressed modestly because she had never had much money to spend on clothes! As for speaking fluent French, she slipped so easily from one language to another when required that she hardly realized she was doing it.

Her heart lurched as Antoine's fingers curled around hers before she had the chance to pull her hand away. Once inside the warmth of the car she had removed her gloves, and the contact was at once exciting and scary. She was such an *idiot*, she found herself thinking furiously. It was just holding hands, and far less than whatever Renee and her hot-blooded Eddie got up to in the woods. At her small intake of breath, Antoine leant towards her. She could feel his breath on her cheek.

'Do I alarm you, *ma petite*? I assure you there is no need. I just want to be your friend – unless you say otherwise. And when I return to Biarritz I would be very happy if you would write as many letters to me as you write to your friend at home.'

'How do you know about that!' she snapped, snatching her hand away from his.

He laughed. 'The little ones are far from discreet, Lisa. They tell me lots of things about their lovely English au pair, even about the time Pierre placed his precious Georges in your bed to try to frighten you. If I had been Georges, I promise I would not have frightened you!'

When they had entered the car she hadn't noticed the smooth way he had slid across the glass partition separating them from the driver, but she noticed it now, and she quickly pulled the panel back, leaning forward to speak to Gerard.

'Do you mind if we leave this open, Gerard? I find the car a little stuffy.'

'Of course,' he answered.

'So tell me about yourself,' she said coolly to Antoine. 'All I know is that you enjoy

110

mountain-climbing and you intend to work with your uncle in Paris soon.'

He leant back, apparently giving up the chase, but she could sense his smile when he answered.

'There's nothing else to know. I am what you see, as transparent as the ocean.'

'Or as deep,' she retorted.

The family seemed overjoyed to see her back. Pierre threw his arms around her neck and kissed her sloppily, and even Dani unbent enough to say she had missed her.

'Not too much,' she added. 'Just a bit.'

Their new tutor was due to arrive in two weeks' time. By then the Christmas decorations had been taken down with as great a flourish as they had been put up, and before the Biarritz family went home Antoine reminded Lisa of her promise to write to him.

'I don't remember promising any such thing. I said I *might*.'

Privately, she was still smarting that Dani had told him so much about her. They were things he had no right to know, such as the fact that she had never had a young man and wasn't looking for one. Which was no doubt a piece of information that was an incentive to Antoine le Blanc to make a conquest of his own. The puritan English girl who was still a virgin. As of *course* she was, Lisa thought crossly, blushing at her own thoughts. Only fast girls gave in to persuasive young men with dark eyes and a wickedly handsome smile.

'But you will. Won't you?' he said, smiling at the door of his family's car, as if he could see right into her thoughts. 'Write to me, I mean.'

'You'll have to wait and see, won't you?' she muttered, wishing he would go before anyone overheard this embarrassing conversation.

She was the hired help, for goodness sake, and she was perfectly sure that these old French families, who were practically royalty compared with her own, wouldn't welcome any romantic liaison between them.

She shivered, pulling her coat around her more tightly as everyone gathered to wish them well on their journey home. It was very cold standing outside the house with the rest of the family, with much chaffing and laughter, and there was more than a hint of snow in the air. The mountains where Antoine would soon be climbing would be full of it, and she admired his adventurous spirit, if nothing else.

She caught sight of his face inside the car window as the car began to move, the wheels crunching on the gravel, and felt an odd little pang of regret. She had thought he was playing games with her, but perhaps her reaction had been too much like that of a Victorian maiden, and perhaps she hadn't given him credit for having genuine feelings for her.

As if to underline her thoughts, he suddenly blew her a kiss as the car swung away. Her face flamed, even though Dani leapt up and down, swearing loudly that the kiss had been meant for her. But they both knew that it had not.

Seven

They corresponded occasionally at first, and then more regularly. In the spring he returned to begin his new appointment with his uncle in the city. Each weekend when they came home from Paris Lisa wondered if his brashness really covered shyness, because the only time he seemed perfectly natural was when he spoke of his beloved mountains.

He talked about them as lovingly as if he spoke about a woman, his voice caressing and sensual. Any woman who loved him could be jealous of those mountains and could never hope to compete – and Lisa didn't want to. But she loved listening to him speak about them, especially when he was his natural self and not trying to impress. Maybe that was the way all young men behaved, but she certainly liked him more when he wasn't trying to be the man-about-town.

Dani had got over her crush on her cousin with fickle speed. When you were eight years old you thrived on being pampered and petted, but she was no longer getting the same teasing attention from Antoine the businessman. She frequently told Lisa that he was dull now, and she wasn't going to marry him after all.

'I can't tell you how relieved I am about that!' Antoine told Lisa in the garden on a balmy September evening.

'Really? I thought you enjoyed being the object of such adoration.'

He laughed back, but his eyes were serious. 'It was not always easy to visit my uncle's house and find a small child desperate to grow up so that I could marry her. I had no such intentions, of course, and especially not now.'

'Oh?' Lisa said, her heartbeat quickening. 'Why especially not now?'

She knew she was being provocative, but it was only a mild flirtation as far as she was concerned. She didn't love him, but at eighteen years old the feelings inside her were no longer childlike. They stopped walking, shielded from the house by shrubbery fragrant with the heady scent of rhododendrons, and he pulled her into his arms and tipped up her chin with one finger so that she looked directly into those fascinating dark eyes.

'Oh, I think you know,' he said softly, 'but if my feelings aren't plain enough then right at this moment I would dearly like to kiss you.'

'You never asked my permission before,' she teased him, remembering the mistletoe, and seconds later she was swept into his embrace. His kiss was sweet and heady on her lips and, despite herself, she wondered if this truly was love.

'Don't read anything into it, Renee, because it's never likely to come to anything,' she confided in her next letter to her friend. 'If a person can fall *in* love, it stands to reason they can fall *out* of love just as quickly,' she continued with her usual pinpoint analysis. 'Anyway, you have no idea how proud these old French families are. However much his mother likes me, she'd never approve of her son marrying a penniless English girl!'

Lisa didn't want to marry him, anyway. She might be in love – sort of – and there might be stars in her eyes, but her feet were still firmly on the ground, and she was sure that for all his compliments and flattery she wasn't the only girl on Antoine's horizon. One of the kitchen maids had wasted no time in telling her so.

'Oh, the dashing M. Antoine has many *amours*,' the girl giggled. 'He has – how do you say it – the big urges and the roving eyes. His mama intends him to marry well, so enjoy the flirtation while it lasts, *non*?'

So she was right. Antoine was a playboy, if a very charming one, and working in Paris must give him opportunities that were lacking in rural areas.

But there was a serious side to him, too, and a year after starting his job in Paris he had an apartment of his own, and rarely came to visit. On one of those weekends that he did, Henri Dubois also brought home a German acquaintance and his wife, and they discovered that the English au pair could converse with them in their own language more fluently than their hosts.

'You're a marvel,' Antoine told her later. 'Aunt Monique was out of her depth with those people. Don't you think you should leave the infant teaching to their tutor and do something useful with your life?'

'The infants, as you call them, are growing up fast. So what do you suggest for me, oh wise one?' she mocked, still exhilarated to have been able to chat so effortlessly with the German couple in their own language.

'Something to tax your brain, such as working as an interpreter or book translator or archivist, or anything you choose. There's a big world beyond this household, Lisa, and if you worked in Paris we could see one another more often.'

'Wouldn't that interfere with your other activities?' she asked, still teasing.

'Has my uncle said something to you?'

'About what?'

'Veronique,' he said abruptly after a brief hesitation.

'Why would your uncle confide in me about any of your friends? I'm only the au pair – the hired help.'

'You should not demean yourself in that way,' Antoine said almost angrily. 'You are a sensitive and beautiful young woman with a unique talent.'

'So who is Veronique?' she demanded, brushing aside everything else.

'The young lady my parents have chosen for me.'

He sounded so pompously Victorian at that moment that Lisa was tempted to laugh until she saw how serious he was. But the little devil inside her couldn't resist teasing him further. She pursed her lips and her eyes flashed.

'I see. So you have been playing with my affections all this time, while you are practically engaged to someone else. You have been taking advantage of me, a stranger in your country and a servant in your uncle's house—'

'*Mon Dieu*, I have done no such thing. Of course I do not think of you as a servant, and never have—'

He realized that she was laughing at him and relaxed.

'So you're teasing me! I thought you were about to denounce me.'

118

'I would never do that, but others might, Antoine. You should be more cautious with your flirting if you have true feelings for this Veronique.'

'Ah, but do I? This is the question I constantly ask myself.'

'And only you can answer it,' Lisa retorted, relieved to feel that she was becoming more of a confidante than a contender for a bride.

It was exactly as she had said to Renee. Falling in love was easy, and so was falling out – once you realized you hadn't fallen for the right man.

'Antoine, we should rejoin the others soon. They'll wonder what we find to talk about all this time. But first, tell me about Veronique.'

Changes in life could sometimes arrive so gradually that you never saw them coming. Three years after coming to France, the Dubois children were at boarding school and Lisa was no longer needed. Her vague plan was to apply to be a teacher in a nearby infant school, and Mme Dubois assured her she could still live with them. Alternatively, she could go to Paris to work. Antoine had become engaged to Veronique, but he had opened her eyes to the possibilities available to her, and she would be foolish not to make full use of her capabilities. But how?

'You have a telephone call, Lisa,' the housekeeper told her one evening.

'Thank you, Mimi,' she said, her heart giving a little leap as always. It might be her brother using the telephone at the news-paper office where he worked now, bragging about his adolescent doings – or, more soberly, it might be news about her mother, who was no longer in the best of health.

'This is Lisa Newman,' she said into the telephone.

The voice at the other end replied in German. She switched at once from her auto-matic French response to an appropriate reply.

'Good evening, Herr Gott.' Her photo-graphic mind registered an instant image of the German couple who had visited the house months ago.

'Good evening to you, my dear. I am calling with a proposition for you, and let me assure you that I have Henri's full approval of my offer.'

Lisa's mind whirled as he rattled on in his quick-fire German manner. She could easily understand the words, but they took her breath away. He manufactured motor cars, many for export, and he was offering her an interpreter's post in a town in Germany that she had never heard of. It was a fantastic opportunity.

But she hadn't been home for a few months now, and to go to Germany would take her further away from everything she knew. The Dubois household was familiar territory to her now, and even Paris, where she had been on a number of occasions, was no longer an unknown quantity. Although, even though she described it all so accurately from her photographic memory, her mother would never understand the attraction of sitting outside on the street in little cafés and watching the world go by, considering it time-wasting frivolity.

For some reason, thoughts of her mother whirled around in Lisa's mind all the time she was listening to Herr Gott, and the *frisson* of anxiety that swept through her mind was like the jolt of a heartbeat.

'Herr Gott, it is very kind of you to think of me,' she said rapidly, 'but I must have time to consider it, and to think seriously about whether I wish to stay in Europe. My mother is getting older...'

'Of course, and I fully understand. But if you find yourself unable to accept there might be another opening for you in Paris. I have offices all over Europe and you would be a great asset with your linguistic skills. This post is not available yet, and the new and expanded office will not be in operation for some time. If you might be interested when the time comes then I can think of no one better suited.'

So if she had time to think about it – and, especially if the new office was to be in Paris,

121

she had a breathing space.

'I will certainly consider it,' she said.

'Then I will follow up this telephone conversation with a formal letter inviting you to be part of my company when the time is appropriate, and you will reply in a similar manner, if you please.'

'Of course.'

Lisa realized how the tenor of the conversation had subtly changed. It was strange how you could almost tell what a person was thinking by the tone of a voice over a telephone. It wasn't simply the words, said in that so-correct German manner, it was the intonation in the voice as well.

She went straight to see Monique, who was busy with her ornate and elaborate flower arrangements in the drawing room. The heady scent of lilies and the exotic hot-house plants Monique grew in her conservatory filled Lisa's nostrils, and was so strong it made her senses swim for a moment. Monique adored flowers to the extent that sometimes the whole house smelled positively funereal.

'I have just had a telephone conversation with Herr Gott,' she said abruptly.

'Ah. I know of this, of course. So you have come to tell me the time has come for our parting, I suspect?' Monique said, her voice regretful.

'Well, not yet. I wouldn't want to work in

122

Germany in any case. The Paris position isn't open yet, and, although it sounds interesting, I'm not sure.'

She was less than her usual confident self. But she didn't *feel* confident. She wasn't sure she was ready to move even further away from her roots, away from everything that was unaccountably calling her back. She had felt this way ever since thoughts of her mother had skidded around her brain.

'Come and sit down, Lisa,' Monique said. 'You look troubled, *chérie*.'

They sat together on one of the elegant sofas, and Lisa thought how kind this French woman was to have taken her in all that time ago, and to treat her almost as a grown-up daughter. But Lisa wasn't her daughter. She had a mother and a brother of her own, and a home that was essentially English with all that that stood for, and the longing to see it at that moment was burning in her brain.

'Before I decide anything, I think I have to go home and see what my mother has to say about all this.'

But she knew what Jess would say. There were still many people in their village – and the whole of England – who would not think kindly about an English girl working for a German company. Even now, fifteen years after the end of that terrible war, for some people the memories were still raw and vivid, and many local people had lost husbands and sons. Renee's father had been one of them.

As for what the staunch Unionist and patriot Ron Newman would have said about his daughter working for the so-called enemy ... Lisa shivered.

'Of course you must consult your mother,' Monique said. 'But remember that although we would be sad to lose you, you are always welcome here.'

'Thank you. But I'm still not sure this is the right thing to do,' she went on delicately. 'Old memories – you know.'

'In France we, too, have bad memories, but we can't live in the past. Enemies can become friends, Lisa.'

Lisa blushed furiously. These people had suffered, too; their cherished capital had been invaded and violated, but they were not slow in holding out the hand of friendship to past enemies, and she felt she was being mildly chastised.

'Take your time to think about it,' Monique went on. 'You will be going home for Christmas soon; tell us of your decision when you return.'

'Thank you. When I do, I will also take up the offer to work at the infant school in the new year for the time being, anyway, as I planned.'

She was half furious with herself for

sounding so feeble, even using the idea of working in an infant school as a kind of safety-net while she considered the wider world on offer. She was normally strong-minded, knowing exactly what she wanted to do, but Herr Gott's offer had thrown a curve into her straightforward planning – which proved that you could never really plan any-thing. Fate had a habit of intervening and upsetting the best-laid plans.

A week later she was on the boat back to England, having been taken to Calais as usual by Gerard. She could get used to being driven about in a limousine, she thought fleetingly. It was a bit different from cycling around Mallory on her old bicycle at home.

It was a chilly December morning. The wind was stripping the leaves from the trees and whipping them over the roads in a frenzy, and the English Channel looked de-cidedly choppy, and greyer than ever.

Gerard gave her a friendly kiss on both cheeks as they parted, and she waved good-bye with the extraordinary feeling that they might not meet again for some time. The feeling was absurd, because she was only going home for a couple of weeks, and she fully intended to be back in the Dubois household for the New Year celebrations of 1935.

She hadn't told her mother she was

coming home so early in December, though Jess would be expecting her for Christmas. This was to be a surprise – and she was keen to hear how Wally was getting on. He had left school the minute he could at barely fourteen years old, and had wangled himself a job at the local newspaper office. He wasn't doing a proper reporter's job yet, and Lisa guessed that he mostly ran errands, but the next time she came home he'd wanted to interview her to get some practice.

After an exhausting journey, including the horrendously rough sea voyage that had made her nauseous, all she wanted was a cup of her mother's home-made soup. It was dark now, and the trees were swaying as the wind whistled through the narrow streets, making her shiver.

A light shone out of Renee's house, but her own was in darkness. Odd, since her mother rarely ventured out at night, unless it was to a church meeting. That was it then. It would be even more of a surprise when she came home – provided the shock of finding someone in the house unexpectedly didn't scare her half to death.

Lisa didn't need a key to get in. Nobody locked their doors in Filbert Street since there was nothing worth stealing. But the house felt very cold, and she was tempted to leave her suitcase and go straight across to Renee's for a warm. Wally was probably out with his pals, too. Never mind. She'd put the kettle on for some tea and have the house cosy when they both came back.

A sudden noise from upstairs made her blood freeze for a second. It was a kind of scrabbling sound, like rats ... or intruders ... or ghosts. Lisa's heart began to thud, and she gripped her suitcase tightly, thinking that if any ghosts or whatever came swarming down the stairs, they'd get it right in the guts...

'Who's there?' she heard a thin, quavery voice say. 'Is that you, our Wally? If it's the doctor, bring him up.'

Lisa bounded up the stairs, two at a time. There would be time enough to light the gas-lamps later, when she had found out what was wrong with her mother.

But through all the instant panic, one thought was searingly clear in her head. It was no accident that had made her come home at this time. It was no twist of fate that had filled her head with the need to be here where she belonged. It was an instinct that went beyond all that. A sixth sense, perhaps, at which so many scoffed, but which Granny Newman had always said existed. Why else would she have travelled all these miles to be here when her mother needed her?

She opened the bedroom door and held her breath as the rank smell of sickness assaulted her nostrils. Why had no one told her about this? In the wavering candlelight by the bed, she saw Jess's face, ashen and gaunt.

'Mum, what's wrong?' she gasped.

Jess lifted her head from the pillow and Lisa could see how much greyer it was since the last time she had seen her, just a few months ago.

'Lisa? Is that our Lisa?'

Lisa rushed across the room. There were too many questions, when all she wanted to do was to pull this frail-looking woman into her arms. But they had never been a kissing or hugging family, and Jess looked fragile enough to break if she did so. Instead, she knelt beside the bed, tugging off her hat and gloves and tossing them to the floor as she grabbed her mother's cold hands.

'Of course it's me, and never mind how I got here. I'm home to look after you, and, from the look of things, not before time,' she said in a choked voice.

They heard the clattering behind them as Wally came charging upstairs with heavier footsteps following behind. The boy's eyes widened as he saw Lisa.

'Crikey, our Lisa, how did you get here?'

'Never mind all that,' she snapped. 'Why haven't you been looking after Mum properly, and why didn't you let me know she was ill?'

'It ain't my fault she didn't want to worry

128

you,' he said shrilly, and then he was none too gently pushed aside as a thick-set man came towards Jess's bedside.

'I'm Doctor Purvis,' he said briefly, glancing at Lisa, 'and you must be the daughter who works in France, I take it?'

'Yes,' Lisa stammered. 'Where's our proper doctor?'

'Retired. And for your information, young lady, I am a proper doctor, and I need to examine your mother, since she is a very sick woman.'

Lisa could see that. Anyone could see that, and she felt shivers of alarm run through her. Her mother was very sick and she hadn't been told. It dawned on her that the doctor's voice had been censorious, as if he was blaming her for not being here to care for her mother. It was a daughter's duty...

As the doctor leant over her mother, she found herself pressing back against the bedroom wall alongside Wally. She wanted to cling to his hand – to anyone's hand – but an adolescent brother wouldn't welcome such feeble behaviour.

'Your mother has severe bronchitis and is on the verge of pneumonia,' the doctor finally stated. 'She needs to be kept warm and in a constant temperature. The fire in this bedroom needs to be lit and kept burning, or else she must have a bed downstairs. She is severely undernourished and she needs proper food and plenty to drink. If the pneumonia takes hold she may need to be removed to hospital.'

He spoke as if Jess wasn't there, Lisa thought furiously. He spoke as if she was already dead – or beyond saving. Before Jess could say weakly that they never lit fires in the tiny bedroom grates, Lisa spoke, livid at his high-handed manner.

'The fire will be lit at once, and there will be no expense spared in keeping my mother warm and nourished. Now that I'm here, I will take care of her.'

He eyed her with ill-concealed impatience. 'Your mother's illness may be a long-drawn-out affair, young lady. How long can we count on your ministrations?'

'For as long as necessary.'

Eight

'There's no possibility of me returning to France now,' Lisa told Renee.

That first evening, once the doctor had left instructions on the medicines and care for her mother, there had been a flurry of activity in the Newman house. There was a fire to be built in the unused bedroom grate, which quickly resulted in everyone gasping and spluttering as decades of soot shot down the chimney, sending Jess into a worse bout of coughing than before. If it hadn't been so tragic, it would have been laughable.

'There was Wally and me, covered in soot, with me mother screaming and struggling to get out of bed and into our Wally's room before we gassed her. If me dad hadn't been so penny pinching and let us light the fires in the bedrooms, or had the chimneys cleaned once in a while, it wouldn't have happened. Lord knows what was up that chimney, anyway, dead birds and all, I shouldn't wonder.'

'Don't,' Renee screeched. 'I hate birds.'

'Since when? You don't object to eating a chicken at Christmas, do you?'

'That's different.'

131

'No it's not. A chicken is a bird, same as every other kind.'

'Yes, but chickens don't escape from their cages in a panic and fly around the room squawking like maniacs and peck you.'

Lisa grinned. 'Whose bird did that then?'

'Eddie's mother has got one of them parrots, and when me and Eddie get married we're getting rid of the thing.'

'What will Mrs Bray say about that?'

'She thinks I'll make such a perfect farmer's wife that she'll agree to anything if I tell her the parrot's making me ill.'

'You'd tell her lies then.'

'If I have to.'

For a moment Lisa forgot why she had come storming over to Renee's, telling Wally to fetch her the minute she was needed.

'I don't believe in telling lies,' she said.

Renee scowled. 'You'd tell a lie if you had to – if someone held a knife to your throat, for instance, and made you tell some deep secret.'

'You've been reading too many penny dreadfuls again.'

'Yes, but *wouldn't* you?'

'I don't know about saving my own skin, but I suppose I'd tell a lie if it meant saving my family. Or my country. It would be expected then. Dad used tell stories about how prisoners of war were tortured to make them tell secrets to the Germans. It would be your duty to tell lies then.'

Renee scoffed. 'I suppose you imagine yourself keeping secrets from the Germans now then.'

'Well, not if I was working for a German company.'

Renee looked shocked. 'Lisa, you wouldn't! It's bad enough you going to France among all those froggies, but working for Germans! My dad would turn in his grave – if he had one.'

'The war's over, Renee,' Lisa said with an edge to her voice. 'If you must know, I've been offered a job in Germany, but I can't think about it for now.'

'Not ever, I should think. But why not now?'

'Don't be stupid. It's because my mother's ill, of course, and I'm staying here to look after her, however long it takes.'

Renee glared at her. 'I'm not stupid, but you've got above yourself, just as my mum always said you would, what with your la-di-da grammar school education and your posh friends. Even your Wally's forever boasting about you and saying that when he becomes a proper journalist he'll probably end up writing a book about his clever sister.'

'Is he?' Lisa said, grinning until she saw that Renee looked really upset now. 'Oh, Lord, don't let's quarrel. I'm just the same as I've always been.'

She shook her head. 'We're not the kids we once were, Lisa, and if I can see that and you can't, I reckon that makes me cleverer than you. So how long does your mum have to stay in bed?'

She changed tactics quicker than blinking, but Lisa found it easier than discussing her fine education, or working for Herr Gott – which seemed impossibly remote now.

Anyway, caring for your family always had to come first. There was plenty of time for ambitious plans. When you were twenty years old there was all the time in the world.

But she knew in her heart that Jess's illness looked like being long drawn out. She wasn't sure how she would cope, and immediately felt ashamed, because her mum was doing the suffering, not her.

'I'm going to see that she stays put for at least a week, while me and Wally get things ready for Christmas. I'll have to go back to France then, to clear up everything, but then I'm coming home to find a job here.'

'Your mum will never agree to that. She's proud of you, Lisa.'

'Is she? She never told me so.'

But she wouldn't. Jess wasn't the kind of woman to whom compliments came easily. Lisa vowed, as she had done once before, that if she ever had children she would always let them know how much she loved and valued them.

134

'What would you do here?' Renee went on. 'You wouldn't want to work in the factory with me, I suppose, but I could put in a word for you if you like.'

'I haven't thought that far ahead,' Lisa said, knowing she would hate it. 'Everything's happened so suddenly.'

She was swallowed up in a cloud of misery. Her wonderful plans were all falling apart, and even though she knew what she had to do, and loyalty to her mother would never let her change her mind, she knew how bitterly disappointed she was at what was happening now.

'You could always teach kids to speak French,' Renee said carelessly.

The thought didn't particularly inspire her. There had been a sense of glamour about working and living in France, which Renee would probably think disloyal to her country. For all her flippancy Renee was surprisingly patriotic, so Lisa never mentioned the possibility of working in Germany again. Renee was also very defensive of her father's memory, and the fact that her mother was now seeing a foreign gentleman she had met at a dance was definitely not to Renee's liking. He was Austrian, but to Renee all foreigners were the same.

'I hate him,' she said, scowling as she informed Lisa. 'He owns a fish and chip shop, and he stinks of chip fat. His hair's so greasy you could slide off it and I reckon he dips his comb in the fish fryer at the end of the day. He pats me on the bottom and calls me "little girl", and he makes my toes curl when he looks at me.'

'Cripes, Renee, he sounds like a real charmer!' Lisa said, starting to laugh.

Renee snapped back, 'It's not funny. Mum's talking about getting married again, and if she did we'd have to go and live above that stinking fish and chip shop. Well if that happens I'll marry Eddie, and go and live at the farm.'

'You can't marry Eddie just to get away from this chap, Renee. You have to love someone before you marry them. You do love him, don't you?'

She shrugged. 'Me and Eddie are all right, and it'll happen someday, so we'd just have to bring the wedding forward. Anyway, when did you become such an expert in love and marriage?'

'Never. That's the last thing I am.'

She wasn't going to mention Antoine again. That had fizzled out good and proper, and Antoine's mama had got her way now that he was engaged to the lovely Veronique, whose parents had pots of money and whose daddy was going to help Antoine in his career. The marriage seemed as far away as ever, but that was the way these families behaved. It was a world away from Renee and her farmer, who couldn't rub two half-pennies together, and even further away from herself and the anonymous love of her life, who hadn't put in his appearance yet.

'What are you looking so moony about?' Renee asked crossly. 'You know I hate it when you get that secretive look on your face.'

'Oh, I was just wondering what to wear at your wedding – if Eddie ever gets around to asking you properly.'

'If my mum decides to marry old fat-face Hans Schmidt, *I* shall ask *him!*'

Christmas wasn't a happy occasion. Jess spent it in bed, and Lisa and Wally made the best of it, taking her dinner upstairs and trying to jolly her along with tempting morsels of roast chicken and mashed brussels sprouts that she couldn't swallow, and a drink of cider that was meant to make her forget her troubles.

'She's not too good, is she, our Lisa?' Wally said when they were downstairs and the determination to be festive had dried up.

'No, but I'm not going to leave you to get on with it, Wally. I'll have to go back to France to fetch the rest of my things, but I've already written to Monique telling her of the situation.'

'Will you be very sad at giving it all up?' he

said uneasily.

'I was at first. But I'm over that now, and there's no choice to be made, is there? I'm quite glad to be home, really. This is where I belong.'

She tried to sound cheerful and to ignore the pang as she spoke. This was her home, and Jess and Wally were her family ... but for all the time she had lived there she knew that France was in her heart. If it wasn't considered blasphemy by some folk, she would have said that if she had ever lived before it must have been in that beautiful country where she felt so at home.

'I'm going to pay someone to come in every day to make the meals for you and Mum while I'm away, and to do a bit of cleaning and washing, too,' she went on determinedly, 'and when I come back I'll have to see about getting a job.'

Wally looked at her as if she had gone completely mad. 'It's only posh folk who have someone in to do their cleaning, and our mum won't like having someone else messing about in her kitchen.'

'She'll have to lump it then. I need to work to earn my keep and I can't be in two places at once, can I?'

It was the only thing to do. She wouldn't earn as much money here as she had in France, but on the advice of Henri Dubois most of her wages went automatically into a savings account. There was no better way to use some of that money than in seeing that Jess had every care.

As expected, Jess objected. But Lisa was taking control now and wouldn't hear any arguments. The child had become the mother, and a good neighbour whom Jess had known all her married life said she would gladly help out and wouldn't even move a saucepan out of place without Jess's say-so.

'You're to help, too, Wally,' Lisa told him. 'You're to fetch the wood and see to the fires, and do any errands that Mum or Mrs Pond ask you to do. No slacking while I'm away, mind. It'll only be for a week at most.'

'You're a real bossyboots, our Lisa. I can tell you were cut out to be a teacher,' he said, but he promised to do as she ordered.

It was funny how a few words tossed out so carelessly could help to make up someone's mind. Maybe it was a fantasy to say that someone was cut out to be a teacher ... but she had enjoyed teaching the Dubois children, and she did have an air of authority when it was needed, even in being an au pair ... and she would miss using the skills that came so naturally.

Wasting no more time, before she went back to France she went to see the headmaster of the local school. She offered to teach the older children to speak French as an extra subject, and was readily accepted.

Sometimes, she thought, as she set out on the long return journey once more, Wally and Renee did have some good ideas.

'We will miss you, Lisa,' Monique said. 'I hope you will write to me often and let me know how things progress with your mother.'

'Of course I will, though I fear the news is never going to be good,' she murmured. 'The doctor says she has been suffering from a chest complaint for a long time, and that it will eventually kill her.'

'And your long damp winters do not help,' Monique observed.

'We do our best to keep her warm and well nourished, and my brother is a great help. He is a young man now and no longer the scallywag he once was.'

Lisa still marvelled at how Wally had shot up and grown in stature as well as common sense since she had been in France. Or perhaps it was just that she was noticing it more because of her long absences.

'And I approve that you have arranged for help in the house,' Monique went on. 'You cannot pull yourself two ways, Lisa, and the post at the local school will be important to you, and to the fortunate children you are going to teach. But I truly hope you will come back to us one day.'

'I want to, with all my heart, and we will always keep in touch if it's what you wish,' she added in some embarrassment.

Monique leant forward and kissed her lightly on both cheeks.

'I do, and I know you are a wonderful letter-writer, so that will be our consolation. Let us not linger over our goodbyes now, for this is only *au revoir*, and our letters will keep us together.'

It was less easy saying goodbye to the children, who now thought of Lisa as their big sister. They clung to her and sobbed, and she couldn't help thinking how different these people were from her own stiff-upper-lipped family. There were no tears from her mother or Wally when she left them, but that didn't mean they didn't love her. They just never showed it the way the French did.

Henri insisted on giving her a farewell gift of the biggest cheque Lisa had ever seen. She gasped in embarrassment as he handed it to her.

'Oh, M. Dubois – Henri – I can't possibly take this—'

'You can and you will, my dear. You will need all the help you can get in the coming months. Take this and use it wisely to give her every care. And one day, God willing, we will see you again. Our home will be the poorer without you.'

'But the children will no longer need me,'

she murmured.

'Ah, but I believe you have taken France to your heart, and there will always be a place for you here. You are in our hearts, too.'

It was such an odd thing to say. It was poetic and passionate and over-sentimental, the way that only a Continental could be without embarrassment, and the words kept running through her head all the way home on that miserable and cold journey back to England. She could speak just as passionately, she admitted, but only when she used the expressive language of the French. How odd that was, too, to think that her native language was the one that suppressed her true feelings! It still charmed her to think that perhaps in a past life she had been a Frenchwoman, which was why the words and phrases and passions came so easily and naturally to her.

She kept such philosophical and fanciful thoughts in mind all the way home. Pushing away the thoughts of parting from the family she had grown to love helped her to stop thinking of her loss of freedom now. It was wrong to feel that way, when she was going home to care for her sick mother, and doing what every good daughter should do. There had never been a moment's doubt in her mind about her duty, but she was also young and healthy and alive, and the feeling of being trapped never entirely went away. She was as much a bird in a cage as that parrot of Mrs Bray's that Renee detested so much.

The feeling of self-pity disappeared the minute she finally reached home in the late evening of a very long day, to find her mother trying to lift a heavy pot of soup from the stove on to the kitchen table in readiness for her homecoming.

'What are you doing, Mum! You shouldn't strain yourself like that – and why isn't Wally here to help?'

'He's out with his friends,' Jess wheezed. 'It's not right to keep him tied to my apron-strings at his age, Lisa. Mrs Pond has only just gone. She wanted to wait for you, but if I don't do a few things for myself I might as well lay down in my wooden box.'

'Please don't talk like that, Mum!'

Lisa dumped her baggage on the floor and crossed the room quickly to fold her mother in her arms, holding her tightly. She was alarmed to realize how thin Jess had become, even in these short weeks since the doctor had first come to see her and made his dire diagnosis.

'We both know it's true, so what's the use of fussing over it?' Jess said, sliding out of the embrace. 'Though I think the good Lord intends to make me stay a while longer before he sends me up among the angels.'

Lisa was alarmed by her words. Jess was a

143

practical woman, but she had never been particularly religious, and all this talk of being with the angels wasn't like her. But she hadn't finished yet.

'I daresay it's a punishment for the way I scoffed at your dad for all his union nonsense. The Bible says a wife is meant to support her husband, and I never did, not in the things that mattered to him.'

'God wouldn't punish you for that. We all thought Dad was fanatical about his union, even me, and I was hardly old enough to know what was going on.'

'Yes, well, I don't want to talk about him any more, so are we going to have this soup or not?'

Her mood changed, and she was once more the mother Lisa remembered, with verbal habits equivalent to picking fleas off a dog. In a strange way, though, this reassured her that Jess wasn't going anywhere yet.

By the time Wally came home she had unpacked the rest of her belongings and felt the comfort of the familiar walls closing around her. The house was warm, thanks to the efforts of her brother and neighbour in keeping the fires burning, and her mother nourished. For the first time she fully appreciated what Henri Dubois had done in giving her the large cheque that would swell the family coffers and keep things going for as long as necessary. She had plans for that money.

'I'm glad you're home for good, Lisa,' Wally told her, when they had seen Jess safely to bed. 'Have you heard the news?'

'What news? Has war broken out while I've been away or something?'

She didn't know why she said it. It was a daft thing to say. There was no hint of war on the horizon, and never would be again, God willing. The war to end all wars had seen to that. The shiver than ran down her spine was just a reaction to being very tired, not a stupid premonition.

'Renee's mum's getting married again,' Wally announced. 'Renee's as mad as stink over it and saying she's not going to live over no fish and chip shop, and she ain't changing her name to Renee Schmidt neither.'

'When did all this happen? I've only been gone a week and I know Renee was worried about it, but I didn't think it was going to happen so soon!'

'The slimy bloke proposed on New Year's Eve, and Renee's mum said yes. They're getting married next summer, and Renee will have to live with them unless she runs away from home,' he finished with a snigger.

Or unless she rushes into marriage with Eddie Bray. She didn't dare say as much, though. With Wally's nose for a story she wouldn't put it past him to start spreading gossip.

'How do you know all that?' she snapped.

145

'Everybody knows it. She's had a real bust-up with her mum, and you know what it's like when they start screaming at one another. The whole street knew what was going on.'

Lisa could imagine it. Dignity and Renee didn't go together. If she hated something, she lashed out about it without a second thought. All their lives it was something that had rankled with Renee, because Lisa could keep secrets and she couldn't.

'I have to go and see her,' she said, scrambling up.

'You can't. It's gone midnight!' Wally said.

'Is it?' She was genuinely surprised. She had been travelling all day and been so tired she could have dropped on her feet, but she had gone through that stage now, and was absolutely wide awake.

'I'll see her first thing in the morning, then, and find out what's going on. She has to be made to see sense.'

'About living over a fish and chip shop? It sounds smashing to me.'

'No. About something else.' And that was a confidence she wasn't about to share with Wally.

Nine

'You've never been in love, so it's none of your business,' Renee said rudely.

'Have *you*? Can you honestly tell me, hand on heart, that you're in love with Eddie Bray, Renee?'

'Can you honestly tell me, hand on heart, that any woman in her right mind can be in love with that German idiot who stinks of chip fat?' she yelled.

'You said he was Austrian,' Lisa said automatically.

'It's all the same, isn't it?'

'Actually, no—'

'Oh, you're always so right, Lisa Newman!'

'And you're always such an idiot.'

After a few prickly seconds, Lisa began to laugh. Here they were, both adults now, still squabbling like the children they had once been. In an instant they were right back to being ten years old, hands on hips and glaring at each other, with neither of them willing to break the deadlock. But one of them had to.

'I'm sorry,' she said, 'but someone has to make you see sense, and who better than your best friend who loves you?'

Renee backed away. 'Crikey, Lisa, I knew you'd get all Frenchified. A girl doesn't tell another girl that she loves her!'

'Idiot! I don't mean anything weird by it. What's wrong with friends loving each other? Even French *men* kiss each other on both cheeks when they meet.'

Renee shrieked in mock horror. 'They *don't*. You're making it up!'

'They do,' Lisa said solemnly. 'So you shouldn't have any objections to your mum getting married again. It's a respectable thing to do,' she added tactfully, because everyone knew that over the years there had been plenty of gossip about the gentlemen friends that Renee's mum had brought to the house, and the number of new 'uncles' that had come and gone for Renee.

'I don't mind her getting married again. Just not to *him*.'

'He hasn't tried anything on with you, has he?' Lisa said, not daring to put it more strongly.

'Good God, of course not! I'd soon kick him where it hurts if he tried any of that nonsense,' she said smartly. 'But if she marries him, I'm marrying Eddie.'

'Does Eddie know?' Lisa asked mildly.

She scowled. 'He says he don't want to get married yet and we're all right as we are. So I'll just have to do something to

148

persuade him.'

When the penny dropped, Lisa felt like shaking her hard.

'That's the stupidest thing I ever heard of, Renee. You wouldn't really get yourself in the family way, would you?'

'I wouldn't get *myself* in the family way,' she said, heavy with sarcasm. 'I'm not the Virgin Mary. I'd need some bally help, wouldn't I?'

Lisa stared in dismay. 'You were always reckless, but this is downright crazy. You couldn't force Eddie like that.'

Lisa wasn't even sure he'd agree. Most of the farm-working community were decent fellows, but she had always thought Eddie was a bit of a yokel, with the finesse of a pig, and the thought of his big fat fingers pawing anyone was enough to make her shudder.

'If there was a baby involved, he'd have to do the right thing by me,' Renee repeated, her eyes bright with hurt tears. 'I thought you'd understand. Hans Schmidt makes me sick. He's always cuddling Mum and kissing her neck and things like that, even when I'm in the room, and I couldn't spend the rest of my life listening to him and Mum – you know – doing the other stuff that married people do.'

'You do have choices, Renee. You wouldn't have to live with them. You could get a living-in job somewhere. It would be better than rushing into marriage before you were ready for it, and you could still go courting.'

Without warning, Renee flung her arms around her and hugged her.

'Lisa, you're brilliant. I always said so, didn't I? Well, perhaps not, but I always thought it. You're the answer to my prayers, and I don't mean that in any soppy way, before you think I've turned peculiar. I'll look for a living-in job and get away from home and that rotten factory at the same time.'

'I'm glad to have been of help!' Lisa said, unwinding the clinging arms before she was strangled.

At Renee's usual enthusiasm, thoughts of leaping from frying pans into fires shot into Lisa's mind, but she wouldn't say so. And if Renee herself couldn't see that an alternative was no more than a small lifeline, Lisa wasn't going to enlighten her about that, either. She'd done enough saintly dabbling in other people's lives for one day. In any case, she had her own future to consider.

She'd never thought of herself as a born organizer, but by the end of January several things had already been settled. She was now teaching rudimentary French to the top classes at the local primary school, and the other teachers were impressed at the way she managed to make learning fun for the children.

She and Renee had scanned the employment advertisements for young women in search of a living-in post, and composed several application letters. And Lisa had arranged for a telephone to be installed in her mum's house.

'What nonsense!' Jess said, outraged, when she heard that a man was coming to install it. 'People like us don't have telephones, Lisa. Who is going to use it, and how can we afford it?'

'*I* can afford it, and it will give me peace of mind to know I can contact you at any time, and you can call me or Wally at work. And before you ask where the money is coming from, it's thanks to my generous bonus, and I'm not going to argue about it.'

It seemed to Jess that this newly independent girl was now taking charge of the whole family. She half resented it and half admired her for it. Even though it had taken her illness to bring her daughter home, Jess thought guiltily, she was still glad that all the French nonsense seemed to be in the past.

'You're a good girl, Lisa,' she said at last, which, coming from Jess, was praise indeed.

'Am I?' Lisa said, smiling. 'Then promise me you'll answer the telephone when it rings, and that you won't be afraid of it.'

Renee's mother wasted no more time in

announcing that she was going to marry her Austrian chap that summer, even though it was obvious that Renee wasn't the only person who disapproved. Hans Schmidt was affable and well rounded, being far too fond of his own fish and chips, and as harmless a chap as could be found. But to some he was still tarred with the tag of being German, or near enough to make no difference, and the fact didn't sit well on older folk. But just like Renee her mother took no notice of what other folk thought, and never had.

A month or so later Renee came bursting over the road, waving a letter in her hand. There was no need to ask what it contained.

'It's from some people called Staples in that big house in the country about ten miles away, and I'm to go for an interview,' she gasped. 'I'd have to help with the cooking and cleaning, and I'd be sharing a room with another girl, but in exchange I'll have all my keep and a small wage besides. What do you think, Lisa?'

'What do *you* think?' Lisa said doubtfully.

'Anything's better than living with a fish and chip smell under my nose day and night, isn't it? Especially with *him*.'

It sounded little more than a skivvying job to Lisa, but as Renee went on to enthuse about the size of the house and grounds they had often seen when they were out on their bicycles she couldn't dampen her enthusiasm.

'Have you asked your mother what she thinks?'

'No,' Renee said with a toss of her head. 'She never asks my opinion about anything, so why should I care what she thinks? Anyway, I may not get the job.'

'You will. I can feel it in my bones,' Lisa told her confidently. 'You can do anything you want to if you wish for it hard enough.'

'Can you tell the future now then?'

'No, but I know determination when I see it.'

She was right, too, because Renee was offered the living-in job at the big house. Her mother didn't object, and even though Eddie apparently didn't like the idea he could go and whistle, according to Renee.

'Does this mean you're giving him up then?' Lisa said with a grin.

'No, but maybe if I'm not around all the time, it'll make him keener. You know what they say about absence making the heart grow fonder.'

'We won't see so much of each other either.'

'We'll still be best friends, though. And don't forget that one day we're going to open those predictions we wrote when we were kids.'

'I thought you'd have forgotten about them

by now!'

'Well, I knew *you* wouldn't. And I'll get my tanner, because I'm darned sure you and this Antoine chap will get married before you're twenty-five.'

'Didn't I tell you he's got engaged to a girl called Veronique? And even if he wasn't, I don't care for him in that way.'

'What way is that?' Renee said as they set out towards the river for a walk.

Lisa laughed. 'You know better than I do! You and Eddie have never been exactly slow in that respect.'

'I ain't let him touch me yet, though. Well, not properly. Not all over, in certain places, if you know what I mean.'

Lisa was going to ignore the arch meaning in her voice, preferring not to know any intimate secrets, despite the fact that Renee obviously wanted to tell her more. But, in a wave of something approaching anger, she was aware again that, for all the so-called sophistication in going to France to work, she was still totally ignorant of the ways of lovers.

It was certainly not something her mother ever spoke about, and despite her schoolgirl curiosity, the biology teacher's additional information had left her more confused than ever. Her sense of inadequacy made her sharp with Renee, who obviously knew far more than she did.

'No, I don't,' she snapped. 'So what has Mister-wonderful-Eddie done to put that sparkle in your eyes?'

'I know you never thought much of him, Lisa, but he's not all about feeding the chickens and milking the cows. He does have his good points.'

She howled with laughter at some secret joke, and Lisa couldn't stand this any longer. She stood up and brushed down her skirt impatiently.

'Well, I don't have time to hear about them, and I'm sure they should be private, anyway—'

Renee howled again. 'Privates! That's a good one.'

'I didn't mean— Oh, never mind. I'm going, so let me know what you decide about the job.'

'I've already decided,' Renee snapped, as Lisa had known she would.

They had already stayed too long at the river, throwing sticks into the water and watching them float downstream on the sluggish current, trying to regain their old easy companionship. By the time they walked home in moody silence, Lisa was thinking about Antoine again. It had been nice while it lasted, and she had been flattered by his attentions. It was a heady feeling to have a dashing young man interested in her. For a while she had thought she was in love ... but he hadn't aroused the passion she knew she was capable of in her heart, and his cool and sophisticated Veronique was welcome to him...

'You never told me about this Vera-somebody,' Renee said suddenly, as if she could read her mind.

'I don't tell you everything,' Lisa retorted. 'It creates an air of mystery. You should try it with Eddie, instead of wearing your heart on your sleeve.'

'There's not much Eddie doesn't know about me – or you! We've all known one another since we were in our prams, like everybody around here.'

'It will probably do him good for you two to be separated for a while when you start your new job then. Let him pine a bit.'

She couldn't put it more bluntly than that without having Renee erupting like a volcano. And there was a whole lot Eddie Bray didn't know about Renee's deviousness, but if she couldn't see for herself that life with him was never going to be a happy-ever-after affair, it was her choice.

As they neared the village they heard the scream of an ambulance.

'What's up now?' Renee said excitedly. 'With any luck it'll be old Schmidt's fish and chip shop going up in smoke, and he'll be as dead as a dodo.'

She was still jabbering when Lisa began

running, her heart pounding. It wasn't a certainty, or even a suspicion. It was more like a premonition...

'It's outside your house,' Renee shrieked. 'It must be your mum, Lisa. Oh God, I wish I'd never said anything about being dead as a dodo—'

'Shut your stupid mouth for once, Renee,' Lisa snapped, even though she was finding it hard to speak at all. She rushed past the neighbours, who had appeared as if by magic all along the street, gathering outside the Newman house, waiting to see what had happened to the woman inside. Lisa pushed past them, and was grabbed by a flustered Mrs Pond.

'She ain't hurt bad, Lisa love, and I picked up that telephone machine and sent for the doctor like she told me. He's with her now.'

'What happened?' Lisa gasped, feeling ridiculous as she grappled with the woman, who seemed determined not to let go of her.

'Your ma was putting some more sticks on the fire when she fell against the fender. I was hanging out the washing, so I didn't hear her yelling at first. By the time I got back indoors and up the stairs she was lying twisted up with her leg bent beneath her. No strength to get herself up again, see? She moaned for me to get the doctor, and then passed out. She was that pale and that quiet,

157

I thought for a minute she was a goner...'

As she paused for breath, Lisa finally managed to wrench out of the woman's grip and ran up the stairs two at a time to where two ambulance-men were already lifting her mother on to a stretcher. She was almost afraid to look at the white-faced woman who seemed to have shrunk visibly since she had gone out that morning.

'Is she going to be all right?' she asked the doctor, her voice shaking.

'She's suffered concussion, and her leg's broken. Her bones are very brittle, and she's also burnt her hands,' the doctor told her as they followed the stretcher down the awkward bends in the stairs. 'My guess is that it happened when she fell; if she was bending down to put sticks on the fire she could have had a dizzy spell. She's suffering from shock now, and she needs to go to hospital to have that leg set, and then we'll see what's to be done.'

'What do you mean, what's to be done?' Lisa stammered as they reached the open door, stunned by this tirade.

'She may need more care than a daily neighbour can give her. Now then, do you want to go in the ambulance with your mother?'

'Of course I do!' she snapped, feeling slighted. Was he implying that she would do anything else? Or that she should be a stay-

158

at-home daughter? But she was no nurse. She might be highly skilled in other ways, but she didn't have the skills to deal with real illness. She tried to ignore the panic in her gut and beckoned to Mrs Pond.

'I'm going to the hospital with Mum. Will you telephone Wally at the newspaper office right away and tell him what's happened, please?'

'Oh, but I'm not sure how—'

'Ask the operator,' Lisa went on coldly. 'It's the least you can do.'

She knew she was being unduly sharp, and that the neighbour had always done her best. It wasn't her fault that she was hanging out the washing – and probably gossiping over the garden fence – when Jess became dizzy and fell.

Once her mother had been taken into the ambulance, Lisa stumbled in to sit beside her, feeling nearly as dizzy herself. Things could change so quickly, almost in the blinking of an eye. This morning she had been so carefree, out walking with Renee, and playing the clever clogs as usual in trying to keep Renee from making a mistake over Eddie Bray.

Now, such things seemed so unimportant compared with the fact that Jess Newman was lying unconscious on an ambulance cot, and looking as pale as death. Against her will, Lisa's imagination was working overtime, filling her with all kinds of dire predictions.

'It's probably not as bad as it looks, miss,' the attendant told her, hearing her choking breath. 'The doc will have given her a sedative, and she's much better like this until they get her leg fixed up at the hospital.'

'She's not going to die then?' Lisa said brutally.

'Lord love you, who ever heard of somebody dying from a broken leg?' he said, joshing her.

Added to a chronic chest infection and the shock of burnt hands, Lisa added silently. But the man was trying to reassure her, and she gave a watery smile.

'Ain't you that girl who went away to France to work?' he said suddenly. 'A bit of a brainbox, my missus said.'

'I'm home now to look after my mother,' she muttered.

'Well, it's probably for the best, since that Hitler feller could be heading us into another war sometime or other, and if he does he'll be greedy to get his hands on France, just like t'other bastard in the last lot, begging your pardon, miss.'

Lisa looked at him properly. She'd thought he was just talking to keep her mind off her mother, but something in his voice caught her attention.

'Are you well up in such things?' she asked,

for want of something to say. She didn't think he looked like a political man, but who knew what anyone was these days? She didn't think of Hans Schmidt as a potential spy, even if Renee did!

'I read the newspapers and listen to the wireless. I don't spend all my time riding around in this death-wagon. Sorry, miss, that's just our name for it,' he added. 'It don't mean nothing, and it looks as if she's coming round now.'

They heard Jess give a small moan, and then to Lisa's relief her mother's eyes flickered open.

'Where am I?' she said faintly, and then she gave a small cry as she tried to move, registered the pain in her leg and passed out again.

'You're on the way to hospital, Mum,' Lisa said, choked, even though she couldn't hear her now. She would dearly have liked to hold her hand, but the sore and reddened skin made that impossible. Jess remained unconscious until after she was wheeled into the hospital, and shortly a small whirlwind came into the room.

'Wally, thank God. How did you get here so soon?'

'Boss drove me,' Wally said tightly. 'How bad is she?'

'They have to put her leg in plaster. She won't be able to walk for weeks, nor do much for herself with her poor hands—'

'You'll have to look after her,' he burst out. 'I'd be no good doing a nursing job, and, anyway, it's women's work.'

'I don't need you telling me what my duty is, and I'll do what I have to, thank you,' she said, just managing not to shout at him.

And then they both started at the sound of Jess's feeble voice.

'Neither of you is seeing to my private needs. I'd rather die before I let a child of mine do such things.'

'Don't talk so daft, Mum,' Lisa told her. 'If you can't do stuff for yourself, somebody will have to help you.'

But she wasn't a nurse, and if her mother couldn't see to her most basic needs she knew she couldn't cope. You couldn't expect a young boy to do it, though, and nor did she want to give up her job, she thought guiltily.

'I daresay the doctor will want to keep you in hospital for a while, Mum,' she went on, 'and then we'll think about what to do.'

'I won't be a burden to you two,' Jess said.

'You're not,' Lisa began, and then stood back as the porters and nurses came to take Jess to the theatre to have her leg set.

By now Lisa could see that Wally was having a hard job not to let his lower lip tremble as Jess was wheeled away. *She* had to be the strong one, the one who held this family together, for however long it took.

Everything else could wait: her career, the dream of going back to France – the thought of one day being a wife and mother herself. It could all wait, and it must.

'Is she really going to be all right, our Lisa?' she heard Wally mutter, and she caught the uncertainty in his young voice. He was still a child in many respects, she thought swiftly, despite his determination to be a newspaperman.

'Of course she is,' she said huskily. 'You don't die of a broken leg, especially somebody as tough as our mum. Once it's mended she'll be as right as ninepence.'

'Except for however long it takes for her hands to heal, and the bloody chest infection. That's never going to get better. *Is* it?'

She was shocked at hearing him swear, and she didn't know how to answer. She wanted to hug him, but she had the feeling that if she did they would both end up like a heap of jelly. They were so consumed with their own fears that the sound of someone behind them made them jump, and the doctor told them to sit down.

'I won't pretend that this hasn't been a setback,' he said. 'The dizziness that caused the accident probably came from the gradual weakness of her limbs due to her taking little exercise and her lack of interest in food.'

'I do the best I can to get her to eat,' Lisa said.

163

'I'm sure you do, but I meant what I said about her needing more care than you can reasonably give her. She needs professional care from now on.'

'We're not sending her away,' Lisa said, remembering graphic tales about places where they sent the disabled, the mentally ill. Once you entered one of those places you never came out and you were forgotten for ever. 'We'll hire a nurse to live in the house. That would be permitted, wouldn't it, Doctor?'

Her voice became shrill and sarcastic. She hated having to ask him, as if her mother was a child who no longer had a will of her own.

'Of course, but—'

'Then that's what we'll do.'

She forestalled him before he could start asking who was going to pay for such a luxury – and she averted her eyes from Wally's face, which was telling her that he was thinking the same thing.

Ten

In the end Jess remained in hospital for several months. Her broken leg had healed, but the fragile skin on her burnt hands took far longer, and the enforced stay in bed exacerbated her chest complaint, so it was early April before she was allowed home. By then Renee was established in her new job, and thinking less about marrying Eddie Bray, and her mother was planning her imminent marriage to Hans Schmidt. With the family doctor's approval, Lisa had plans of her own.

Between them, she and Wally could easily cope with any demands that Jess made during the night. The telephone was their lifeline, and Jess was adamant about not wanting a stranger sleeping in the house. Mrs Pond was a good neighbour, but not qualified in anything remotely medical. So a day nurse was required.

Miss Tweed was a home companion with nursing experience, and came with good references. She was of indeterminate age, with pepper-and-salt hair and no-nonsense spectacles.

'Nobody's dreamboat,' Wally called her in private, using the latest Hollywood jargon, but it didn't matter as long as she did her job and got along with Jess, which wasn't always easy. However, she and Miss Tweed hit it off remarkably well after a couple of hesitant weeks. Wally was soon calling her Tweedy, and Lisa didn't have to give up her job, although she would have done so in a minute.

'You're more use at school,' Renee told her. 'Mind you, I doubt that the kids need to learn French. Not many will be going to France the way you did.'

'They might if there was another war,' Lisa said without thinking.

'What put that idea in your head?' Renee, who rarely thought about anything outside her immediate horizon, was genuinely astonished.

'The newspapers! The wireless! Adolph Hitler, who some people are calling a fanatic, including our Wally!' Lisa said, heavy with sarcasm.

'What does that shrimp know about anything?'

'He keeps abreast of what's going on in the world. He's no dummy, Renee.'

'So this worry-guts thinks there'll be another war?'

'I don't know. I certainly hope not. It would put the kybosh on the Olympic

Games next year, anyway.' There had been hints of her being invited by her French 'family', and staying with the Gotts in Germany, though she hadn't mentioned it to anyone else yet.

'I thought you'd done with playing games with that Antoine chap.'

Lisa sighed. 'Is that all you can think about? It's got nothing to do with Antoine. The Olympic Games are in Berlin next year. The family I work for are planning to go and I'd hoped to go with them. I'd be away for two weeks though, so it will all depend on Mum.'

She crossed her fingers, praying for this small respite some time in the future. By now the prospect of remaining at the village school for ever stifled her. If Tweedy was a friend as well as a professional home companion by then, Jess surely wouldn't object to her sleeping in the house for two weeks. Lisa desperately hoped she would get the invitation, although the letters from Madame Dubois had not formally said so yet.

'Well, we'll open our envelopes before you go to any soppy games,' said Renee, whose idea of physical exercise meant private games for two, and who refused to even talk about Lisa going to Germany. 'So get a move on and find the man of your dreams. You're far too good looking to wait years to get married!'

'I told you—'

But Renee's butterfly mind was already elsewhere, and Lisa knew the outcome anyway. This time next year she wouldn't be married, and Renee would be well on the way. She shivered, unwilling to acknowledge that the letters they had written all that time ago could be anything more than childish guesses – not wanting to think they could be a prophesy that her future husband was not yet destined to put in his appearance.

By the spring and summer of 1936, Jess wasn't getting any worse, and Lisa was optimistic that she was going to live for years under the tender care of the tireless Miss Tweed, who had now, as Lisa had hoped she would, become more a friend than an employee.

On a bright sunlit day in May, on one of Renee's days off from her living-in job, they went down to the river and opened their envelopes.

'Well, well, Miss Clever Clogs,' Renee said excitedly, 'you weren't quite right after all. I'm not married yet, though me and Eddie did get engaged at Christmas. But not everybody knows your name, like you said they would!'

Lisa pulled out the letter that had arrived that morning, and it seemed spooky that it had come on this particular day.

'You'd better read this then,' she said.

After one glance she scowled. 'You know I can't read that German rot.'

'Sorry, I forgot. It's from Herr Gott, who once offered me a job in Germany. He says he's never forgotten me and he's still eager to employ me in his new Paris office. Meanwhile, I'm invited to stay with him and his family for the duration of the Berlin Games, along with the Dubois family. What do you think of that?'

'So a German chap remembers your name. It's hardly the same as having everybody knowing it!' Renee said.

Lisa laughed. 'Ah, but when you write a prediction you should be prepared to bend the rules a bit! I'm amazed that he even remembers me after all this time, and especially that he still wants me to work for him.'

'So what's stopping you?'

Her smile faded. 'Mum. Wally. Life.'

'Cripes, Lisa, your mum's settled with this Tweed woman, and if you can afford to keep paying her don't let that hold you back. Your Wally don't need you to baby him, though wild horses wouldn't get me living in Germany.'

'I told you, it's in Paris, and I'd be an interpreter, selling motor cars to foreign dealers. I'd be in my favourite country, not too far away from the Dubois family.'

'It must be fate then,' said Renee, who didn't believe in such things.

'It must be,' said Lisa, who did.

She *had* to go to Berlin for the Games. Jess was surprisingly agreeable, and Lisa realized how dependent her mother had become on Miss Tweed. Despite the similarity in their ages, Miss Tweed had become almost like a mother figure to Jess. Wally was doing well at his job now, and he and Miss Tweed had adopted a friendly banter between them. There was no reason for her to miss the Games.

But fate didn't always play fair. A few weeks later she was coaxing the small boys in her class with their French pronunciation when the headmaster's secretary told her she had a telephone call.

She knew at once what it would be about. If it hadn't been a gut instinct, the look on the woman's face would have told her. She rushed out of the room, leaving the secretary to deal with the class of wide-eyed children.

In his office, the headmaster silently handed her the telephone.

'I'm so sorry, Lisa.' She heard the gulps in Miss Tweed's voice. 'One minute we were sitting in the garden chatting normally, and the next minute your mother gave a gasp and slumped over in her chair. She didn't say a word. There was nothing I could do, and the only consolation I can offer is that she never suffered. I'm so very, very sorry,' she repeated, parrot-like.

With her heart hammering fast, Lisa forced down the sense of shock and grief. Miss Tweed was highly competent, but right now she seemed to have lost her composure.

'Stay calm, Miss Tweed. I'll come home right away. Have you called my brother? And the doctor?'

'Not yet. I thought I should speak to you first,' the woman stammered.

'Right. But now I want you to call Wally, and then the doctor. Please do it as soon as you put the phone down, Miss Tweed,' Lisa repeated firmly, registering in an instant that she was the head of the family now, and any decisions were hers to make.

It was a weird time to be having such a thought, but, for a fraction of a moment, it delayed having to accept that Jess was dead, that she and Wally hadn't been with her and that they had to go through the ritual of a family burial all over again. Then she put the phone down, sobs tore at her throat and seconds later she was weeping in the comforting arms of the headmaster.

Wally was stronger than she could have imagined. She was the older sister, but he assumed the mantle of the man in the family, almost without Lisa realizing it. He

171

was home before her, and was comforting a wretched Miss Tweed, who was wailing that she didn't know what she could have done to prevent it.

'For goodness sake, Tweedy, do you think we're blaming you?' Lisa snapped, unconsciously using Wally's pet name for her. 'It's a blessing that Mum had someone with her at the end whom she liked and trusted. If it couldn't be Wally or me, then we're both grateful that it was you.'

She turned away, knowing there were things to be done. The formalities of death had to be attended to, and such things had always been taken out of her hands, until now.

Wally spoke jerkily. 'The doctor hasn't been yet, Lisa, but shouldn't we get Mum indoors and out of the sun? She should be lying down and made more comfortable.'

Lisa didn't know whether to laugh or cry or be horrified. Jess hadn't liked too much sun, but it couldn't harm her now. Sitting up, or slumping over, or lying down, she was still dead...

'Wally's right,' Miss Tweed said. 'We must get the dear lady on to her bed ready for when the doctor comes.'

Then it would be the laying-out woman, and the undertaker and his men, all coming to do their gruesome tasks ... and Lisa didn't want to see her mother, with all the life gone out of her, and know that it was real...

'Come on, sis,' Wally said quietly, 'we can't leave her all on her own.'

He was wiser and stronger than she was at that moment. He was already a man, taking charge, and moments later they carried the frail body of Jess Newman indoors and laid her reverently on her bed to await the arrival of the doctor.

And in the midst of it all, shameful and guilty though it was, came the thought that Lisa didn't really have anything to stay in England for now, except for Wally, who was a man and could take care of himself...

'It's not that I didn't care for Mum,' she told Renee later, 'because of course I did. But with Dad gone, and then Gran, and now Mum, it's time I thought about myself, isn't it? Or do you think I should stay here and look after Wally?'

'Of course not!' Renee said bluntly. 'He's big enough to take care of himself. Besides, perhaps the Tweed woman will be his mother from now on.'

'He already has a mother. *Had* a mother. Oh, you know what I mean. She's not a replacement for Mum.'

'Why not? Don't bite my head off, but why not ask her to stay and be a home companion for Wally? She did everything a mother did, didn't she? She did the cooking and

173

cleaning and washing and ironing. She's a perishing angel, if you ask me. Even if you don't go to France, you could do with somebody in the house to do those things, Lisa.' She gave a grin. 'Besides, she's old enough and ugly enough so that people wouldn't think it odd for her to be looking after a good-looking chap like your Wally.'

'I can't think about that now.' *Nor make jokes about it, either.* 'We've got the funeral to get through first.'

It wouldn't be solely her decision, anyway. The two other people were the principal ones involved, but Lisa found herself watching them and wondering if it was feasible ... and how soon she could tactfully get around to saying it.

A week later, it was taken out of her hands. The funeral was over, the neighbours had dispersed after cups of tea and murmurs of sympathy, and the three of them were alone. Miss Tweed cleared her throat awkwardly.

'I'll be looking for another post as soon as possible, but I would just like to say what a privilege it has been looking after you both, as well as your dear mother. I shall miss you all.'

Wally looked startled. 'Miss us? Where are you going?'

She smiled wanly. 'Oh, there are always places for someone like me, always folk who need someone with no attachments to cook and clean for them. You don't need to worry about me, Wally.'

'But what about us? *We* need you, Tweedy! Why can't you stay and cook and clean for me and Lisa?'

He didn't mean it in any demeaning way, and she didn't take it as such, but she flushed darkly, glancing at Lisa. 'I don't think that's my decision.'

Lisa knew she had to choose her words carefully. Wally had just lost his mother, and, if what she wanted came to pass, he would be losing his sister, too. She hadn't given that aspect too much thought until this minute, and now wasn't the time to bring it up.

'If you are agreeable to the arrangement, Tweedy, I know we would both prefer you to stay. You've become part of the family.'

'Then of course I accept,' the woman said with obvious relief. 'And your mother always said that one day you would return to France, Lisa.'

Before she had a chance to reply Wally spoke up.

'Of course she must go back to France. It's where her heart belongs, and we'll be all right, won't we, Tweedy? Besides, I'll be able to get the low-down on any stuff that's going on in Europe for the paper. She'll be my own private spy.'

'You're such a ninny,' Lisa said, choked because these two were making it so easy for her to do what she so dearly wanted.

'And you're far too clever to waste the gifts that God gave you,' Miss Tweed said, which made her feel like weeping all over again.

She agreed to finish the school term and leave for France in early July. By then the shock of Jess's death would have faded a little, and the new order in the house would be established. She would have time to inspect the choice of apartments M. Dubois had found for her in Paris, and look over Herr Gott's new office just outside the city, then she would spend a week at the Dubois family home before they all went to Berlin for the Games. Then she would begin her new job.

'You've got it all mapped out, haven't you?' Renee said jealously. 'Everything's going your way now.'

'Except for losing my mother,' Lisa retorted, wondering what was nagging her now. 'What's up? It was your idea to suggest asking Tweedy to move in permanently, if you remember.'

'I know, but I never wanted you to go away again.'

'I don't see why not. You've got your new friend at work, and you've got Eddie. You won't miss me!'

'Yes I will. Sophie's a blabbermouth and I don't tell her everything. And me and Eddie don't always see eye to eye about things.'

Lisa knew that if she said there were plenty more fish in the sea besides Eddie Renee would snap her head off, and if she sympathized she'd start hearing intimate things she didn't want to know.

'Well, you can't expect to get along with people all the time, not even best friends. We've certainly had our moments. How are things with your mum now, by the way?' she asked.

Renee shrugged. 'All right, as long as I don't have to see *him* too often. He keeps wanting me to live with them, but I'd rather go on sharing my poky little room with Sophie, thanks very much.'

'So what are you grumbling about?' Lisa said.

She wished Renee would finish with Eddie Bray once and for all. Their relationship had been on and off for so long they were like an old married couple, bickering half the time and sickeningly lovey-dovey for the rest of it. Love shouldn't be like that – or so she believed. But she wasn't wasting precious time thinking about it. A new life lay ahead of her, and she intended to make the most of it.

She arrived in France to find the ever-faithful Gerard waiting for her with the limousine. She asked after the family and relished hearing all the news.

'The Biarritz relatives are preparing for Antoine's wedding in December. He and his bride will be moving there, and he and his brother are taking over their father's business. Dani expects to be a bridesmaid, but Pierre's more excited about going to the Games in Berlin. They're like little adults now.'

'They always were, even though they're only eleven and thirteen,' Lisa said dryly, making them both laugh. 'Will you and Mimi be going to Berlin?'

His face clouded. 'I fear not. Mimi's not well enough to travel these days, and I would not want to leave her for so long, so M. Dubois will drive himself.'

'I hope it's nothing serious!'

Gerard gave an expressive shrug. 'No more than the march of time. But we were sorry to hear about your mother, Lisa.'

She noticed how neatly he turned the conversation and didn't press him any more. And once they arrived at the house and she was hugged by Mimi, looking exactly the same as before, Lisa was reassured – and curious. But there was little time for speculation as she was greeted like a long-lost relative, and she realized again how amazingly easy it was to slip into the role of pseudo-Frenchwoman.

The house was bathed in sunlight on this perfect July afternoon. The flowers were in fragrant profusion, seeming to welcome her with every breath she took. Everything was dear and familiar, her room was the same as before, and as the children who were no longer children escorted her in she burst out laughing at the sight of the glassy-eyed, green fabric frog that squatted on her pillow.

'You decided not to frighten me with the real Georges then!'

'The real Georges died,' Dani said with callous cheerfulness, 'so I made this one for you instead, to keep you company.'

'Very thoughtful of you.' Lisa grinned back, thankful that these little adults were no longer precocious little monsters.

'Did you know Antoine and Veronique are getting married?' Dani went on, watching her. 'I'll show you a picture of the dress I'm going to wear. Are you sad Antoine's not marrying you instead?' she shot out.

So she hadn't changed that much. She had always liked to shock. But there was no longer any hint of her own childish crush on her cousin.

'I shan't be sad at all. Antoine and I were just friends, and I haven't met the man I want to marry yet. And before you start asking any more questions let's go downstairs or your mama will wonder what we're doing.'

All the talk downstairs was of the coming Games, and how wonderful it would be to see the vast stadium that was going to house

179

it all.

'There's a new innovation this year,' Henri said. 'There has been a torch relay all the way from Olympia, where the ancient Games were begun in Greece, of course. It's been carried through seven countries to reach Germany, over several thousands of kilometres, and the final runner will light a flame at the stadium to burn throughout the Games.'

'And the Games will actually be shown on television,' Monique added. 'There will be twenty-five huge screens in theatres in the city, so that local people can watch them free of charge.'

'I made a chart of all the countries the torch goes through,' Pierre said, not to be outdone. 'It begins in Greece, and goes through Bulgaria, Yugoslavia, Hungary, Czechoslovakia and Austria, until it reaches Germany.'

'My goodness. I'm impressed that you have been paying such attention to home-work, Pierre!' Lisa teased him.

'I've impressed on him that it's an impor-tant occasion for Germany,' Henri said. 'Bringing countries together in the name of sport is something in which we should all take pride.'

Lisa glanced at him, sensing the slight change in his voice. It was well documented by now that Chancellor Adolf Hitler, whose job it would be to open the Games, had no love for other races. Wally, too, through taking a keen interest in the newspaper archives as well as in current affairs, was well versed in the fact that Herr Hitler had a strong belief in Aryan racial superiority. But this historic event, which brought nations together in true sportsmanship, would surely mean that all such prejudices must be put aside.

Lisa sensed that for all his friendship with Herr Gott, and the fact that many French and German businesses had dealings with one another, Henri Dubois was not a great lover of the German chancellor. She didn't have the temerity to ask him, but she could ask Mimi. After enquiring about her health, she was told that it was no more than rheumatics that plagued her, but it made sitting for long hours, even in a vehicle such as the Dubois limousine, very uncomfortable.

'So what do you think about Herr Hitler being the ambassador for the Games, Mimi? Will he make a success of it?' Lisa asked, hoping the question was innocuous. After all, everyone was aware of the unprepossessing appearance of the man and his rasping voice.

To her surprise Mimi's face darkened. 'Perhaps. But he is a dangerous man with his rigid opinions, and I see violence ahead, if not now then in days to come.'

'I didn't know you were a clairvoyant!' Lisa teased, ignoring the little chill at her words.

Mimi paused. 'Well, perhaps that's too strong a word for it, but I do sometimes see things. If I had been born in another century I would probably have suffered the same fate as Joan of Arc.'

She spoke so complacently that Lisa wondered if she had really heard the words at all.

'Do you mean it?' she said at last.

'Oh yes,' Mimi said. 'I knew you would come back to us in time to go to Germany, just as I knew that M. Antoine was not the one for you.'

'Why didn't you tell me at the time then?' Lisa said, not sure if she should be having this bizarre conversation. Mimi was an ordinary middle-aged woman, not the kind of person you imagined having second sight.

'You don't tell people things until they're ready to hear them, and sometimes it's wiser to say nothing at all.'

Lisa watched Mimi stiffly walk away, the rheumatics rather more obvious, and she felt an unaccountable shudder. It was as if the sun had gone behind a cloud, instead of shining in a brilliant blue sky, with no hint of impending violence or anything other than a beautiful summer's day.

Eleven

The limousine taking the Dubois family to Germany covered the kilometres smoothly. They were arriving at their hosts' house a week before the Games, which gave them ample time to relax and explore the countryside. To Lisa, the Gotts' house was little short of a palace. The heavy, excessively ornate furniture was not to her taste, but, having been brought up in a small house attached to a dozen others in an English country village, it was vastly different from what she was used to.

It was a pleasant visit, but she was glad when the opening day of the Games arrived and they had something specific to do. Any boredom vanished as they drove to the city stadium on the first of August for the opening ceremony of the Games, through streets that were bedecked with German flags and swastikas. A month earlier, a civil war had broken out in Spain, and Hitler was no doubt thanking his stars that these Games, accorded such prestige in Germany, had not gone to Barcelona, as was first planned.

All that was forgotten now, in the blaze of

glory heralding the arrival of the Olympic torch. The newspapers were calling it a symbol of friendship, uniting all the nations taking part. Four thousand athletes paraded around the stadium behind their flags, some giving the Nazi salute to Herr Hitler as they passed, but many others merely giving him the 'eyes right'.

Lisa had spoken to the chauffeur's wife at various times now, and recalled her unease about these so-called peaceful Games. Discovering Mimi's Jewish background, Lisa understood why she and Gerard hadn't wanted to come to Germany.

'Adolf Hitler is a man with a devil's black heart, Lisa,' Mimi often repeated, with a rare venom.

'Why do you say that?' Lisa had said the first time, startled by her passion.

'Because I feel it, *here*,' she said, pressing her hand to her chest. 'He is evil, Lisa, and one day everyone will know it.'

'You're scaring me now!'

'I don't mean to. But perhaps after all it is not such a bad thing to be frightened of what we cannot control.'

Lisa was remembering that conversation more than she had intended to throughout the Games. It was obvious that Herr Hitler wanted his country to win the most medals; that he considered his compatriots to be the 'Master Race' – even though he wasn't even German, but Austrian, and some still thought him a ridiculous little man.

He was also the people's champion, since the twenty-five large television screens throughout Berlin enabled local people to watch the Games without paying a fee. It seemed he could do no wrong, and Mimi must be mistaken.

All the same, despite all the excitement, including the one unpleasant moment when Hitler refused to shake the hand of the black American athlete Jesse Owens, the Dubois party were glad to leave when the Games ended, to return to the comparative calm of the French countryside. Crowds of people still thronged the Berlin streets, as if loath to turn their backs on what had been such a spectacular event, and vehicles crawled for many kilometres before leaving the city environs.

A sudden scuffle in an alleyway alongside the main road resulted in shouting and screaming as several youths brandishing hammers chased an elderly man and his sobbing wife, and it was only brought under control by the man's supporters chasing the youths away.

'What was all that about?' Lisa gasped. 'Who were those poor people, and why were those ruffians hounding them?'

'There are several Jewish bakeries around

here, and I daresay the youth of the Master Race decided they had had enough of them. It happens,' Henri told her.

Lisa stared at the back of his neck, which was noticeably redder now. Monique murmured something to him, which Lisa could not hear, and the next moment the glass screen in the limousine had slid into place, separating those in the front seat from those in the back.

'Maman always does that when she doesn't want us to hear the gossip,' Dani complained. 'She thinks we're not old enough to know what's going on.'

'What *is* going on?' Lisa said, thinking that if this child with the too-knowing eyes knew what was happening then she had a right to know it too. The street incident had shaken her more than she expected.

'I expect it's about Mimi being upset one night when Maman was trying to comfort her,' Dani said, suddenly all conspiratorial.

'What does Mimi have to do with this?'

But instantly she knew. Mimi was Jewish...

Dani shrugged, too young to see the significance of what she was saying, but too canny not to love the way she was about to shock somebody older.

'Maman saw Mimi in the garden. She was crying and Gerard was holding her tight. They're married, you know,' she added.

'Yes, I do know,' Lisa said impatiently.

186

Lisa raked her mind about something Wally had told her a long time ago, something about the Nuremburg decrees Hitler had made regarding Jews being barred from teaching and farming and broadcasting, as well as various other occupations, including journalism, which had enraged Wally. Jews were also forbidden to marry Aryans, or to have extramarital relations with them.

At the time Lisa remembered shutting him up, saying he was far too young to talk about such things, even if he was in the newspaper business, where scandals were openly discussed. Now she wished she had listened to him more. Because suddenly it was personal. Mimi was Jewish, and Gerard was not. But they lived here in France, where such things were not frowned upon. To Lisa the sight and sound of those old people being openly persecuted in a Berlin street had now become personal too.

'I don't know what it was all about really,' Dani went on regretfully, 'except that Mimi had two sisters in Germany and now they've gone to live in Belgium. Mimi was crying because she thought she'd never see them again, and Maman said that we should be extra nice to her because she had such a cross to bear. What do you think she meant by that?'

Lisa made light of it. 'Having you home for the holidays, I should imagine!'

But she wished feverishly that if only that were all that it was ... and she meant to phone Wally as soon as she returned to her flat in Paris, where she could be undisturbed, to report first-hand news about the Games and to find out more.

'I knew you never listened to me,' Wally said, his voice crackling over the wire.

'Well, I'm listening now. What do you know about it?' She refrained from calling it the 'Jewish situation', because it seemed so ghastly for an entire race to be condemned by a dictator. There were already some who whispered that Hitler was a monster whose activities should be curbed ... She broke off her thoughts to listen to what her brother was saying.

'Sis, since last September, when Hitler declared them no longer German citizens, the Jews have had no rights in Germany. Many of them have fled the country rather than be hounded in their own homes.'

'But why?' Lisa said, shocked.

'Who knows what goes on in a fanatic's mind?' Wally said. 'He wants Germany to be a pure race, though there are many who would argue that his methods are anything but pure. It's even on record that German servant girls have been dragged from their beds and told not to return to Jewish employers.'

'So that makes what I saw all the more real,' she said slowly.

'What did you see?' Wally said, his voice sharpening, and she imagined how his newspaperman's nose for a story was quivering.

She related the small incident quickly.

'Come home, sis,' he said quietly.

'What?'

'You're getting mixed up with all kinds of people. This Herr Gott, for instance. What do you really know about him?'

'I know he manufactures motor cars! He's not one of Hitler's henchmen! Why should I come home? None of this will affect me.'

'It may affect the whole of Europe eventually, and maybe even the world. Come home, Lisa. I'm sure English firms need interpreters too.'

He sounded so adult now, so mature. He was like a father figure, worrying for her, and she felt a huge rush of affection for him.

'Wally, this is my home now,' she said, 'but I promise I'll be back for Christmas. We'll want to be together then.'

She didn't say that it would be the first Christmas without Jess, but she didn't need to. It was unthinkable that she would join in Antoine's wedding celebrations when there would be a grieving little household in England. She was glad she was living independently now, so Monique would see nothing strange in her wanting to go back to England

189

instead of joining them in Biarritz.

'Wally, I have to go now,' she said firmly in the small silence that followed her mention of Christmas. 'Say hello to Tweedy for me, and take care of yourself.'

'You too, sis,' he said, and then the line went dead.

She knew it didn't pay to dwell on things that did not concern her, or could not be changed. World events may be of major interest to Wally in his profession, but not in hers. Her job was to do the best she could for Herr Gott, to make new friends in the country that she loved, using her skills to the best of her ability.

'You pompous ass,' she muttered out loud, her mouth twitching at how important she made herself sound, when she was no more than a cog in Herr Gott's business machinery. 'Still, Mum would be proud of me – except for the fact that I was working for a German.'

The sudden image of her mother had the most unexpected effect. One minute she was mocking her own self-importance, and the next she had dissolved into a heap in her armchair, weeping for her mother and the days that were gone and could never come again.

Most of the office staff where she worked were German, imported, as they called it, from other offices in Germany. There was one French girl, but Lisa was the only Englishwoman, and treated with a little hostility at first, although that changed when they discovered she was good at her work and ready to make friends. It was the best way, Henri Dubois had advised her. It always takes the breeze from the sails. Smile at them all, and they'll be obliged to smile back.

It usually worked, provided they didn't think she was some inane countrywoman who grinned all day long, as she commented to Wally on her weekly phone call home. By then, in mid-October, she was looking forward to travelling home for Christmas using the new sleeper train and ferry crossing between Dunkirk and Dover, which would take her as far as Victoria in London without changing.

'As long as you're happy,' Wally said cagily.

She picked up the nuance in his voice at once.

'What's wrong? You're not ill, are you? Or Tweedy?'

'We're fine. I suppose you haven't heard about yesterday's Fascist march through London led by Sir Oswald Mosley and his Blackshirts.'

'No, I haven't.'

Wally would have been avidly interested, of course, both as a journalist and because of his sister's involvement with the German

191

firm. Not that Herr Gott's business had anything to do with the Fascist movement. She hoped.

'Come home, Lisa.' Wally repeated his old theme, suddenly urgent, unable to disguise the anxiety in his voice.

'Why? This march took place in London, didn't it, not Paris! It sounds as if I'm safer here!' she said.

'It turned into a riot. Mosley was wearing a military uniform and jackboots, which was enough to incense those who opposed him, and his posh car soon had its windscreen smashed. But that was only the start. Glass was flying everywhere, bricks were hurled at the police and lorries were overturned. There were loads of arrests and injuries, and a Jewish tailor and his son were thrown through a plate-glass window by these Blackshirt thugs.'

Lisa's heart was thumping by now; she was all too aware why Mimi hadn't wanted to go to Berlin for the Games, where the Jews were being so discriminated against.

But this had occurred in London. This was England.

'Are you still there, Lisa?'

'Yes. I'm just finding it hard to believe.'

'Believe it,' Wally said grimly. 'This is only the start.'

'The start of what?'

'Your guess is as good as mine, sis.'

But it wasn't. Wally might have a young reporter's enthusiasm for dramatic events, but he had a sensible head on his shoulders, and more of an insight into current affairs than she ever would. For a moment she felt as if the image of a shadowy something was staring her in the face, an image more horrific than she could ever imagine. Something that was still too vague to comprehend, but which sent an icy shiver down her spine.

She went home for Christmas, after a flying visit to the Dubois', in the rickety car she had now acquired and learnt to drive, to deliver Antoine and Veronique's wedding gift. And by then England had more to think about than a fanatic in a military uniform and jackboots.

Every newspaper carried the story that the King had abdicated for the love of a divorced American woman, Mrs Simpson, and that his brother, the Duke of York, was the new King George the Sixth. The Duchess of York was now Queen Elizabeth, their two daughters were the princesses Elizabeth and Margaret Rose, and ten-year-old Princess Elizabeth was the new heir to the throne.

Reading the numerous and varied accounts of the abdication crisis and its consequences helped to fill the many hours it took for Lisa to reach home. All the talk was of the scandalous royal affair and its conclusion, and the country's opinion seemed divided over the whole thing.

As the train carried her westward from London, Lisa sat back and closed her eyes, half listening to the gossip all around her, and trying to imagine what such a decision to abdicate must have meant to King Edward. A king had to be passionately in love to give up his crown for a woman, and to some it would be the most romantic thing. To others it was clearly a national disgrace and betrayal.

She discovered how strong Miss Tweed's feelings were on the subject almost before she had got her coat off and warmed her toes by the fire. Wally wasn't home yet, and Tweedy fussed around her like a mother hen.

'You'll have heard the news and seen all the papers then?' she said, seeing a copy sticking out of Lisa's coat pocket.

'I could hardly miss it, nor the way people were talking about it!'

'Well, I daresay it keeps them off the subject of war for a while,' Tweedy said tartly. 'Personally I think it's a scandal. The man should have had more control of himself, and not thrown his poor brother into such a situation.'

Lisa started to laugh at such down-to-earth comments.

'You can hardly refer to the new king as

somebody's poor brother, Tweedy. Have you no respect for the monarchy?'

'Did the King?' she countered. 'All he cared about was his lady-friend, and a divorced one at that.'

'Well, I'm far too tired from my journey to discuss it right now,' Lisa said firmly. 'I'm sure Wally will put me in the picture. The house looks marvellous, by the way. You've got a really artistic touch with Christmas decorations, Tweedy.'

Miss Tweed's stern face relaxed. 'And you've got a clever way of turning a conversation when it's not going your way, miss!'

'Have I?' Lisa said innocently. 'All I want is to enjoy Christmas with my family, and I suppose it's far too late for me to stir the Christmas puddings?'

'Far too late, but you can still help to decorate the cake.'

Only when she had unpacked and was going downstairs to the kitchen, where the delicious smell of the evening meal was wafting around, did her footsteps falter. She had been determined not to let the memories of all those other Christmases spoil things: when the house was a real family home; when her mother was preparing the meal, and her father was still strong and alive, and Grannie Cissie had a say in everything ... but the sweet ghosts still lingered, despite her resolve.

Then Wally burst into the house, bringing a breath of frosty air with him, and the ghosts were gone. He hugged her tight for a moment and then let her go.

'Good Lord, I swear you grow another inch every time I see you,' Lisa said weakly, hoping she wasn't turning into her mother with such a remark.

'And you grow more beautiful,' he said cheekily. 'That Antoine of yours doesn't know what he's missing.'

'Oh, I think he does. And he was never mine, anyway. I just borrowed him for a while until Veronique came along.'

'So who's on the horizon now?' Wally asked.

'No one! And it's none of your business, anyway.'

But she was smiling as she said it, because it was so good to be home, to be talking in her native language instead of French or German, and to be quite sure that the watchful spirits of Jess and Ron and Cissie were still here.

'I saw your friend Renee the other day,' Wally said over supper. 'She's all agog over this abdication thing, of course, and obviously thinks it's the most romantic thing in the world. She was always such a ninny.'

Lisa was indignant. 'Renee's just soft hearted, and she never sees the bad in anyone – well, except her stepfather.'

'Oh yes, Herman the German,' Wally commented.

'That's not his name.'

'It's what some of the village kids call him, though. He's not well-liked around here, and Renee's well out of it, if you ask me.'

'I didn't,' Lisa said, feeling oddly unsettled at his implication. 'Anyway, she's still my friend, and I want to see how she's getting on just as soon as I can.'

Miss Tweed cleared her throat, sensing the small friction between them.

'So how is the French family, Lisa?'

'Very well. Dani paraded in her bridesmaid frock before I left, and M. Dubois has promised to send me some photos when I return to Paris. I can stay home for a couple of weeks, if that's all right,' she added.

'Why wouldn't it be?' Wally said. 'This is your home, isn't it?'

Well, it was and it wasn't. Lisa had a strange feeling about it that never quite went away. It wasn't just that Tweedy and Wally got along almost as well as mother and son now, it was more that Lisa knew she had moved on. All these years away from the pastoral Somerset village where she was born had changed her after all. It wasn't that she didn't love it here, but life never stood still, and the time came when you had to move with it.

She soon discovered what Wally had meant about Renee being almost besotted by the romantic news of a king giving up a throne for love. It was almost sickening, the way she went on about it, never mind the whole country being thrown into turmoil at the effect it might have on the people and the government.

'Oh well, as long as the new man does a good job, we shouldn't worry too much, should we?' she said pithily, as cynical as Tweedy.

'The *new man*?' Renee echoed. 'How can you be so disrespectful, Lisa?'

'I'm not,' she said crossly, 'but I don't see what difference it will make to us. To me and you – and Eddie. I suppose he's still around?'

'Of course. We're engaged, you know we are. And when did you become so hard? You're turning into a proper old maid, Lisa.'

'Thanks! I suppose only my *best friend* could tell me so.'

They glared at one another, and then began to laugh, the way they always did when the tension between them ran too high. It was their safety valve, the one that meant their friendship was far bigger than any petty argument.

'You're not going to miss being at the froggie wedding of the year, then?' Renee went on.

'Of course not. And don't call them that. They're good people, and Antoine means nothing to me. If you must know...'

'What?' Renee said as she hesitated. 'Have you met someone else?'

She was too gullible, too easy to fool, and Lisa knew she was about to do it, if only to let her know she wasn't turning into a proper old maid...

'Well, there's a chap at work who's quite nice and I've been out with him once or twice.'

'I knew it! Come on, then. Details!'

Lisa laughed, already wishing she hadn't started this. 'His name's Johann and he has blond hair and blue eyes—'

'He sounds German,' she said, disapproval oozing out of her.

'He is but that doesn't stop him being a nice person. In any case, he won't be at the Paris office much longer. He's going back to Berlin in the new year to take up a new post, so that's that,' she said, nettled at this reaction. Though she should have expected it from Renee.

But she liked Johann. He made her laugh, and he made her feel alive, reminding her that she was nothing like a proper old maid! He made her feel sensations she hadn't known since Antoine. She didn't yearn for romance, but Johann made her realize that such feelings were never dead and buried for ever, and only needed the right person to bring them to sizzling life again. Maybe Johann wasn't the one and maybe he was. In any case, there could be no future for them if he was returning to Berlin, because Lisa knew she wouldn't follow him there. The brief incident in the street after the Olympic Games had intensified her distaste at the thought of being under the thumb of such a dictatorship.

'Just as long as you don't go and live there,' Renee said, as if she could read her thoughts. 'That would really be a sell-out, wouldn't it?'

'I definitely won't. So have you and Eddie decided to set the date? Do I have to buy a new hat yet?'

Renee brightened. 'End of next summer with any luck. You've got to be my brides-maid, and I shall refuse to get married without you there.'

God, it was tempting ... but Renee looked so flushed with happiness that not for all the world would she dampen her glow. If Eddie Bray was the one she wanted then who was she to say he was a farmyard oaf?

She hugged her friend. 'Wild horses would not keep me away.'

Nor that nasty little Adolf Hitler ... though why his name flashed through her mind just then, she couldn't have said. And she just as easily flashed it away.

Twelve

Lisa considered 1937 to be a year of big events, both personal and international. In February Johann went back to Berlin, and she hardly missed him – which proved to her that their relationship had been going nowhere. That same month Antoine's younger brother, the quiet Alain, volunteered to fight in the Spanish Civil War, and not long afterwards the news came that he had been killed.

The family grief, so soon after Antoine's wedding, was indescribable. Monique told her on the telephone that her sister was inconsolable, and the family closed in on themselves to the exclusion of everyone else. Lisa made no attempt to intrude, apart from sending flowers and inadequate condolences.

She was guiltily glad she was no longer so closely involved, since sharing other people's grief was the most exhausting of emotions. It wasn't that she didn't care. She admired Alain's strength of character in supporting a cause when he had no need, and hoped she managed to convey such thoughts in her letters.

In May came news that the giant German airship, the Hindenburg, had exploded in a raging ball of fire as it was preparing to land in New Jersey.

Wally Newman phoned his sister, his voice hoarse with a journalist's natural excitement, mingling with horror at such a story.

'Have you heard the news? Passengers and crew have been killed, and it was like an inferno as the thing blew to pieces in front of those waiting to see it land. What a scoop for any reporters there!'

'Wally!'

'Sorry, sis, but you know that's the way we are. Whatever makes news, it's our job to report it. Anyway, the coronation will make happier news next week.'

'How callous you are.'

'No I'm not. Just realistic. How many of the crowds in London next week cheering their new King and Queen, will give a thought to the Hindenburg disaster? It will already be yesterday's news, Lisa, and that's human nature.'

She supposed so. There was always something terrible going on in the world, but hopefully there was always something good to counteract it. She mentally crossed her fingers at the thought.

Wally promised to send her some newspapers with the pictures of King George and

Queen Elizabeth's coronation at Westminster Abbey, and a few weeks later they arrived in a bundle at Lisa's flat.

What he had said seemed to be true. Except for those most intimately concerned, most people had already forgotten the Hindenburg disaster, and the scenes in the newspapers were of a smiling King and Queen with the little princesses on the balcony, wearing their crowns, the perfect family unit.

A month later, in June, came the news that the ex-King Edward, now the Duke of Windsor, had married his American lady in Tours, and hundreds of French sightseers were there to watch, knowing that the couple were to settle in France. There was nothing like a celebrity wedding to draw excited crowds, especially one as controversial and poignant as this one.

But there were more personal things for Lisa to think about. In September Renee was finally getting married to Eddie Bray and Lisa would be her chief bridesmaid. Sophie, Renee's workmate, was to be the other. They were to choose their own frocks in pale blue, and, provided they each wore the small floral headband Renee had given them, they were free to choose their own style.

'I know you won't want to bother with fittings and all that nonsense,' she wrote, easily committing the chief bridesmaid's appearance to one of far less importance than the bride's. Which it was, of course, and Lisa read on.

You always look lovely, Lisa, so just be there to stop me having the jitters. I didn't think I'd have them, having known Eddie for so long, but this is different. When we walk out of that church, we'll know each other *intimately*, if you know what I mean. Oh, and I'm not having *him* give me away. I've asked my Uncle Frank from Uphill to do it. I'm not having any old Fritz taking an important part in my wedding, and Mum can either like it or stay away. She won't, though, even though we had an unholy row when I first mentioned that I'd already asked Uncle Frank.

Lisa was laughing by the time she came to the end of the letter. Renee's bubbling excitement was obvious now. Eddie Bray apparently made Renee happy, and if he was her choice who was she to put a spanner in the works?

But choosing her own dress, with her workmate Marie on hand to help, inevitably made her think about her own lack of prospects.

'Do you think everyone has only one soul-mate in the world, Marie?' she asked, as they sat at the nearest riverside café for some welcome coffee and cakes, the blue frock now boxed and wrapped.

Marie shrugged. 'If that were true, there would be fewer second marriages and more widows in the world. No, I just think that neither you nor I have found the right one yet. But he'll come along one day, you'll see.'

'Let's just hope he's not the same one, then,' Lisa said, poker faced, which met with no response at first, and then Marie began to laugh.

'Ah, you English, you do love your little joke, don't you!"

Renee's wedding day was bright and sunny, a lasting legacy of summer and the promise of a warm autumn. Lisa had offered her flat to the newlyweds for a week's honeymoon while she stayed in England, but, predictably, Eddie had refused.

To a farmer there were always pigs and hens to be fed, and cows to be milked, and he couldn't spare the precious time away from the farm for such shenanigans, he told Renee pompously.

It didn't bode too well for the future, but Lisa knew better than to blight the occasion by saying so. Renee was cheerful enough at leaving her live-in job, to become what she called 'a lady of leisure', though Lisa couldn't ever remember such a phrase being applied to a farmer's wife.

At least Mrs Bray's wretched parrot had perished some while ago, and Renee had flatly refused to marry Eddie if she ever decided to get another one. Surprisingly, his mother had agreed.

It was a small wedding, since Renee had few relatives apart from the puffing and red-faced Uncle Frank from Uphill, but she had also invited Wally and Miss Tweed, so it was a jolly wedding party who sat down to a slap-up do, as Eddie called it, provided by his mother at the farmhouse.

'Not quite your cordon bleu, is it, sis?' Wally whispered to her, as they surveyed the hunks of pork pie spread out on the side table.

'No. And I'm glad you haven't forgotten your French,' she said with a grin.

'Well, you never know when I might need it.'

Before she could query this odd remark, Uncle Frank hammered on the bridal table for a bit of hush, and made a little speech among much laughter and a fair bit of farm-yard humour, before asking the bridegroom to stand up and be counted.

Lisa couldn't help comparing this homely wedding, with the bridesmaids in their mis-matched frocks, and the farmhouse setting, to the photos of Antoine and Veronique's, in the posh surroundings of an elegant French church and swish hotel. And *then* going off to some exclusive little hideaway in the country for their honeymoon.

But Renee looked so luminous and happy that she willed away the disloyal thoughts. It didn't matter where you were married, or what the circumstances. All that mattered was being head over heels in love with the man beside you. And these two had it all. How could anything be wrong in a world when love was the only thing that mattered?

Back at work the following month, she received some newspaper cuttings from Wally that were more than disturbing. They told of the second skirmish involving Sir Oswald Mosley in a week – the first had been in London – where costermongers, barrowboys and the like tried to bar the way of thousands of Blackshirts, some of them women, rallying to Mosley's Fascist cause.

This incident had taken place in Liverpool, where he was preparing to address a crowd of thousands. Bricks, bottles and other missiles were thrown at him as he stood on the roof of his loudspeaker van, until a stone hit him on the head and knocked him unconscious.

Apparently the government had refused the Labour party's appeals to ban these extreme right-wing marches and rallies, and, according to Wally's accompanying letter, the country was already in some kind of turmoil, and Mosley was doing nothing to stem it.

Since the French newspapers were just as avid for gossip as any others, Lisa was already aware of the final item in Wally's cuttings. It concerned the Duke and Duchess of Windsor, and claimed that the royal couple had been fêted when they arrived in Berlin for a meeting with the German chancellor, Adolf Hitler, and other Nazi leaders. The visit was being called an occasion to study social conditions and housing problems in Germany.

'What possible business can these exiles have with German social and housing problems?' Wally wrote, disapproval of the couple plain to see.

> I tell you, Lisa, the world is going crazy, and now the government is considering a plan to erect air-raid shelters in towns and cities, which Mr Churchill has been urging for the past three years. If that doesn't mean war is imminent, I don't know what does.

She caught her breath before reading on.

Can't you see how vulnerable you would be, working for a German firm, especially in Paris, when France will be its nearest neighbour if war breaks out? Or should that be when war breaks out? Please think seriously whether a highly paid job is going to be worth it in the end.

It was the most serious letter she had ever received from Wally, especially in the skilful way he avoided actually begging her to come home this time, but left his meaning perfectly clear.

By the end of the year the plan for air-raid shelters to be erected had been approved by the government. Then, as if to underline how all-powerful the German chancellor was becoming, Lisa's German colleagues told her a law had been passed in Germany stating that all children not educated and drilled to believe in the Nazi regime risked being taken away from their parents.

'This is a very bad law,' the young office worker called Viktor commented. 'It takes away the right of every parent to bring up their children in the way they wish. Instead, they will virtually belong to the state, as Herr Hitler demands.'

'You don't agree with everything he says then?' Lisa asked him mildly.

'We don't all have these fanatical ideas, Lisa.'

'But perhaps it is best not to voice your thoughts too loudly,' she suggested.

'Perhaps that is so,' he agreed.

It was sad for a vigorous and normally outspoken young man like Viktor to have to be so cautious, even with his colleagues. But he had a family in Germany, and she could see that it would be unwise for him to protest openly.

Viktor spoke intelligently on many subjects: music and literature and the arts. He wasn't stuffy, though, and when he asked her to a dance one Saturday evening she accepted. Dancing was all the rage in the nightclubs now, and it seemed ages since she had dressed up for anything other than Renee's wedding. Besides, it was a chance to forget Wally's portents of war, and to enjoy herself.

She wore a pale-green frock that set off her red hair, now coiffed into a chic Parisian style, which accentuated her startling green eyes. A thick cream-coloured cape did double duty as a coat, for the December night was chilly, even though they would travel to the nightclub in Viktor's automobile. The moment he saw her, it was obvious that he was smitten by the sparkling girl who greeted him, contrasting so vividly with the more businesslike girl he knew at the office.

'Lisa, you are truly stunning tonight,' he said.

She was flattered. 'And you are a credit to the Fatherland,' she countered, admiring the expensive dark suit and elegant tie with its gold pin at the centre. At the office he was sometimes teased about his father being a count and having pots of money, and tonight's apparel would seem to verify it.

'Oh, I think we shall both make quite an entrance,' Viktor laughed. 'Your carriage awaits you, madame.'

He held out his arm, and as she moved towards him he pulled her into his embrace. Seconds later his mouth was on hers, and although she instinctively made to struggle, he held her fast. Then she was no longer resisting – and registering that nor did she want to as his hand caressed the nape of her neck, sending a delicious tingling throughout her body.

When the kiss ended, his lips were still touching hers as he murmured against them, sending waves of erotic feelings through every part of her.

'My apologies, *liebling*. I promise I won't take such liberties again.'

To Lisa's amazement he stood back a pace and drew his heels together smartly, his fine brown eyes begging her forgiveness. She spoke as evenly as she could, considering the way her heart was racing.

'Don't be silly, Viktor. It was only a kiss. What's a kiss between friends?'

'Then you don't condemn me for it?'

She was suddenly more angry than amused. For heaven's sake, the man had just *kissed* her, leaving her in no doubt that he found her desirable, and awakening passions in her that had lain dormant for so long – and now he was apologizing! But since his ardent enthusiasm seemed to have waned so quickly, she had no wish for him to see how that kiss had affected her.

'I shall only condemn you if you don't take me dancing as you promised. Or do you intend that we should stand here feeling embarrassed with one another for the whole evening?'

'Of course not,' he said, clearly relieved.

'Then let's go,' Lisa said, and daringly gave him a small peck on the cheek.

Because she really liked him. And if liking should one day turn to love, no one but a fool would refuse it. On the other hand, said the more logical part of Lisa's brain, if it was foolish to fall in love with a German in Europe's present unstable conditions, then they could just as easily remain good friends, even kissing friends.

But he made no further attempts at seduction. He was the ultimately correct young man, as polite as only the Germans could be when it was demanded of them. After a highly enjoyable evening, when they had danced the night away and he returned her home, exhausted, he ran his finger down her cheek.

'We must do this again, Lisa.'

'Of course. We had fun, and I enjoy your company immensely, Viktor.' And that was as far as she would go towards saying she would have no objection if he kissed her again, either.

He did so chastely with restrained passion, and yet with all the promise that what was between them was still to come – if they both wanted it. After he left Lisa leant against the door of her flat for a few moments, her eyes closed, wondering if she really did. It was one thing to be respected, which, of course, was what every girl welcomed. It was quite another to have felt that erotic glow of passion in herself, and then have it so quickly extinguished.

She knew she didn't love him. It wasn't the same, and it was certainly no substitute. Her instincts told her that Viktor was not a highly sexed man, nor the type to sweep a girl off her feet. That first kiss, ending with an almost clumsy apology, told her so. If she insisted on just friendship, and pleasant company on evenings out together, she had the feeling that he would have no objections. In a way she felt cheated. No girl wanted to be violated by a man, but neither did she want one who was so ready to settle for friendship rather than love. He might even be afraid of love. If not, why hadn't he approached her in the office before now? There had been times when she had caught him looking at her, and times when she had heard others laughing behind his back. It seemed to explain so many things about the decent young man who was more interested in music and literature and the arts than having a red-blooded relationship with a woman.

She didn't think for a moment that he preferred men to women, but she had a strong suspicion that he was more comfortable without all the sex stuff, as Renee would call it.

Renee. Now there was a girl who knew all there was to know about love. Who was the clever one now? And what the heck did it matter? she asked herself angrily, as she got ready for bed. There was more to life than love and marriage – except for those who wouldn't mind a bit of it for themselves.

'I wouldn't say we're a couple,' she told Renee, home for another Christmas season, 'so don't go reading anything into it. But now you're an old married woman I know you won't be happy until I'm in the same honey trap as you! His name's Viktor, and we go out together or in a group most Saturday nights, dancing, or a poetry reading. I like him, but that's all.'

'Good God, is he a nancy boy?' Renee said bluntly. 'You should ditch him, Lisa, and look around for someone who'll keep you warm at night.'

'I'm perfectly happy as we are. Viktor's good company.'

Renee looked at her silently. 'Sometimes I worry about you, Lisa. You've become more French than English in your appearance – and very nice it is, too. But if you're hob-nobbing with all these German folk, God knows where it will end.'

'I work with them so I can hardly ignore them. Though there's been an undercurrent in the office lately.'

'What kind of an undercurrent?' Renee was persistent, as always.

'Oh, nothing much, rumours mostly.'

'Well come on, you can't leave it there! What kind of rumours? Has your Viktor found himself a boyfriend on the side?'

Lisa burst out laughing. Renee was a bit much, and she had got even bolder since marrying Eddie. That was life on the farm for you, she thought uncharitably. All that mucking out of pigs and cattle and seeing nature in the raw.

'Leave Viktor out of this. No, rumours are flying about the Paris office being closed down, and everyone moving to Germany. We don't know how true it is, but Marie is flatly refusing to go anywhere, and as for me, I just don't know.'

'Of course you know! You'll refuse as well. Crikey, Lisa, it's bad enough for me having Herman the German as my so-called step-father, and you working with some of them, but to go and live amongst them would be the end.'

'The end of what? Our friendship?'

'I didn't say that, but it might, if you want me to be honest.'

'When were you anything but?' Lisa said testily, wondering how the dickens they had reached loggerheads again. 'Look, it's not going to happen, so let's talk about some-thing else.'

'Is that a promise?' Renee badgered.

'Yes it is,' Lisa said, her head suddenly clear. 'It definitely is.'

'Thank God you've seen sense over that, anyway,' Wally said.

She hadn't mentioned it at all until it was nearly time for her to return to Paris, knowing he would object. But his reaction made her hackles rise at once.

'I didn't need to see sense, as you call it. I've never had any desire to live in Ger-many. I don't know why everyone suddenly seems to think I'm about to go cavorting with the enemy – not that they are the

216

enemy, are they?'

'Not yet!' Wally said, his words heavy with meaning. 'But everyone knows it's going to come sooner or later, Lisa. We're heading for a war with Germany, and the last thing I want is for you to be stuck in the middle of it. Leave your job while you've got the chance. Find another one in France, if you must, but being employed by a man who is a potential enemy won't do you any favours in the future.'

She stared at him, annoyance quickly turning to fury. 'Sometimes I think you're all stark raving mad! Herr Gott is the nicest of men—'

'And a potential enemy, darling.'

It was the endearment that caught her up short from launching into a tirade. As far as she could remember, he had never called her darling in her life before, and it seemed to underline the depth of his concern for her. While she was still torn between surprise and emotion that he had called her 'darling', her fury dissipated as quickly as it had come.

'You're dead serious, aren't you, Wally?'

His laugh was awkward, as he had only just realized himself how he had addressed her. He tried to make his tone more teasing.

'Of course I am, and I know it's a bit below your principles to take advice from a kid brother, but this time, Lisa, just for once I wish you would.'

She was moved more by his restraint than all that had gone before.

'I promise you I'm listening, and I'll heed your advice, whatever I decide to do. You may be my kid brother, but I respect what you say. I'm not giving you any more praise, though, or your head will get too big to go through the front door.'

Thirteen

Wally habitually sent her newspaper cuttings now, some from the local rag which had his name beneath the articles. He always underlined some of the headlines he thought would interest her, such as when it became compulsory for schoolchildren to practise gas-mask drill. The newspaper pictures of the little mites in their cumbersome gas masks was sad and depressing.

In March Hitler announced the so-called 'spring cleaning' of Austrian Jews, when professional jobs were stripped from them, and theatres and music halls no longer engaged famous Jewish artistes such as Richard Tauber.

'It's appalling,' Lisa told Henri Dubois on one of their occasional meetings in a riverside café. 'How does Mimi feel about all this?'

'She says very little about it,' Henri replied. 'She has a wonderful protector in Gerard, but if France ever came under Nazi rule it would take more than a strong husband to keep her safe.'

'What do you mean if France ever came

under Nazi rule? You can't be serious, Henri. You're scaring me now.'

'It's good to be scared,' he said bluntly. 'The worst thing any of us can do is to be complacent.'

'Then you think I should heed what my brother says?'

'If he advises you to go home, I would not stop you, Lisa.'

She hadn't expected this. He knew how much she loved her adopted country and how much she wanted to stay for ever. She was thrown off balance by his words. In any case it all seemed so unlikely. It was a perfect spring day here in Paris, the river Seine flowing serenely by the Left Bank where they ate their lunch at a pavement café. The sun shone, and there was no hint of war clouds overhead, or of a ruthless invader who would crush this beautiful city and country.

'What would I do in England now? I love my life here, and it's been my home for too long for me to want to leave it.'

'If the Germans invaded then you would be an alien, Lisa. An enemy.'

'But my German colleagues are my friends. Herr Gott is my friend as well as my employer – and your friend, too.'

She was starting to find this conversation unreal and more than a little ludicrous. But Henri looked anything but amused. He took her hands in his.

'Lisa, my dear, friends can just as easily turn to enemies if the state dictates it. Friendship will count for nothing then. It will not be of the ordinary man or woman's choosing, but that is how it will be. Has there been any talk of your office staff being relocated to Germany?'

'Talk, yes. There's always talk,' Lisa said, becoming more disturbed now.

'If that happens, would you work in Germany?'

'I would not!'

'Good. It would be most unwise if you did.'

She realized they were both speaking in short, staccato sentences now, as if they were seeing a future that didn't bear discussing fully. He released her hands, and she felt the small chill of the river breeze as the link was broken.

She spoke uneasily. 'I could always work for you again, Henri!'

He didn't reply, and she could see what he was thinking. If Britain went to war with Germany and France was invaded, why would a Frenchman risk his life and family by harbouring an enemy of the invaders? But this was crazy talk and crazy thoughts. It was implying that war was a certainty, not a game of chance between leaders ... not a game at all.

'If the office closes down, then I shall

return to England, at least for a while,' she said, before she had time to think. 'I'm sure my old school will find me work, or I can always apply for a post as a housekeeper or something!'

'You would be sorely wasted if you did,' Henri said, his voice stern. 'But I'm glad you've made the decision, and you need have no fear about your apartment. If you leave for any length of time, I will see that it is leased on a temporary basis until you return. Which, of course, you will, my dear.'

He may have been trying to boost her spirits, but she returned to the office that afternoon in a daze. She had expected a pleasant hour with her old employer, and instead she had practically received a directive to return to England for her own safety. She could recall every word they had said, and sense the unspoken ones, and she couldn't ignore his urgency. Did he know something she didn't? But why would he? He was not a government man.

She tried not to covertly watch her colleagues, wondering if they knew any more than she did, and knowing she dare not ask about such a sensitive subject as a possible war. These people were her friends, even though she wasn't especially close to any of them, except Victor.

She had never sought to form close friendships, and she wondered if that had been through some sixth sense, some premonition, that it wouldn't be wise. And she almost hated Henri for putting such unwelcome ideas into her mind.

'What's wrong, Lisa?' she heard Marie say. 'That's the third time I've spoken to you, and you seem to be in a daze. Did your gentleman friend ply you with too much wine at lunch?'

The thought of the devoted Henri plying a lady other than his delightful wife with wine banished the disturbing thoughts from her mind.

'No! I'm just feeling a little distracted today.'

'Then you need to be taken out of yourself. That is how you English say it, is it not? You and I should go to the theatre tonight. What do you say?'

'I say it's a splendid idea,' Lisa said.

Anything to brush away the morbid thoughts would be welcome. And perhaps she could probe Marie about her own plans, should the office close down.

It wasn't hard to do. Marie was adamant that she would work in her family's café near Lyons. She didn't like office work, anyway, and said she was only the dogsbody, unlike Lisa, with her clever brain and her ability with languages.

'You're much more than a dogsbody, and you shouldn't run yourself down,' Lisa protested, at which Marie burst out laughing.

'Oh, you English and your funny phrases. How can I run myself down!'

'What I mean is, don't demean yourself.'

'Is it demeaning to work in my family business then?'

'No, but you're a valuable person in the office. If not, Herr Gott would have fired you long ago. He won't tolerate staff who don't pull their weight.'

'Well, I would be sad to leave such a good company. The German fellows are fun, and so are you, but I wouldn't work in Germany.'

'Nor would I. I will be sad to leave the company too, and even more, to leave France. But I believe it is becoming inevitable.'

In September the Paris office closed, and all employees were offered the chance to relocate to Berlin. Most of them agreed. In no time at all, it seemed, it was as if the office had never existed, such was German efficiency once a plan was decided. Marie left for Lyons and Lisa had time to catch her breath.

But events in Europe escalated when German troops marched into Czechoslovakia to occupy part of the country. This action had supposedly been ratified by the Munich Agreement, signed by Mr Chamberlain and other European leaders, as an attempt to guarantee the peace of Europe. Though how the affirmation of peace could be allied with an army taking over part of another country wasn't clear in the minds of many people.

Wally spoke to his sister on the telephone with barely disguised rage. 'Mr Chamberlain appeared on the balcony of Buckingham Palace with the King and Queen, as if this agreement was something wonderful. These dictators think nothing of ordinary people who have lost part of their country. I tell you, Lisa, it's the thin end of the wedge. Come home. Please.'

'I am coming home,' she said quietly.

'Thank God,' he replied after a startled second, his tone saying more than words how relieved he felt.

'Yes, but I shall have to find a new job, won't I? Any ideas, or do I go back to school?'

'Why not? There's a whole generation there since you left, all eager to learn French. I'm not so sure about German, though. I'd give it a miss for the time being.'

He was teasing, but it didn't disguise his feelings. He wanted her safely home from a tyranny she couldn't even imagine, yet. She was touched by his concern for her, even if that comment about a whole generation of children eager to learn French since she left had given her a little shock.

'You'd better tell Tweedy to get my room aired for me in a month's time, then,' she said, her brain working like quicksilver now. 'I'll spend some time with Henri and Monique when I've settled everything here, and then I'll be home.'

Her heart gave a little flip when she said it, and she couldn't quite tell whether it was of gladness or sorrow. One part of her would always be glad to go home, and to breathe the fresh green countryside in the little Somerset village where she had been born. She could never quite escape the tug of it, however much she loved France. But if England was her natural home, France had become her chosen one.

'Stop it,' she told herself, when everything in the apartment was packed into boxes. 'You're getting maudlin and it Won't Do!'

For a moment she could almost hear the ghost of her old headmaster, Mr Davidson, in her head, admonishing her for being feeble when it was not in her character, and telling her she could do anything she put her mind to.

And so she could, she thought. Working for a German firm in Paris wasn't her only option, and now that she didn't have to turn up at the office every morning, she could take a leisurely drive to the Dubois home. Henri had already offered Gerard's services to drive her back to Calais for the ferry to Dover, and the plan was that she would leave her car with the family until she came back to reclaim it. That was something she had insisted on, leaving Henri in no doubt that someday she would return. The little car was there waiting for her, like a talisman. One day she would return.

Monique greeted her like a long-lost relative, and she was immediately absorbed into the more relaxed life of the countryside. The children were away at boarding school now, but had left notes for her, wishing her well back in England.

'I'm not going for good,' she told Monique in the garden one balmy afternoon. 'I will be back, I promise.'

'We all pray that it's soon, Lisa. You've become like another daughter to us, but if it was not safe for you to be here we would not wish you to stay.'

'You think the prospect of war is definite then?'

'It is too much of a possibility to ignore it, and it would be foolish to bury our heads in the sand.'

'That's what my brother says. At least he'll be pleased I'm going home!'

'And you are not, *chérie*?'

Lisa's shrug was as expressive as that of any Frenchwoman. 'How can I be? My whole life is here, and now everything will be changed. But I know I have to adapt, and I will. I've faced changes in my life before, so this will be just one more.'

She gave a short laugh. 'Oh, take no notice of me, Monique. I'm just feeling sorry for myself, that's all. Isn't that feeble!'

'No one could ever say that about you. You are a very strong person,' Monique told her. 'How old is your brother now?' she added.

'He's eighteen.'

Even as she said it, a tremor ran through her. Wally was no longer a boy, but of an age to go to war, if war came. It was something she hadn't acknowledged until that moment. The tremor became a shudder, and Monique commented at once.

'I think we should both go indoors now. The late-afternoon soon grows cold at this time of the year.'

But not as cold as the chill that was gathering around Lisa's heart.

When she left France it was an emotional parting. None of them put it into words, but it was obvious that they were all wondering when they would meet again. By now, Jews were fleeing from the harsh regime in Germany, and Mimi had decided that if and when war was declared she would go at once to stay with her sister in Belgium, with Gerard's fervent agreement.

Fear and resentment of the Nazis was having an escalating effect everywhere. Even

Renee had become almost hysterical in her last letter, saying that her stepfather had changed the name of his fish and chip shop from Schmidt to Smith, in order to appear neutral.

'It didn't do much good,' Renee wrote. 'He's had paint thrown at the windows and people jeering and taunting outside at night. I don't know why Mum stays with him. I told her to come and live with me and Eddie on the farm, but she says she don't want to wallow in cow's muck.'

Lisa couldn't imagine how Renee's flashy mother, in her high heels and mincing walk, would find life on the farm. But her smile had faded as she'd read on.

'I worry for her, Lisa. If there's a war, what's going to happen then? They might take him away and lock him up, but what about her, seeing as how she shares the same name? Will they think she's one of the enemy as well? I'll be that glad to see you when you get home, Lisa, so we can talk like we used to. I'm not much good at writing letters, as you know.'

She seemed to be doing pretty well, thought Lisa, and her anxieties were plain to see. She and her mother had always managed to jog along without the need for either of them to bother too much over what the other was doing, but if Renee was really worried then that worried Lisa, too. But Renee was the last person on her mind as she left Gerard at Calais. She hugged him like the old friend he had become, and on an impulse she told him that if ever he thought Mimi's background put her in real danger she must come to England and Lisa.

Although she had begged none of the others to come to Calais to see her off, she felt bereft as she boarded the ferry, wondering when she would ever see any of them again. Part of her told her not to be foolish, and that this was only a temporary parting until the craziness in the world had righted itself again. And another, more realistic part of herself said that she was doing the right thing.

But if she parted from her French 'family' with her spirits in turmoil, she was greeted by her English one with no less delight. Tweedy wrapped her arms around her and Wally cleared his throat half a dozen times in a fair imitation of her father's favourite way of avoiding showing emotion.

Ron Newman had only ever got really roused over his blessed union meetings, but Wally was less inhibited now than Ron had ever been, and hugged his sister just as tightly as the housekeeper did.

'So now we're a real family again,' Tweedy said huskily, 'that is, if you'll pardon me for including myself, Lisa.'

'Good heavens, of course you're part of the

family, Tweedy. And don't think I'm going to be taking over in the house. As soon as I've got my breath back I'm going to look for a new job.'

'You're back to stay then?' Wally said, challenging her.

'I'm back to stay,' she said, mentally crossing her fingers as she did so.

The chance of a job came to her, rather than the other way around. Wally had already contacted her old school, and a letter from the headmaster arrived a couple of days later, inviting her for an interview for a rather unusual post.

'What do you suppose that means?' she asked Renee that afternoon, when she had cycled over to the Bray farm to see her. Renee was looking puffed-up and blowsy, both from Eddie's mother's stodgy cooking and from being three months pregnant. 'And why didn't you tell me about this before!'

'Which do you want me to answer first?' Renee said crossly. 'I haven't got a clue about the job, and I didn't tell you about the baby because we weren't sure until recently. I thought I was putting on weight with all Mother Bray's puddings.'

'But you're pleased, aren't you?' Lisa probed, as she registered the dark shadows beneath Renee's eyes and the fact that she

231

was looking anything but the contented bride.

Renee scowled. *'They're* pleased, but they don't have to look all blown up like a blasted whale, do they?'

'Good Lord, Renee, it hardly shows, and you've got a long way to go yet.'

'That's what I mean. What am I going to look like by the spring when I can hardly waddle about?'

'Well, you got what you wanted, didn't you? Marrying Eddie, I mean.'

The scowl got deeper. 'Oh yes, helping around the farm is so exciting! You got all the glamorous jobs, Lisa, not me. You've travelled. Met people. Done things. Eddie wouldn't even take me to Paris for my honeymoon. All he wants to do in the evenings is jaw with his dad about cattle and pigs and boring stuff like that, while I'm supposed to sit around and knit bootees with his mother and await the little arrival, as she calls it.'

'So what do you suppose the headmaster wants to see me about?' Lisa said, trying hard not to laugh at the picture Renee was painting, when it was clear that Renee's whole life now centred around grumbling about Eddie and her in-laws and the life she had chosen, and as usual Lisa was the sounding-board she had been missing all this time.

'How should I know? And guess what Mother Bray wants us to call the little arrival. Beatrice if it's a girl, after her mother, and Cyril if it's the boy they all want. I ask you. Why can't we call it something modern, like Margaret Rose, after the princess! Anyway, I hope it's a girl to spite them all,' she added.

Lisa could no longer contain her laughter. 'Oh, Lord, Renee, you do me a power of good!'

'Do I?' she said blankly, and then her face relaxed into her familiar grin. 'You cheer me up as well, Lisa. I'm ever so, *ever* so glad you've come home. You'll come over to the farm again soon, won't you?'

'Of course,' Lisa said in a choked voice. 'As soon as I've had my interview I'll let you know what's happening.'

'Oh, all right,' Renee said vaguely.

The minute she arrived at the school and was shown into the headmaster's office, Lisa knew this was no ordinary interview. As well as Mr Davidson, there were three official-looking people in the room.

'Lisa, let me introduce you. This is Mrs Wallington, one of our school governors, and Miss Granger and Mr Thorpe are concerned with children's welfare, especially fostering displaced persons.'

'I'm not equipped to foster children,' she

233

said nervously.

'No, no, my dear, that is not why we've asked you here,' he said, 'although some home visits might be appropriate, even desirable.'

'Can we first set out our suggestions?' the other man broke in. 'Miss Newman, you have a unique talent, and you are well aware of the situation in Europe, of course.'

'Of course,' she said dryly.

She didn't know where all this was leading, but she was becoming acutely aware that if she needed a job, they needed her more.

'Miss Newman – Lisa, if I may,' Miss Granger took up the role of spokesperson, 'we are in the process of evacuating Jewish children from France and Belgium, and from Germany, too, when we can, although that is a delicate matter.'

'Is it?' Lisa said.

'If war is declared they would be in an invidious position here,' her colleague said. 'But, naturally, those who are already here need to go to school. We have about a dozen in our area at present, and none of them speaks English except for a smattering of phrases. This is where you come in. You would be our liaison, and your job would be to sit in on their lessons as an auxiliary teacher to assist them at all times. You must understand how hard it is for these small children, to be taken away from their homes, and to feel alienated even more by not understanding the language fully.'

'Don't you have a French teacher then?' Lisa said.

'We do,' Mr Davidson said. 'But it's not the same as having someone who has lived and worked in France for so long.'

'Where do these children live now?' Lisa asked.

'Some of them are fostered, but it isn't easy for either side, as you can imagine. The rest are being housed and cared for by our department. We try to keep them together as far as possible, and in a congenial atmosphere in the country. As yet, there are not too many, but in time there could be an avalanche.'

The words spoke volumes. Lisa didn't want to imagine floods of children fleeing from the Nazi regime – and what if war came? Would their own city children be sent to the country as well, for their own safety, as had been hinted?

'Do you want to think about it, Lisa?' Mrs Wallington asked.

'There's no need. Of course I'll take the post, and I thank you for offering it to me,' she replied with dignity. 'When do you want me to start?'

'I'm really proud of you, sis,' Wally said later.

'Are you? Oh, I know it's all in a good

235

cause, but for my own part I can't help feeling it's a backward step. It's what I was doing before I went to France!'

'But not with these poor kids who have been obliged to leave their homes and families,' Wally said. 'You'll be a link with their past, Lisa, and that makes you very special.'

'Cripes, you'll have me blushing soon, but I suppose you're right, and I shall do my best to get them used to our ways without forgetting their own.'

'I could do an interview with you for the paper when you're settled, about your valuable work,' he offered.

'No, you couldn't,' she said at once. 'The last thing these children need is for you to draw attention to them. Leave well alone, Wally.'

She soon discovered she was in a strange situation. She was truly a link between these bewildered, frightened evacuees and the rest of the schoolchildren, who didn't quite know what to make of them, and the harassed teachers. As well as being a go-between in all their lessons, she mopped up tears, and hugged, and reassured them in their native language, which seemed to be their main source of comfort. And finally she realized she was doing something vital in rehabilitating them.

Fourteen

A month after Hitler entered Prague and declared that the old republic of Czechoslovakia no longer existed, the British government made plans for several million British city children to be evacuated to the country. By now, thousands of air-raid shelters were being constructed in the event of war.

Lisa regularly visited Renee, even though an uncomfortable pregnancy was making her short tempered and ready to argue about every new piece of propaganda information.

'Why don't they start this blessed war instead of all this messing about? It's like pushing pieces around on a chessboard – not that I'd know anything about that! But why don't they get on with it?'

'Do you want to see all our young men sent away to fight?'

'Of course not. Eddie will be in a reserved occupation on the farm, anyway.'

'Oh well, that's all right, then.'

Renee ignored her sarcasm. 'No, it's not. Sometimes I wish he'd join up and wake himself up a bit.'

'What's happened to love's young dream?'

Lisa said with a grin.

'You can laugh, but marriage is not all it's cracked up to be when you have to live with in-laws who won't let you do anything, and your husband comes in from the fields stinking of cows and muck every day.'

'Good Lord, Renee, you must have known what to expect as a farmer's wife.'

'I thought I'd have something to do besides twiddling my thumbs and trying to knit baby clothes, which I'm hopeless at!'

'But you wouldn't really want Eddie to go away to war, would you?'

'Yes. No. Oh, I don't know. Sometimes I just wish he'd go away.'

She looked so sorry for herself that Lisa lost patience with her.

'You should feel lucky he wouldn't have to go away and fight. Tell me that if the worst happens and my brother has to go.'

She tried never to think about it, even though Wally seemed to think it would be a great adventure. If the time came for young men to enlist voluntarily she was sure he would be at the front of the queue. The excitement of being a war correspondent had been mentioned more than a few times, though with his luck, he'd said cheerfully, they'd probably put him in a tank regiment instead.

'Lisa, I'm sorry,' Renee said. 'I wasn't thinking.'

'You never do. If something doesn't concern you personally, it just goes in and out of your head, doesn't it?'

'Am I really that shallow?'

Her dismay made Lisa swallow her instant retort.

'Well, I'm sure it's just because you're uncomfortable with the baby. Once it's born, you'll see things differently.'

But she mentally crossed her fingers, as she so often did when Renee was in one of her gloomy moods.

There were times when Lisa cursed her photographic memory. All the way home, cycling through the lanes, the trees burgeoning with fresh spring leaf now, she could picture Renee's miserable face. Marriage to Eddie obviously wasn't as wonderful as she had anticipated. Renee had always expected things to go her way without having to work for it. But life wasn't like that. Lisa only hoped that once the baby was born she would feel happier and more fulfilled.

Her thoughts were interrupted by another cyclist coming towards her at a fair rate. As if she had conjured him up out of thin air, Wally slewed to a stop in front of her, his bicycle wheels spinning and sending the dust flying.

'Are you trying to kill somebody?' she yelled.

'I'm out on a job,' he yelled back, 'but I wanted to tell you the news that's just come through. The government's conscripting men over twenty, and there's to be a national register for all men under twenty-one.'

'Is this supposed to thrill me?' she said, sobered at once and knowing exactly what that gleam in his eyes meant.

She had seen it all before, in her father's eyes, when he was hell bent on attending – and disrupting – some rally or other.

Wally's youthful confidence spilt over. 'I can't wait to get into uniform.'

'Well, you're still only nineteen, so don't go getting any daft ideas, Wally.'

He ignored her, neatly mounting his bicycle again and whizzing past her before she had the chance to say any more.

'I won't. Or, then again, I might. See you later, our sis,' he called out.

She knew he'd be getting the very ideas she'd hoped he wouldn't. There would be no stopping him, nor thousands like him. They wouldn't wait to be conscripted, and they would only see the glory in going to war and none of the tragedy and futility of it all. It might be admirable as far as patriotism was concerned, but Lisa had lost the rest of her family, and she couldn't bear to lose Wally as well.

She was angry with herself for having him practically dead and buried before he had even joined up. She put such dire thoughts out of her mind as she cycled home, head bent over the handlebars as if to shut out all the hateful images of war.

Indoors, Tweedy was preparing the evening meal, and as the smell of cooking teased her nostrils, for one sweet, breathless moment it was as if her mother was there, doing the same homely chores. Lisa blinked away the sudden rush of tears as Tweedy turned from the stove, her hands covered in flour, and, uncannily, tuned into Lisa's mood at once.

'Well, you look as flustered as I feel,' she said cheerfully. 'Nothing wrong with that young lady at the farm, I hope?'

Lisa looked at her mutely. She rarely cried, but in seconds she was blubbering into Tweedy's accommodating shoulder for no good reason other than she wished for the impossible: that her mother was still here, and her dad and her gran, and that she was still a child and that things never had to change.

'Renee's fine,' she said, when she finally extricated herself, feeling foolish as she noisily blew her nose into a handkerchief.

'Good.' Tweedy was a great one for not asking unnecessary questions, which Lisa considered one of her strong points. 'Then let me get on with this pie or that young man of ours will be complaining when he gets home.'

'We do love you, Tweedy,' Lisa said impulsively. 'You know that, don't you? You've made this house into a home again.'

This time the hot colour rushed to the woman's cheeks. 'That's the nicest thing anybody ever said to me, considering I never had a family of my own.'

'You do now,' Lisa told her, and turned away before they both became too sentimental for comfort. She hardly knew what was the matter with her today. Perhaps it was seeing Renee so discontented when she had everything she had ever wanted. Perhaps it was the memory of Wally's eager young face at the thought of going to war. Perhaps it was because she had no one of her own to love.

She wasn't weird. She wanted love as much as the next girl. She wanted to have a young man who would hold her and kiss her, and tell her she was beautiful, even if she was not – not in any film-starry way, anyway. She was just ordinary, but even ordinary girls fell in love and got married. They had babies ... At the thought her mood changed at once, and she wiped her hands almost viciously on a towel.

What right did Renee have to be so downright miserable when she had it all? When, for all any of them knew, they might all be hurtling towards a war that nobody wanted, and there might be no more tomorrows for any of them to make love. And women like

Lisa would never have known what it was like, ending up like those poor unmarried women whose sweethearts were killed in the Great War, lonely, frustrated and alone.

'My God, what's the matter with you?' she whispered into the air.

An insidious little inner voice whispered slyly back: *You need a man, that's what!*

Renee made it her new crusade. It would give her something to do, and it would show Lisa what she was missing. Eddie's farmer cousin wouldn't mind teaming up with Eddie and his wife and Renee's friend for a night at the pictures.

'You should go,' Tweedy said. 'You don't have any social life at all.'

Coming from someone who rarely left the house except to do the daily grocery shopping, and was perfectly content with her lot, that was a laugh.

'And you do?' she asked mildly.

'We're not talking about me. Your friend is expecting her first baby, and you don't have even have a young man on the horizon. Was there anyone in France? Don't answer that if you think I'm being too nosy.'

'I'm not a nun, Tweedy. I've had a few men friends, but you can't make yourself fall in love, and I'm not getting married and having babies just because my friend's done so. I always said I wouldn't get married until I was at least twenty-five, and I'm nowhere near that yet.'

'You're already twenty-three, aren't you?'

'A mere child,' Lisa said airily. 'And until Mr Right comes along, that's the way I'm going to stay.'

She knew Eddie Bray's cousin Jake wasn't going to be the one. He was big built, like Eddie, with pale ginger hair and eyelashes, light blue eyes, and a tendency to fiddle with an unfamiliar tight collar when he was nervous. Away from the business of the farm he was constantly nervous. But he was eager to please, which made him more like a unkempt, lovable puppy than a contender for marriage.

'So what do you think?' Renee asked later in the cinema. Their escorts had gone to buy ice creams in the interval, and the bloke at the organ at the front of the house had risen up like a phoenix and was blasting their eardrums with popular tunes. 'Are we likely to end up as cousins-in-law?'

'Not a chance! Jake doesn't make me feel amorous in the least.'

'Shame.' Renee scowled. 'I always said you were hard to please. But will you come out with us again if I can arrange it?'

'Don't you even like going out with your husband without other people around?' she teased.

'That's about it,' Renee muttered.

'Oh, Renee,' Lisa began, half in exasperation, half in alarm, and then she caught sight of the tortured look on her friend's face. 'Look, I'm really sorry if things are so bad for you—'

'It's not that,' Renee gasped. 'I'm getting terrible griping pains. I think something's happening, and I'd better get out of here quick before I pass out.'

She certainly looked as if she was about to collapse as she clutched her stomach. They shuffled past the other people in the row, ignoring their complaints, and reached the aisle just as Eddie and Jake came back with the ice creams.

'Where are you going?' Eddie grumbled. 'We've queued up for these for ages and they're near to melting already!'

'We've got to get her to a doctor,' Lisa ordered. 'There's something wrong, and it could be the baby.'

She had to agree that Eddie could be forceful when it was needed. He wasn't slow in understanding what was going on, and he hustled Renee out of the cinema as fast as she could manage, and shoved her unceremoniously into his old car.

'I want my mother,' Renee whimpered in between yells of pain.

'I'm sure it's best that you see the doctor first,' Lisa said quickly, thinking that a fat lot of good Renee's feckless mother would be.

'Shut up, Renee. We're going straight to the doctor,' Eddie shouted. 'And try to keep quiet, for God's sake. I'm sure all this bellowing's not good for the babby.'

'That's all you care about, isn't it?' Renee sobbed. 'You want me to be like one of your prize cows, dropping one every year.'

'Well you're not much good for anything else lately, with your whining.'

Lisa couldn't believe she was hearing all this sniping. They used to be so lovey-dovey, and now they sounded as if they hated each other.

'You can drop me off at the pub, Eddie,' Jake piped up. 'I'm not much good with doctoring, and Lisa can come with me.'

'Don't be stupid,' Lisa snapped. 'Do you think I'm going to desert her now? Do as he says, Eddie, and then come into the back seat with me, Renee.'

When she did so they held each other's hands tightly. Renee's face was ashen with pain and fear. Lisa was sure Renee was in danger of losing the baby, and if that happened she wondered what the future was going to be for her and Eddie, since there didn't seem much love left between them. It was hard to feel positive when Renee kept bleating every few minutes, and Eddie kept cursing her from the driving seat.

She and Eddie spent the next few hours at the doctor's surgery, wondering what was going on behind the closed doors from where they could hear Renee's screams. Eddie smoked an entire packet of cigarettes, until the small waiting room was blue with smoke and making Lisa feel ill – but she didn't dare try to stop him.

'The doctor will take good care of her, Eddie,' she kept repeating.

'We want this babby,' he said savagely once. 'We want sons to carry on the farm after me dad and me have gone. It's been a Bray farm for generations, see?'

Lisa bit her tongue hard at such insensitivity. Her gran always said that giving birth was a time between life and death for a woman, and although Renee was nowhere near her time it seemed highly likely that something of the sort was happening to her now. And a young woman's life was more important than providing this oaf with a son. She had never realized before what a cold, self-centred man he really was.

Nor could she see Renee being willing to provide sons in the plural after this experience. But by the time the doctor appeared again his hands were bloodied and he told Eddie there was not going to be a son this time, nor any other time. Renee's insides were damaged, and an ambulance was on its way to take her to hospital, where they would perform an operation so that there would be no more babies.

'No!' Eddie shouted. 'You can't do that. She'll be able to have more babbies, and it's not your say-so. This won't stop her.'

The doctor spoke coldly. 'I'm afraid it will, Mr Bray. Unless you want your wife to die, I'd advise you to take heed of what I'm telling you.'

To Lisa's horror Eddie blundered out of the doctor's surgery without even going to comfort Renee, and the next moment they heard his car wheels screech away down the street.

'He's very upset,' Lisa said quickly, covering her shame at witnessing such inhumane actions. 'I'll go to the hospital in the ambulance with Renee.'

'And you'd better contact her mother. The young woman will need to be in hospital for a while, and she'll need friends and family to rally around her.'

He didn't say that the husband would be less than useless, but he didn't need to. Any idiot could see that.

'Can I see her while we wait for the ambulance?'

'Of course. She's had a sedative and she's very tired, but she's young and she'll recover in time.'

On the examining couch, curled up like a foetus herself, Renee smiled tremulously at Lisa.

'I never really wanted babies, anyway,' she

said in a thready voice. 'And I don't want Eddie, either. Not any more.'

'I'm sure you'll feel differently in a week or two, Renee, when you've got your strength back.'

She shook her head. She had been sweating so much that her hair stuck to her scalp in rats' tails, and her eyes were huge and dark in her white face.

'He's an animal, just like the rest of them on the farm, and I never want to see him again. I *mean* it, Lisa. He ran out on me, didn't he? He couldn't even be bothered to come with me to the hospital. I want my mum,' she finished on a sob.

'I'll telephone the shop as soon I see you settled in hospital,' Lisa promised. 'I'm sure she'll be here to see you as soon as she can.'

'Will you go to the farm and get my things? I'll need a nightdress and a flannel and toothbrush,' she said, her voice beginning to slur as the sedative took proper hold. 'And you can tell him I'm moving in with my mum when I'm better. I'd rather put up with the Jerry bloke than go back to that pig.'

Wally and Tweedy were shocked at the way her evening had turned out.

'The poor girl's really lost her baby then,' Tweedy said.

'I'm afraid so,' Lisa said, declining to tell her how vitriolic Renee had been about the whole thing. People would expect her to be upset, not relieved that she had had a miscarriage and was unlikely to have any more babies. 'She'll be in hospital for a few weeks and then she's going to stay with her mother to recuperate.'

There would be time enough for the scandal to break that Renee Bray had left her husband and preferred to live with her flighty mother and her Jerry husband than with an old, established Somerset farmer's family.

Renee's mother brought the second shock to Lisa, when she turned up at the house one evening to say that Eddie had sent round all Renee's things and told her she could stew in her own juice from now on.

'He's a real bastard, Lisa, and God forgive me for using such language, but it's like our Renee said. Him and his family only wanted her for breeding purposes, and now she can't have no more babies he's done with her. After all the time he chased after her, too.'

Lisa resisted saying that Renee had done her fair share of chasing, since it didn't seem the time for comparing notes.

'And she'll be staying with you when she comes out of hospital?'

Renee's mother tossed her head. 'Only for a bit. You know she and Hans don't get on, and I know there's a lot of folk around here who don't like him either,' she began to whine, 'but he's a good man, Lisa, and he's no Nazi-lover.'

'I'm sure he's not,' Lisa murmured, not wanting to get into a discussion about Hans Smith, or whatever he was calling himself now. 'So what's Renee planning to do, if she's not going to live with you permanently?'

'I suppose she might try for her old job with those Staples people if they'll have her.'

It was a good solution. The atmosphere between Renee and her stepfather would be explosive, and a living-in job had suited her. All the same, she was her friend, and Lisa would always stand by her.

'She can come here for a week or two, until she gets back on her feet,' she offered without thinking.

'Would you do that, love? She'd like to be with you, I'm sure.'

The relief in the woman's eyes was almost nauseating. Anything to get Renee off their backs, Lisa thought in annoyance.

But in the end she had to admit that Renee wasn't the easiest of guests, and nor did she take to Tweedy's homely house rules. So it was a relief when her friend announced that she was going to try getting her old job back, and moved out a week after she had moved in.

'I still worry about her. It's almost as if the wedding and the baby had never been, as if

251

she's somehow completely blocked it out of her memory,' she told Wally.

'It's not your worry, Lisa. She deals with things in her own way, and there are more important things to worry about than the antics of that young madam.'

'I wouldn't call them antics,' she began, but she knew what he meant.

The King and Queen had visited New York to attend the World's Fair in June, and Wally had said cynically that newspaper reports of such interesting activities as British royalty dining with the Roosevelts were meant to allay fears of impending war.

In August Hitler and Stalin signed a non-aggression pact, alarming the Western powers – not that ordinary people quite understood why. But by the end of that month, as predicted, trainloads of children had left major towns and cities for the country, sent away by their parents for safety, and labelled evacuees.

There was no averting war now, despite the feverish attempts of Neville Chamberlain to do so, and on September 3rd the long-expected announcement was broadcast that Britain was now at war with Germany.

'I know it's almost blasphemous to say it,' Wally told his womenfolk, 'but it's almost a relief now it's happened, and we can stop all this hedging. Let's get out there and beat the Hun into a bloody pulp, I say.'

'*Wally!*' Tweedy said sharply. 'You're much too young to talk like that.'

'I'm not too young to go and fight,' he retorted. He looked at his sister guardedly. 'I'm not a coward, sis.'

After a long minute, she said flatly, 'You've already done it, haven't you?'

'I leave for the barracks in a week's time,' he replied, and despite the uncertainty in his eyes there was no hiding the excitement in his voice. 'Me and half a dozen lads from the village have signed up together.'

While Lisa was still dealing with the turmoil in her stomach at the thought of her little brother going to fight a war, it was Tweedy who put her arms around him and hugged him.

'We're proud of you, aren't we, Lisa?'

'Of course we are,' she said swiftly, and was rewarded with a smile.

'Promise me you're not going to be fretting about me all the time then.'

'I just want you to come home safely, that's all, and not take any daft risks.' And if that made her sound like a mother hen worrying over her chicks, she didn't care. He was the only chick she had.

'Don't worry,' he said again, full of confidence. 'Jerry's got us to face now.'

What? A group of lads, still wet behind the ears, Lisa thought immediately, and then revised such shameful thoughts. Wally was taking control of his life. No longer her little brother, but a man, ready to face all comers.

And God willing the conflict would be over quickly, not dragging on like the war to end all wars that hadn't done any such thing. She sent up a swift prayer to the Almighty, sure that He wouldn't have any objection to a personal prayer for one young man, as well as for the rest of humanity.

Fifteen

Henri Dubois didn't need sources close to him to know that Hitler would eventually invade France. Even before war had been declared, the Nazis had invaded Poland, and it was certain that the low countries and Scandinavia would be next. Unless he was stopped, the whole of Europe would be under Hitler's control.

Henri's older brother lived in French-speaking Quebec in Canada, and by the beginning of 1940 Henri's family had left France for their farm. The Dubois house was closed up, save for quarters for himself. Gerard chose to stay, but Mimi and her sister also left Belgium for Canada.

'We won't see one another for a while, *chérie*, and none of us knows how long that may be,' Henri told Monique, 'but the children see this as a great adventure, and so must you. Beau will enable us to keep in touch as much as possible, and in our thoughts and our hearts we will never be parted.'

He could be eloquent when he chose, which was why he was the spokesman in his elite special group when important decisions had to be made. Such activities were never referred to at home, but Monique knew that he was involved in something far greater than mere city business. Lisa, too, had realized long ago that there was far more to Henri than appeared on the surface.

As her brother Wally would have said: he was 'in the know'.

After a quiet start, in what was called the phoney war, Britain had its share of battering in the first grim months of the new year. Bombs rained down on London and the south coast of England, and by then Henri's prophecies had come true. Hitler had invaded Denmark and Norway, then Belgium and the Netherlands, and the Nazis had swept into France, pushing back the British troops.

Wally Newman was 'somewhere with the forces', and Lisa could only speculate where that might be. In her heart, she was sure he would be in France. She ached to be there too, impossible though it was. Unofficially, Wally had realized his ambition to be a war correspondent. He sent regular reports to the local newspaper, heavily censored before they gave any news that might help the enemy. But when she saw his name beneath one of his articles she knew he was still all right, and the editor was pleased to have one of their own in the field of battle, as they termed it.

Lisa worried constantly about him, until Tweedy told her in no uncertain terms than she should get on with her own useful life and leave him to enjoy the excitement he craved.

'Excitement! Is that what you call risking your neck every time you come into contact with the enemy?'

'It's his life, Lisa.'

'And it could be his death.'

Tweedy looked exasperated. 'I don't know what's wrong with you lately. Even Renee has left that posh mansion now, and gone to work in a horrible munitions factory in Bristol, sharing digs with Lord knows who. At least you've got a nice home and you're doing good work helping those poor little evacuee children.'

Lisa sighed in annoyance. 'Well, that makes me sound wonderful, doesn't it! Wally's doing his bit, almost certainly in France where I'd dearly like to be! Renee's making munitions, and probably in danger herself from the German bombs. And what am I? Nothing but a glorified schoolteacher doing good work, and not even properly qualified at that!'

'With your gifts, qualifications on bits of paper are unnecessary. You know that, and the people who employ you know it too.

Now stop mithering and help me get the tea, if that's not too humble a task for you, madam.'

'You're a bully, Tweedy.'

'So I am, but somebody's got to do it,' she said calmly, which started them both laughing.

It wasn't that Lisa didn't enjoy her work, but she felt frustrated at not being able to do more, when she did have skills that could be useful. She toyed with the idea of joining the ATS as an interpreter, but what could be more important than helping the displaced children who relied on her so much?

Here in the Somerset countryside the war sometimes seemed far away. They didn't have the blistering air raids that bombarded London and the south-east. Bristol hadn't suffered much yet, and the bombs that did reach Bristol and the Avonmouth docks were like the dull rumblings of distant thunder in Mallory.

The village was isolated and virtually cocooned, and only the appearance of the tape criss-crossed over every window and the obligatory black-out curtains that the air-raid wardens inspected regularly made it seem as if there was a war on. But with food rationing starting people were encouraged to grow their own food. 'Digging for Victory' became the current phrase, and the new Prime Minister, Winston Churchill, had the knack of making everyone do as he asked.

Some folk with corrugated Anderson shelters in their back gardens put earth on the rooftop and planted cabbages and lettuces on them, partly to disguise the steel monstrosities, and also to show that they were doing their bit for the war effort. The Newmans had an Anderson shelter now, although Tweedy flatly refused to go into it unless absolutely necessary, since she didn't see how something smelling of damp earth and resembling a tin coffin would save them if a bomb hit their house. 'Cripes, Tweedy, talk about being cheerful keeping us going! Old Adolf doesn't have "come and bomb us" marked on our roof!'

'I don't think that madman cares who he bombs.'

Lisa's grin faded. She was right, of course, but you had to see the funny side of things sometimes, or you would go crazy.

Confidence in Mr Churchill was high, but the war wasn't going well for the British. As the year went on, Wally's letters and reports to the local paper became less frequent. Tweedy said he'd be too busy trying to win the war single-handed to spend much time writing letters. But when the news came that despite all their efforts the British were evacuating Dunkirk with thousands of little ships plying back and forth across the

English Channel to get them out of France as the enemy advanced, the prospects of peace looked very dark. The evacuation of Dunkirk was called a triumph by political pundits, but everyone knew it was a disaster for the British and a triumph for the Germans, despite the fact that it had all been stage-managed so speedily and stealthily.

Things continued spiralling downhill. In June Italy declared war on France and Britain, and four days later Paris was invaded by the Germans. Lisa was choked with emotion when she heard the news on the wireless. The beautiful city that she loved was now in the hands of those monsters. The fanatical Nazis were set on overrunning every other country, and nothing seemed capable of stopping them.

A week later, Wally arrived home in the middle of the night, tired and dishevelled. He had landed in England from Dunkirk on one of the little ships then hitched his way home. They managed not to ask questions until he had recovered, and then they got disappointingly few real answers.

'I'm just glad to be home in one piece,' he said grimly. 'At least for now.'

'What do you mean? You've got some leave, surely?' Lisa said, thinking she would have him here for a few weeks at least.

'I'm going back as soon as possible, sis. We don't have cushy holidays like you civvies.

Once I've given a first-hand account to the news editor and got my breath back I'll be off in a day or two. You don't think we've abandoned the front for ever, do you?'

'So what was it really like?' she persisted, ignoring the sinking feeling in her stomach at his words.

'Hell on earth describes it fairly well. Chaps who were your friends moments ago dying in front of you or being blown to bits.' He took a deep breath, clearly not wanting to see the images in his mind, nor to linger on them. 'Coming home, I saw that Bristol's had its share now, plenty of bomb damage, and barrage balloons over the Downs. Didn't you say Renee's there now? I should not worry about her, though. She'll always come bouncing back like a bad penny.'

Lisa didn't miss the way he turned the conversation neatly away from the fighting in France. She vaguely remembered how older people said that was the way it was after the Great War. Once the men came home again they were as tight as clams. Except that Wally would open up to his precious newspaper and she would have to read all about it second-hand. She felt an unreasoning jealousy for all the people who would read Wally's words at the same time as she did. But with one more look at his tired young face she abandoned such thoughts.

'I daresay you'll want a bath, Wally,'

Tweedy said briskly. 'I'll light the boiler for your water, so help me bring the bath in from the yard, then me and Lisa will stay in the parlour and you can have the kitchen to yourself while you clean up.'

'Thanks, Tweedy. I daresay I am a bit niffy,' he said, with a grin that was more his old self. But he wasn't that any more. He was older, more mature, having seen things that no young man should see. Lisa ached for him, and for all those like him, for having their youth snatched away from them.

He stayed for three days, restless to be back in France. She knew the feeling well, but his was the need of the hunter, a leonine, physical need to fight and conquer. Just like Hitler's, she thought, furious that even for an instant she had classed them together.

She was determined not to cling to him when he left. She couldn't have done so, anyway. She simply went to work one morning, and when she returned he was gone. But when his graphic version of events appeared in the local newspaper, it was a kind of comfort after all, and she was inordinately proud of him.

A month later, the government ordered all signposts and street signs to be removed, to confuse the enemy in case of invasion. It made the war seem frighteningly near, and when, in September, the London Blitz began in earnest, it seemed as if the Germans were inexorably winning.

On one of Renee's flying visits home, she told Lisa she was fed up with the factory and was joining the ATS, determined to do something more glamorous.

'You mean you fancy yourself wearing a uniform,' Lisa said.

'They say girls like men in uniform, so why not the other way around? Come with me, Lisa. It would be a laugh.'

'You're daft. How can you call being in the ATS a laugh? What are you planning to do, shoot Germans?'

Renee hooted. 'They don't send girls to the front line. No, I expect I shall serve tea and biscuits in the canteen, or something equally cushy. But I'll be meeting blokes at the same time. I might even be a nurse,' she mused.

'Haven't you forgotten something?'

'You mean Eddie, I suppose. He's more interested in his cows than me.'

'You're still married, Renee. Does the ATS allow married women?'

'I shan't tell them. I shall change me name. I'll call meself Renee Garland after that film star in *The Wizard of Oz*.'

She was so positive, and as unlike Judy Garland as it was possible to be, that Lisa began to laugh. Knowing Renee, she would probably get away with it.

'How's your mum?' she asked her.

Renee scowled. 'All right, I suppose. I don't see her much now she's living with her Jerry bloke.'

'Austrian,' Lisa murmured automatically. 'And she's not just living with him. He's her husband.'

'I'm surprised they haven't taken him into custody yet. A lot of good it'll do her when they start roughing him up,' Renee said angrily. 'Nobody's going to be as fussy as you about where he comes from.'

'You can see into the future, can you?'

'I can see that much. They had a firework pushed through the door of the fish and chip shop the other week, and if Jerry hadn't been in the shop it could have sent the whole place up in smoke.'

Lisa changed the subject, hoping she wasn't proved right. Renee's mum was known as a flighty piece, but nobody wanted to see anything bad done to her; by now the story being circulated was that Hans Schmidt, or Smith, was Swiss.

By the time Renee left she was determined to join up under a false name. It was easy enough these days, she said. You just said you had lost all identifying papers when you were caught up in a bombing raid. Plenty of chaps did it, changing their names and saying they were older than they were, and the army was keen enough to have them, so why not her!

*   *   *

By the latter part of the year, food rationing was tightening everyone's belts. Only
essential occupations were allowed petrol
coupons. The hazy late-summer days of
going to the seaside at Burnham or Weston-
Super-Mare for the day in a family friend's
car were a nostalgic memory now.

The Blitz was in full spate in London,
especially in the East End, where entire
streets vanished overnight in the onslaught.
Many other cities were targeted as well, and
in the west the war came to Bristol with a
vengeance. Local newspapers reported first-
hand experiences of ravaged homes and
orphaned children, and as Lisa read them
her heart ached.

She could recall Bristol instantly from the
time she and Jess had been there for her first
interview with Henri Dubois all those years
ago.

'It says there are bombs falling every night,
and fires and rubble everywhere,' she told
Tweedy. 'I remember Wine Street, and that
seems to have gone up in smoke. Theatres
and churches have been hit, too, and people
who weren't even caught up in the bombing
are being wounded by shrapnel. I'm glad
Renee's away from there after all. Life will
never be the same again, will it, Tweedy?'

'Nothing ever is after a war,' Tweedy
replied sadly. 'War changes the way we live,

and it changes people. Some come out stronger and some go under. And some never come out of it at all.'

Lisa shivered. 'Goodness, how gloomy we are tonight.'

She glanced at the clock. She spent several evenings a week teaching English to the foreign evacuee children now, giving them extra lessons in a group as well as in their normal school classes, where they tended to cluster together.

'It's time I went. Don't spend all evening reading the papers, Tweedy.'

'I shan't. It's too depressing. Besides, I've got to get on with my socks.'

Lisa grinned. Tweedy diligently struggled with the 'knitting socks for soldiers' campaign. She was no knitter, but she was determined to do her bit.

They all were, Lisa reflected, as she cycled to the village hall, where the children gathered for their extra lessons. In their own ways, they all helped the war effort, including cycling along the country lanes with their headlights covered in brown paper to shield them from enemy planes above, through streets that were as black as pitch when there was no moonlight. It was a wonder there weren't more civilian casualties from accidents in the enforced darkness.

By the time she got home again, her eyes were strained from peering through the gloom, and her throat ached from repeating the same words over and over again. Some of the children were angels and eager to learn, but others were little monsters who had no intention of learning English at all.

An unfamiliar car was parked near her house, and that was a novelty in itself. Some people could always obtain petrol, she thought, unaccountably irritated as she put her bicycle away in the back yard and marched indoors. Tweedy was at the stove, her eyes apprehensive, her voice wary.

'Lisa, there are two people here to see you in the parlour.'

Any minute now she would start to wring her hands as if this were a Victorian melo-drama, Lisa thought, and she sounded very unlike her usual efficient self.

'You shouldn't let strangers into the house, Tweedy, especially after dark.'

Idiotic thoughts of spies descending on their quiet little village and going straight for Lisa Newman's house flitted in and out of her head. They all knew about careless talk costing lives, but as she didn't have a pistol to confront these visitors she supposed she had better go and see what they wanted.

'I'll be right behind you, Lisa,' Tweedy whispered.

'I'm sure that won't be necessary,' she muttered as she opened the door to the parlour. And then her heart leapt.

'Henri!' she almost shrieked. The next moment she had flown across the room and was clasped in his arms.

She was instantly embarrassed. He was a good friend, but still her old employer. Her mind whirled. Monique and the children were living safely in French-speaking Canada. So why was he here, instead of going to them...?

'What are you doing here?' she stammered next.

'Don't be alarmed, *chérie*. Nothing's happened to the family. Allow me to introduce you to Etienne Arnaud, my colleague.'

Lisa hadn't even noticed the other person until the tall young man rose from an armchair and shook her hand. She registered him quickly, knowing she could recall his image easily enough later. He had a rugged, almost swarthy face, which spoke of long hours in the open air. He was not Hollywood handsome, but his lean and hungry look was typically French, and far preferable to chocolate-box heroes. His eyes were dark and very intense.

'*Enchanté, mademoiselle*,' he said, releasing her.

'In English, I think, Etienne. Or perhaps not,' Henri added, seeing the ghost of Tweedy's apron from the kitchen beyond.

As he reverted to French, Lisa sat down abruptly, aware of the tension here, aware that this was no ordinary visit, and nor could it be in these uneasy times.

In Wally's words: something was definitely up.

'Please tell me why you are here,' she said, following his lead and speaking in French. 'Assuming that all is well with the family, I am sure it is not for your health, even though the Somerset air can do wonders for all kinds of ailments.'

Her voice faded as she realized how inane she sounded, while these two looked so solemn. A shiver ran through her. Why were they here, and why now, when France had fallen to the Germans, and the Paris that she loved was being violated?

Henri said, 'Please understand that you are perfectly at liberty to refuse what I am about to say, Lisa, but I beg you to hear me out before you make any decision.'

His companion was saying nothing as yet, but his eyes never left Lisa's face, and she felt the heat in her cheeks. She was hot and dusty after cycling home from the village hall, her hair had fallen out of its pins, and here was this young man, so elegantly French despite the working clothes both he and Henri were wearing, she noted now in some surprise.

Her heart skipped a beat at the stranger's gaze, and she was briefly annoyed with herself for paying attention to such things.

'You had better tell me what this is about before I burst with curiosity, then,' she told Henri, almost curtly.

He smiled for the first time, glanced at Etienne, and spoke directly to him.

'I warned you that this little one has a mind of her own and is not afraid to use it, Etienne.'

'Then let us hope it does not hinder our cause,' came the unexpected reply.

Lisa's eyes sparkled. The damn cheek of the man! He was an uninvited guest in her home, and he had the nerve to criticize her without knowing anything about her. But she guessed that Henri Dubois would have told him far too much already.

She sat silently, her lips pursed, an un-bidden shot of adrenaline running through her. Whatever these two had in mind, she had the certain feeling there would be sparks flying between herself and the self-assured Etienne Arnaud.

Tweedy knocked on the door and, without waiting for an answer, she brought in a tray with three cups of cocoa and a plate of biscuits. She put it on the table and left in the same stiff-backed way. Whatever else went on in the world, British good manners were not to be ignored.

'You did not want to leave France, Lisa,' Henri stated.

'You know I did not,' she said.

'Would you wish to return?'

'Of course. Someday.'

Etienne leant forward. 'Not someday, mademoiselle. Now. Tonight.'

She caught her breath. The man clearly enjoyed using shock tactics, but she refused to show alarm, as Henri put his hand on his companion's arm, and continued speaking in measured tones.

'Lisa, you know what is happening to our beloved France, and to Paris. Officially we have surrendered to the Germans, but un-officially there are many who are resisting, and doing all that they can to undermine their authority.'

'And there is a place for me in this?' she said, quick to understand and quick to respond.

'Knowing you, *chérie*, I cannot imagine that you would want to be denied it.'

In the same instant, caution rushed into her mind. 'But how can I? You yourself urged me to leave Paris. My brother too. France is surely a dangerous place for an English-woman now.'

'But not for one who can pass herself off so superbly as a Frenchwoman.'

At his words she felt another rush of excitement in her veins. She was still aware of Etienne staying silent, just gazing at her, as if to gauge every nuance of her changing moods. As if also trying to assess whether

271

she was up to whatever task was involved, she thought, with a flash of anger.

'What is it you want of me?' she said quietly.

Sixteen

As they unfolded their plans, Lisa realized she was to return to France with them almost immediately. And Etienne became more vocal.

'We must return under cover of darkness while there is no moon,' he said. 'We can give you no more than a few days to make your arrangements.'

Lisa bristled at his high-handed manner. He was undoubtedly a charismatic man, and would be a dynamic leader in whatever he did. But they needed her, not the other way around, and she glowered at him.

'Henri said I was at liberty to refuse,' she said, more sweetly than she felt.

'But you will not,' he retorted. 'Will you, mademoiselle?'

Of course she would not. He knew it and so did she. Henri cleared his throat, aware of the frisson of antagonism between these two.

'Lisa, if I did not think that you would agree, I would not have asked.'

The message was clear. She now had full knowledge of how the loyal French were resisting the Germans by every means

273

possible. She could forget this plan, or she could sabotage it. But if Henri knew her well enough to trust her completely, his compatriot did not.

'Of course I agree,' she said steadily. 'But I must have these few days.'

'Good. And you will explain that you have been offered a government translation post somewhere in the south-east of England, and that you leave almost immediately. Caution is a necessity these days, and no one will question it.'

'What of the brother?' Etienne said, his voice brusque.

Lisa was really beginning to dislike him now. However important he was in his organization, she held the strings. She could still refuse. He looked at her intently, and momentarily it was as if they were the only two people in the room – in the world – and she swallowed the swift retort.

'My brother will know what everyone else knows,' she said. 'If that is your wish, Henri?'

Her hands were damp as she spoke directly to him. She told herself it was because of this daring undertaking, but the basic part of her brain told her differently. It was because of *him*.

They quickly turned to the practicalities. The hired car would take them to the coast in two days' time, where they would board a small, fast boat for France under cover of darkness. Lisa would discard her British clothing and don the complete French outfit that Henri had brought for her. She would have no British identification, no toiletries or handbags or anything that might identify her nationality.

That was the whole skill of deception, and, as always, it was the tiniest details that were important. The final details were the new identification papers that had already been prepared. She gazed at an old photograph of herself on the supposedly well-thumbed papers.

'Were you so sure of me?'

'I was sure that you would not let us down,' Henri said.

'And I am to be Lisette Arnaud,' she said. *His* name.

She was suddenly alert. 'You do not expect me to pose as your wife?'

The thought was at once too alarming and too enticing to be comfortable.

'Sadly, no,' Etienne replied, seeing right through her. 'Charming though I find the notion, we are to be cousins, Lisette.'

His voice caressed her new name as if to tease her. He had been so serious until that moment, but now he smiled, his mouth widening, the laughter lines around his eyes changing his face completely, enough to make her heart pound.

★ ★ ★

'I won't be able to keep in touch very often, Tweedy,' Lisa told her. 'I'll be doing an important job for the war effort, and it's all a bit hush-hush.'

Those words covered a multitude of deceptions. Anything that was hush-hush on behalf of the war effort was treated with respect and not questioned. Over the next two days her story was readily accepted, but she had had a hard job not to change her mind as some of the displaced children clung to her and wailed at the thought of losing her.

But this was more important than personal feelings. Once she had been driven to the coast she would change her clothes and finally shed her English identity. She would become Lisette Arnaud, living at her cousin's farm well to the south of Paris and away from her old haunts. Besides living at the farm, she was to work at a patisserie owned by a M. Lamont, whose premises were frequented by the sweet-toothed Germans, and were not too far away from the buildings that the Germans were already occupying as headquarters. Her job was to flirt discreetly with them, to collaborate and gain as much information about their plans as possible, risking the wrath of those who would see her as a traitor.

She was supposedly a simple French girl, unable to speak German. There were risks involved, and Henri had not underestimated them, if she was caught passing on information to the growing Resistance movement, with which Henri and Etienne were now heavily involved.

'Collaborating with the enemy is treason,' Etienne had said. 'You must be careful at all times. French girls who throw themselves too blatantly at the enemy soldiers have been spat upon. In extreme cases some have had their heads shaved and been paraded publicly for all to see their shame.'

'You paint a pretty picture,' Lisa muttered, finding it too graphic for comfort.

'No. Just an honest one. I tell you this for your own safety, and because you are valuable to us. We have no wish to lose you.'

God, he was a cold fish! How could she ever have thought him attractive when those dark eyes bored into her. She was valuable to them, provided she did what they asked. If she failed she knew they would deny all knowledge of her – except that it would be difficult to do, since she was meant to be Etienne's cousin.

She realized now what a huge risk they took in making her their accomplice. If she was ever suspected of spying and then interrogated, they would surely bring in her 'cousin' for questioning too, and the whole operation would be in jeopardy. For the first time she knew not only what they were asking of her, but how much trust they were placing in her.

Oh well, if the French didn't get her for collaborating, the Germans would get her for spying, she thought, attempting to make light of it. And then she caught sight of their faces, and abandoned such flippant thoughts.

'I will never let you down,' she said.

It was the weirdest sensation to be crossing the English Channel at night, with not only the throb of the boat's engine and the swish of the waves to break the silence, but the distant sound of gunfire and the drone of aircraft. The craft they were in was small and cramped, and she shivered despite the thick dark coat she wore now. She felt Etienne squeeze her hand, aware of her nerves.

'I will be as much of a cousin to you as your own,' he said, so quietly that only she could hear.

'Thank you,' she mumbled, taken aback by his surprising understanding As if he knew – as he must – how much this was costing her, to leave all that was safe, to head straight into danger.

But she was also going back to the place that had been home to her for so many years. She was capable of living, breathing and acting as a Frenchwoman, and never had those skills been more necessary – even though it meant being a closet friend to the enemy.

'We go straight to the farm so that you can familiarize yourself with it,' he went on. 'We will then explain your role more exactly, and we shall visit M. Lamont in a few days. The work at the patisserie will not be arduous,' he added, a smile in his voice now. She couldn't see his face, but she could picture every line of it.

'Will he know why I am there?'

'Oh yes. He is one of us. The place has been closed for renovation for some time, so it will not seem strange to the Germans to see a new assistant.'

'And I am to live at your farm,' she repeated.

At his home. In close proximity to him.

'Of course. We are family members.'

It was a bizarre conversation in the middle of the choppy English Channel. She ignored the way her stomach was starting to heave and concentrated on everything she was being told, easily committing it to memory.

'What do you farm? Pigs? Cows?' she asked, trying to disregard the fervent urge to throw up over the side of the boat and disgrace herself.

'None of that,' Etienne said. 'I grow the finest grapes in the district.'

There was no mistaking the pride in his voice now. He wasn't all steel then. He had

279

the Frenchman's passion for doing something he loved, and the arrogance to know that he did it well.

'Do you have the final product of your grapes?' she asked.

'Naturally. We will sample it to revive us after the journey. You may already know the wine, Lisette. Arnaud's Red is full blooded and bold to the taste.'

And why did she sense that he was not only referring to the wine...?

'I look forward to it,' she murmured, wondering if it was only the Channel crossing that was making her feel light headed.

But you didn't start to fall for a chap in the middle of a war, did you? And what divine decree was there to say that you did not?

A well-remembered figure awaited them at the small dark inlet where the boat landed in the early hours of the morning.

'Gerard!' she breathed gladly, instantly on familiar territory.

'It's good to see you, Lisette.' The name startled her, until she recalled that she had always suspected he and Henri were more than employer and chauffeur. He must know why they had arrived back on French soil in so clandestine a manner.

She wondered how far this network stretched – and how organized it actually was. Were there small pockets of resistance as was rumoured, or was there some larger organization controlling what these partisans did to undermine their invaders? It was never referred to in detail in wireless broadcasts or newspapers, unless it was in coded messages, since secrecy was the means by which they operated.

Her excitement began to grow, diminishing her fears, at least for the present. There was no ostentatious limousine waiting for them now, and the boat had vanished into the night.

'We must not attract attention,' Henri said, 'and you might feel more at home in this little vehicle, which I apologize for commandeering, Lisette.'

Gerard opened the doors of her own small car. In any case, she knew she would feel far too jittery to drive into the city, even if it were allowed. She realized she was now under orders. It was at once frightening and exhilarating.

'If I am to live and work outside Paris, I won't be needing a car, will I?'

'No,' Etienne answered, 'there's a bicycle for you at the farm. You are fit enough to cycle to the patisserie each day, but also into the city when you wish.'

She began to feel as if this was all a dream. It was unclear whether Henri or Etienne was actually in charge, but what was clear was that Etienne was her main contact, her pseudo-cousin, and she had to be totally familiar with his home and background. It was a bizarre situation, but one that she suddenly relished.

Perhaps she was a latent actress, and, if so, this was the biggest part of all. In fact, she thought, quickly coming down to earth, it had better be.

'What are you thinking?' Etienne asked her quietly, in the cramped rear seat of her car as it trundled off in the night in the direction of Paris. The dull sound of distant gunfire that rattled her nerves wasn't in her imagination, either.

'I'm thinking I must play my part well,' she said.

'You must, and you will. If you fail, we all fail.'

He sounded so dourly *French* that she gave a shaky, uncomfortable laugh. 'I am surely not that important.'

'Each one of us is important, so never underestimate what we ask you to do, and never question it, however disagreeable it may seem,' he said. His hand squeezed hers for a fleeting moment of reassurance, no more, but enough to send a wave of sensation through her veins. She had bemoaned the fact that she was doing nothing substantial for the war effort, yet here she was, in the most dangerous place of all for an English girl to be, in the company of a charismatic Frenchman whom she would get to know very well in the days ahead, and her sense of adventure was fast coming to the fore.

'I won't let you down,' she said again.

She couldn't see his face clearly in the car's dim interior, but she knew he was smiling. As before, she could instantly picture every line of his face, his dark eyes that could be expressive or enigmatic in a moment, his mouth, curving and widening in that smile...

'I know you won't,' he said lightly, totally unaware of her sudden rush of turbulent emotions.

Dear God, Lisa thought frantically. In these circumstances, it would be madness to have any romantic feelings towards Etienne, however wildly attracted she was to him. And she couldn't deny that oh yes, she definitely was!

But it wouldn't be so wrong to show a certain amount of affection for her 'cousin'. It would be perfectly natural. And again she wondered whoever took account of circumstances when it came to falling in love – or mere infatuation.

'Are you all right, Lisette?' she heard Henri say, and she realized she was breathing heavily.

'Perfectly, thank you,' she managed to say, as the actress in her took over.

By the time they reached the sprawling stone-built farm she was very tired. It was not yet dawn, but Henri and Gerard were to snatch a few hours sleep before leaving. Helene, Etienne's middle-aged housekeeper, provided a token meal of bread and cheese and hot coffee, and they all drank freely of the delicious wine known as Arnaud's Red. Then Lisa was shown her bedroom.

'Be sure to tell me if there is anything else you require, mademoiselle Lisette,' Helene said.

The use of her new name alerted Lisa that Helene was either in the know or had been told the fiction that she was Etienne's cousin. She suspected the former. In the world of espionage and resistance, people needed those around them whom they could trust absolutely. As the words came into her mind, she shook her head slowly. So much had happened so quickly that her head was still reeling.

But through it all came a small feeling of warmth that she was back where she felt she belonged, and also in the same country as her brother. There was always a chance that they might meet ... but even if that happened she knew it would be unwise, if not impossible, for them to acknowledge one another. As each new thought arose, the ramifications of what she was undertaking made her shiver anew.

But she threw off her anxiety for a few moments while she examined her room. Lit

by oil-lamps, it was comfortably old fashioned, with rose-patterned wallpaper, heavy,
solid furniture and a wardrobe large enough
to hide inside. She wished the thought
hadn't entered her head and she opened its
doors to dispel the picture, and then she
gaped.

Inside was a complete set of clothes for
every occasion and season. A quick glance
told her they were all in her size. The drawers
in the dressing-table contained underwear.
She wondered who had chosen it all, and
who knew or had guessed her size so well.
Such efficiency was unnerving. But it had to
be Helene, after seeing Henri's many photos
of her. She would have been the person to fit
out her bedroom with these intimate gar-
ments, not Etienne Arnaud ... Somehow she
managed to get a couple of hours sleep in
the unfamiliar bedroom before the sound of
birdsong roused her. She was definitely in
the country, she thought with a small feeling
of bliss, before she awoke properly and
remembered exactly where she was and why
she was here.

A bathroom led off her bedroom, complete
with soap and towels and bowls of heady
pot-pourri. The old stone farmhouse had
been modernized to some extent, for which
she was grateful. The thought of wandering
down a passage and finding Etienne emerg-
ing from a bathroom would have been a

shock, to put it mildly.

She bathed quickly, then donned a suitable blouse and skirt, stockings and shoes, and brushed her hair, swathing it into a chignon at the back of her head. Her reflection in the mirror told her she looked completely French. Everything she wore was French. Her thoughts and her emotions and her dreams were French. The transformation was complete.

'Good morning, Lisette.'

Henri greeted her when she found her way downstairs to the big farmhouse kitchen, fragrant with the smell of strong coffee and hot croissants.

'Good morning,' she said evenly, refusing to admit how her heart flipped with his easy use of her new name. No one would address her as anything else now.

'We will have a brief meeting this morning, and then Etienne will show you around the farm and vineyard and wine cellars. In due course you will visit the patisserie. You will find the city much changed, Lisette,' he added sadly.

Then their host joined them, asking if she had slept well, as if this were an ordinary visit, instead of the most extraordinary one she had ever experienced.

Later, in the big old parlour, and still feeling as if she were living in a dream, Lisa listened to their plans for her, and for their cause.

'Albert Lamont is to be trusted in all things,' Etienne said. 'He is a likeable, fatherly figure, the kind of man the Germans probably see as a bit of a buffoon, but don't be fooled, Lisette. His mind is as sharp as a razor.'

'But what am I actually supposed to do?' Lisa said.

'I have explained. The Germans like their sweet things, and visit the shop for cakes and pastries. On no account are you to address them in German, or show that you understand their language, apart from good morning and goodbye and a few basic words. Do not be precise with your accent. You are a Frenchwoman serving them under protest, but making the best of it. Is that understood?'

She resisted the desire to salute and merely nodded.

'And?'

His eyes softened for a moment. She would have been a fool if she didn't recognize desire when she saw it. It was quickly hidden, but it was there, she thought, a shiver of excitement running through her veins. It was definitely there.

'And you will collaborate by accepting any invitation that comes your way. I am sure such invitations will come,' he said, confirming her feeling that he was just as aware of her as she was of him. 'Go dancing or to a cinema, or to one of the officers' clubs in the city – especially that. It will be easy to say you do not wish to be seen too openly with them, and they will agree. You will listen and observe, and report back to us any small piece of information you overhear. At all times you will be careful, and not allow yourself to be blatant when your country-men and women are around. Discretion is the most important word in your vocabulary from now on.'

'Is that all! It's hardly infiltrating a German stronghold and having access to secret documents, is it?' Lisa said, disappointed at how feeble it sounded, and ignoring the fact they weren't actually *her* fellow countrymen and women...

Henri laughed. 'I fear you have been read-ing too many spy stories, Lisette. It is from these small pieces of information that the whole picture is built up. A careless word here, a laughing word there, especially when officers have had a little too much to drink, can be of enormous help to us, and to our allies.'

'You still have the chance to refuse, Lisette,' Etienne said.

She looked at him. 'You know, and I know, that I do not, and will not.'

His smile was the warmest she had seen it,

lighting his face as his hand reached out and patted hers, and a feeling akin to electricity bolted through her.

'In any case,' Henri began, and she was instantly alert to the nuance in his voice. She *knew* there was something else. 'You will probably not work at Lamont's for very long, Lisette. Your main role will be here with Etienne.'

'Why send me there in the first place then?' And why did she have the feeling that this was all part of some master plan?

'To establish your presence, Lisette. The Germans will get used to seeing your pretty face at the patisserie, but because of the Allied bombing in the city I know that they are considering commandeering this farm for an out-of-city barracks. We pray that it won't happen, but we will have no choice in the matter if they do, in which case you will help your cousin to cater for their needs.'

'You will expect me to be a glorified servant?' she said indignantly.

'Would that bother you?' he challenged.

She wanted to say yes! She hadn't become an accomplished teacher and valued interpreter to end up as a skivvy to a group of enemies in an occupied country. But one look at the way her cousin's mouth broke into that sensual smile again, she found herself capitulating to a greater force. Just like France.

Seventeen

She soon discovered why Etienne was so against having his farm commandeered by the Germans. Everyone resisted as fiercely as possible, of course, but it wasn't only on account of his own pride. It was because the farm was playing its own role in what was happening behind the scenes.

There were many rooms in the rambling old farmhouse, including attics and cellars, as well as the extensive vineyards and wine cellars that formed part of the Arnaud estate. Etienne's carefully selected workers were involved in the secret Resistance movement that was still haphazard at present, but which Henri prophesied would one day be countrywide and help to rid France of the invaders.

Arnaud's farm had a pivotal role in housing crashed British airmen, who would be flown from there back to England under cover of darkness with as much coded knowledge as the Resistance people could gather. Lisa's fraternization with the Germans, however slight their conversations seemed, would help to build up a network of information to be sent back to England.

'I hardly think they will give away anything important!' she protested.

'A pretty girl can always get information out of a man if she flatters him enough, and all young men like to be flattered, even Germans,' Etienne told her, with barely disguised contempt. 'They are also heavy drinkers. You will encourage them in this, which is when they will open up to you. With your excellent memory, you will repeat everything to me accurately, and we will do the rest.'

She fumed silently. His compliments were so back-handed as to be almost laughable. But she recognized that he was deadly serious and she knew she would do everything that was expected of her.

As they cycled towards Paris a few days later, Lisa was shocked to see so much bomb damage in and around the city. The sound of gunfire was ominously close, and she was relieved to find the patisserie in a quiet suburb in the city, in a different district from where she had once worked.

It was unnerving to see so many German soldiers in the streets, some patrolling in their goose-stepping march, others lounging around in cafés and squares, so obviously the victors. Yet it was not so long ago that she had worked freely here with Germans who had been friends, not enemies.

But now she had to be their friend in a different way. She had to listen and spy and report. And who knew what else might be necessary?

'Second thoughts?' Etienne asked as they entered a cobbled side-street.

'Are you a thought-reader?' she flashed at him. 'If so, you are wrong. I have only a deep sadness that it is necessary to do this at all.'

'Spoken like a true Frenchwoman,' he said.

She looked at him steadily. She was not a true Frenchwoman, and yet in every way she knew she must think and act as if she were. It would not be difficult. It was the way she had thought of herself for years, she admitted.

'Have I said something to amuse you?' Etienne said without even glancing at her. 'Your gaze burns into my soul.'

She mocked him. *'Mon Dieu!* How very melodramatic you are!'

He turned to her then, and not by a flicker of a smile did he acknowledge her teasing. 'And how beautiful you are. As I said before, I think you will have no problem in attracting our enemies.'

Lisa wondered if she had heard aright. He said it so calmly, as if he were assessing a piece of fine porcelain. So *insultingly* calmly, she thought furiously. She was not made of porcelain, or glass, or anything so inanimate.

She was a flesh and blood woman, and just for a moment she doubted if any woman had the capacity to tame this cold fish of a man!

She almost laughed out loud, wondering if she was mixing her metaphors, just to distract herself from the fact that, cold fish or not, he was undoubtedly charismatic, and the understated bravery in his enterprise helped to make him that way. But this was not how she wanted to think about Etienne Arnaud.

He was her contact in this organization, no more. What he did with any information she could give him she didn't want to know. It would be far better if she didn't know. She could work that much out for herself. She could also work out that she had been brought here to be nothing more than bait to the Germans, and it was hardly complimentary.

'This is the place,' Etienne said, when they reached a small patisserie. 'It has been well frequented by the Germans, including a number of officers who seem to regard it as their property. You have an air of class about you, Lisette, and make no mistake – you'll be noticed.'

'Right,' she said through clenched teeth, not sure whether to hate this man or admire him for his very coolness. Then his voice warmed.

'Come and meet M. Lamont. Hold your

chin high, and be my cousin, my naughty little cousin who was once the bane of my life when we were children.'

He smiled, and for one moment Lisa felt her heart stop as he repeated the history he had created for them, inventing the children who had never existed, but whom she and everyone else had to believe were part of her life.

She liked Albert Lamont on sight. As she had been told, he was a jovial man, whom she could no more imagine to be dynamic in the world of espionage than Father Christmas. But that was the secret of their success. Who would ever suspect...?

The patisserie was not strictly a café, but, as was usual in France, there were tables and chairs for those who wished to sit and chat over their delicacies. One of them was occupied by two German officers.

'So this is Lisette,' M. Lamont said, beaming. 'I've heard so much about you, *chérie*, that I feel I know you already. But you are such an elegant young lady, and I'm sure all those tales Etienne told me about your playing childhood tricks on him cannot be true!'

She gave a cheerful laugh. 'My cousin likes to exaggerate, M. Lamont, but he was never above teasing me in return! It's the way families behave, *non*?'

She hugged Etienne's arm affectionately, playing along with the fantasy, enjoying the sudden gleam of satisfaction in his eyes, especially as the two German officers were looking their way and making comments.

'This one's an improvement on some of the local wenches,' one said, to which the other gave a more earthy reply.

Lisa understood them perfectly, but there was no way she would let them know it. From the small squeeze on her arm, she knew that Etienne understood them too, and probably M. Lamont also. It was obviously something she would have to get used to. Officers or not, these men in an occupied country were probably starved of female company, and again she felt a shiver, wondering how far she would need to go in her deception.

'You'll see that she comes to no harm, Albert,' Etienne said. 'And if she becomes too much for you, just let me know. She's not too old to be spanked!'

Lisa gasped, and then heard the chuckling at the table, realizing that the Germans knew enough French to follow Etienne's words very well. The nerve of him! He had painted an unsavoury image of her that she didn't care for one bit. But she realized that was the intention. She was the once-naughty little cousin who had played mischievous tricks, and probably wouldn't mind having a good time. And these days the Germans were the ones with all the money and the means.

'Why don't you go home and leave me to start work, cousin?' she said lightly, 'or M. Lamont will think I'm here under false pretences.'

She winked at Etienne as she spoke, and he laughed back, giving her a kiss on both cheeks and holding her close as he did so. She tried not to look startled. It was all part of the playacting, and she must accept it. But as he playfully slapped her backside before he left she had a job not to slap him back.

'I'll come back for you at six o'clock. I prefer that you don't cycle home alone,' he told her, loud enough for the Germans to hear, making it clear that he intended looking after his 'cousin'. Impulsively, she tossed her head.

'I'd be all right on my own! Or I could always find someone to escort me.'

She allowed a small smile to curve her lips as she glanced at the Germans, and then looked away again as Etienne scolded her.

'You'll wait for me, do you hear, Lisette?'

'I hear,' she said resentfully, and then threw her arms about his neck and kissed him on the cheek. 'Oh, all right! I know you mean well, but I can look after myself, truly! I'm not a child any more.'

She watched him go, and then turned to M. Lamont, wondering if she had gone too far. But she also knew that they had been sweet, heady moments when she had been held close to him, and the game they were playing had only just begun. She didn't let herself question just which game she was thinking about ... the daring, dangerous one where she risked her life as well as being branded a traitor ... or the other one, in the intimate, pseudo-family world of Etienne Arnaud.

'What do you want me to do, M. Lamont?' she said quickly before her thoughts strayed too far.

'Firstly, I want you to call me Albert,' he said affably, 'and then I suggest you clear the table of the two gentlemen while I attend to my work in the back room. If they want to stop and chat there is no hurry this morning.'

By the time the officers left the patisserie she had learnt from their halting French that they had their headquarters in one of the city's best residences, and were missing the girls back home in Germany, but wouldn't mind a little female company when it was offered. She had laughed, knowing full well what they meant, and kept her voice teasing as she said it was not worth her while to be seen with the enemy, or to make sport after curfew.

'But there are always ways and means,' one

of the officers said, tapping his finger to his nose in a ridiculously secretive gesture. 'I'm sure a lively young fraulein like yourself can get away from that pompous cousin of yours one evening, and we could show you a good time. Do you like dancing?'

'Yes, of course!' Her heart was thudding, wondering if this was all too easy.

'Then we will collect you from an arranged rendezvous on Saturday night, and take you to a private club where there is music and dancing, and then drive you home. I'm sure the hawk-eyed cousin will have no objection.'

He continued to speak in fractured French with his heavy accent, and it was all Lisa could do not to laugh out loud. But that would be fatal.

'I'll think about it, Herr Lieutenant,' she said, in her best flirtatious manner. The officer caught her hand, caressing it very slightly.

'Don't take too long then ... Lisette. And I'm Kurt.'

She released her hand quickly. He went too fast – but perhaps not. She had a job to do, and she had better remember it, however distasteful she found it.

'I'm sure something can be arranged,' she said with a smile.

'Good. Then I shall return on Friday to arrange a meeting place.'

He stood up, clicking his heels smartly before he left, his fellow officer following with a leer on his face. Lisa didn't like him, and Kurt seemed the better of the two. At least he hadn't been the one making the lewd comments earlier.

'You did well, Lisette,' she heard Albert Lamont say. 'Etienne will be pleased that you made contact so soon. Now, while we have a few quiet moments, come to the back room and I will give you a few more details of our operation.'

She moved as if in a dream, knowing she must keep her wits about her, but suddenly wishing herself anywhere but in this situation. This was no Boys' Own fictional adventure, such as Wally used to read about in his comic books. This was real life – or death.

The Germans weren't the only customers in the patisserie and several times during the day Albert disappeared with one or another contact masquerading as a customer to the back room, where Lisa presumed there was a report to be made. After her short attack of nerves earlier she wondered just how much good all this was doing. They must think it worthwhile, but it was oddly depressing to think that this was how a war could be won.

The scream of an air-raid warning followed by a shatteringly loud bombing raid somewhere to the north of them made her revise her thoughts quickly. It was a bizarre situation. Her own countrymen were bombing this city that she loved, in order to smoke out the enemy – and they were the people she had worked with not so very long ago, and whom she now had to cajole into giving her vital information about their movements and plans.

For a moment she felt disorientated, wondering exactly who she was, and if she would ever have a real identity again. In that moment she longed for England and home with a passion. And then she saw Albert ushering someone into the back room, almost certainly another of his contacts, and she knew she was doing this for England as much as for France. She may be only a tiny cog in a huge machine, but even tiny cogs were important to keep it running smoothly.

Etienne was pleased to hear about her date for Saturday night, and during dinner that evening he gave her instructions.

'You will stay at Lamont's until the officer collects you, and he will return you there later. You will sleep in Albert's spare room and cycle back to the farm in the morning.'

'You don't think there will be anything urgent that I will have forgotten by then?' she asked sarcastically.

'I know you will not. I can be sure of it.'

'Are you so sure of me?'

'I trust Henri completely, and I am quite sure he has found us the most competent of women for our needs.'

And what about your needs? What about mine?

She bit back the thought, glad that she hadn't said it aloud. But to be considered the most competent of women wasn't exactly glamorous, she thought indignantly, and found herself glaring at Etienne over the dining table.

'I think I have insulted you now,' he said calmly. 'But I have already called you beautiful, and if you want me to add that I think you are amazing and exceptional and also very brave, then I will. But don't expect to hear me say it too often, Lisette. It may get in the way of what we are trying to achieve.'

'And if I say that you are amazing and exceptional and very brave too, will that get in the way of anything?'

She didn't know why she was goading him in this way, nor why she longed to see some of the passion of which she was sure he was capable. He had to be cold and calculating in his work, but she had also been held in his arms and felt the beat of his heart next to her own. She had felt his kiss on her cheeks, and she knew there was a real man beneath the facade. That was the man she wanted to know.

'It might ... complicate things,' he said at

301

last. 'Oh, and one more thing, Lisette. When we have *visitors* you will continue to be my cousin at all times. It is best that no one knows any different.'

By visitors, she knew he meant any British airmen he would be sheltering here until they could get back to England. So far she had seen no evidence that any were here right now, but that was probably the best way, she thought. What you didn't know and couldn't see, you couldn't reveal to the enemy. And when Etienne slipped out of the farmhouse after dinner she neither knew nor asked where he went.

But that night, lying in the bed that was becoming familiar to her now, she wondered how long two passionate young people living in the same house could continue to be indifferent to one another. And just how wrong it would be if they were not.

She stared at the small window, through which she could see dark scudding clouds that hid the moon, and wondered how many British planes would be flying over France and Germany that night, desecrating beautiful cities and country villages – and how many German planes would be doing the same to Britain on the whim of a power-crazy dictator. It was all so mad, and so futile.

Long before Christmas that year the news

had filtered through that Bristol was being continuously bombed. How Etienne had got the information Lisa didn't know, but that was part of his job.

It stirred up all kinds of memories inside her; like the day she and her mother had gone there to meet Henri and his wife, and begun a chain of events that had led her here, and that Renee had gone there to work to get away from Eddie, and had presumably now joined up as Renee Garland and was somewhere safe ... and the childhood pledges she and Renee had made so long ago when they were ten years old.

And now she was twenty-five and still not married, as she had predicted. But perhaps she was on the brink of falling in love. Perhaps.

She moved restlessly in the big bed. It wasn't Kurt she was thinking of at that moment, although by now she was seeing him on a fairly regular basis, and was accepted in the officers' club where there was music and dancing on Saturday nights. They had followed this routine for a few weeks, and he always respected her wishes when she insisted that she must return to Lamont's before midnight.

This was well after curfew, but escorted by a German officer she knew she would be safe – provided none of the local French people saw her and reported her for their own brand of justice. There was danger at every turn, but there was a kind of exhilaration in it, too, especially as Kurt seemed to enjoy the games they played in keeping her well out of sight until she was safely behind closed doors.

She turned over in her bed again, thankful that at least Kurt seemed to be a gentleman as well as an officer. He was very correct and well mannered. A few kisses were all he demanded of her – and were all she intended to give him, Lisa thought fiercely. Anything else should be kept for the man she would marry.

A sudden noise alerted all her senses. In ordinary times it could have been dismissed as little more than a small animal scuffling in the grass, or a rustling of leaves on a windy night. But this was no ordinary time, and a sixth sense told Lisa full well that something was happening. She crept out of bed and went across to the window, which she kept partially uncurtained so that she could see the sky.

It took a few moments to get accustomed to the darkness outside, and at first she could see nothing unusual. The air was cold and frosty and very still. There was nothing that could have made a noise ... but then she saw the moving shadows at the far end of the yard, and she shrank back so that no one could see her. Excitement bubbled through her. It had to be Etienne out on a mission to bring back some airmen, and she would desperately have loved to be out there too.

If they were British it would surely reassure them to hear her English voice, but she knew such a thing would never be allowed. At all costs, no matter whom she was with, it had been impressed on her that no one was to be trusted with her true identity. She was to forget she had been born in a small Somerset village and had a family of her own.

From now on Etienne was her family. Just as quickly as the excitement flared, it died. On no account was she to wander in forbidden reaches of the old house or the wine cellars and make herself known. She was Lisette Arnaud, Etienne's cousin, who officially had no knowledge of his undercover activities. Both Henri and Etienne had insisted that it was for her own safety.

Then she realized that the brief activity outside had stopped. The night was still once more, and Lisa went back to bed filled with frustration. She wanted to do so much more. She had *expected* to do so much more. She did so little, for all that Etienne told her that her meetings with Kurt and his fellow officers were important. She felt that she was contributing nothing. Where was the danger, the excitement, in smiling and chatting to Germans while they whirled her around the dance floor to the irritatingly bouncy

German music?

It must have been a hour later when she heard the small tap on her door, and she sat bolt upright, her heart thumping. Assuming it would be Helene, the housekeeper, though with no idea why she would be coming here at this hour, Lisa sped out of bed and opened her door a crack.

The corridor was dimly lit, and she was wearing only a nightgown, even though it was primly buttoned to the neck. But she couldn't miss Etienne's smile as he took in her appearance, her hair loose and tangled from sleep.

'What do you want?' she almost hissed.

'Just to reassure the vision at the window that all is well, *chérie*,' he said very softly, 'and to bid my beautiful cousin goodnight for a second time.'

His arms were around her before she could move a muscle. She was pressed tightly against him in her cotton nightgown, her breasts flattened by his embrace, her senses rocked by the unexpectedness of it. He was cold, smelling of the outdoors, like an immensely sensual animal, she thought faintly, and then he was kissing her mouth and she was kissing him back just as passionately without any heed of what tomorrow might bring.

Eighteen

Next morning, Lisa wondered if it had really happened. Not that anything much had happened. It was just a kiss ... if such a meeting of lips, bodies and senses could ever be called just a kiss. Encompassing all but the act itself, it was the sweetest seduction, and it had tipped her over the brink, just as she knew it must.

Etienne had gone out very early, and she had no option but to eat breakfast alone and cycle to the patisserie without seeing him. He was obviously regretting his visit to her room, she thought, with a mixture of outrage and misery. He didn't love her. She was merely useful to him, and from now on any cousinly playacting on her part was going to be strictly curtailed. While they had a job to do, never by one glance or one touch would she betray her feelings for him.

She had to assume that Etienne felt the same, since he made no reference to what had passed. It was both a relief and hugely insulting, but she admitted that he was ultra-professional in whatever he did, whether in his vineyard business or his undercover

307

work. She was kept well away from the upper part of the house, where the uninvited guests stayed, and she had no connection with any wireless transmissions sending coded messages to England.

Although she knew of these things now, she began to feel more and more excluded, and on one of Henri's regular monthly visits early in the new year she exploded, almost weeping with rage, feeling that Henri was the only one with whom she could really be herself – whoever that was now.

'Why am I here? What good am I doing? I'm no more than a shop-girl, apart from the time I'm paraded in the German officers' club like some trophy for Kurt and his colleagues!'

'Has he been troublesome?' Henri said, calm as ever.

She glared at him. 'No, he has not! He is the most insufferably correct, polite German I have ever met. And of course I'm glad about that! I've no wish to get into any personal entanglements. He even shows me photos of his wife and children. It's not his fault that I'm living an unnatural life!'

She stopped, ashamed of her outburst. If she was living a so-called unnatural life, how much more were they? Etienne would surely have preferred a peaceful life here on his farm; Henri was thousands of miles away from Monique and the children; and Kurt, too ... she couldn't miss the look in his eyes when he spoke of his wife and his little blond-haired daughters.

'I know it's hard for you, Lisette,' Henri went on. 'We all long for the day when peace comes again, and I daresay that goes for the Germans, too.'

She didn't miss the faint note of derision in his voice. But they weren't all bad. Henri knew that as well as anyone. He'd once had good friends in Germany, done business with them, and it was only one madman who had been the cause of all this...

She nodded slowly. 'I know I'm being foolish, but I just wish I could do more. The officers are used to me now, and they are indiscreet when they have drunk a lot, but whether what they talk about is any use to the war effort, heaven knows.'

He became authoritative. 'I assure you that it is, and the battle has only just begun. Just go on doing what you're doing and take every care.'

She remembered those words when she noticed another girl at the officers' club looking at her quizzically one Saturday evening. She was vaguely familiar – a friend of a girl she had worked with in the Paris office, perhaps, though she couldn't be sure. Moments later she saw the girl, Claudine, whisper something to the officer with her.

He strolled across to where she was chatting with Kurt, and, without warning, addressed her loudly in English.

'How do you like the winter weather here in Paris, miss?'

She didn't flinch, even though her heart was racing. Kurt put down his glass of beer and stared at them. To Lisa's horror, the officer then gripped her arm and repeated the question. She gave a little cry as his fingers bit into her arm. She tried to shake him off, and in rapid French she let out a stream of expletives that would have done justice to a navvy.

The Germans didn't understand it all, but they understood enough to break out into raucous laughter at such blasphemies coming from the mouth of such an elegant Frenchwoman. Kurt pushed the man away, and his comrades jeered and told him to take more water with his drink, and the small incident passed. But it had shaken Lisa all the same. She had lived and worked in France, and in Paris, and she knew she always ran the risk of being recognized.

She was confronted by the girl in the women's cloakroom. Here it comes, she thought. The denouncement. Visions of being paraded through the streets of Paris, of having her hair shaved, and worse, sent trickles of icy fear through her. And then the girl spoke softly.

'You did well tonight. It will be noted.'

Alarm bells rang through Lisa's head. Claudine spoke in English now, in a sweet, Home Counties accent, allying herself at once with the girl who was masquerading here. Lisa spat out a bit more venom, knowing she must keep up the pretence, trusting no one, especially not this girl, who could be a spy for either side.

Claudine's face went a vivid red, and then she let out an answering stream of abuse. It didn't shock Lisa. You didn't live in a country for all these years without being aware of the colourful and unsavoury words of the language. She turned her back on Claudine and went on applying lipstick to her mouth with steady hands as the girl flounced out.

It had to be reported to Etienne that evening. She repeated all that had happened, as well as the overheard conversations between the various officers. He listened gravely, and then he nodded.

'As the girl said, you did well tonight, Lisette.'

Lisa started. The words were too similar. No ... they were *identical* to Claudine's.

'Am I missing something? Is there something I should know? After all these months, was this just a *test*?' She felt bitterly hurt and disappointed. Had he so little faith in her that she had had to be put to the test?

'Lisette, we constantly try our people so

311

they do not falter. It would be fatal if they did. It is a case of keeping the strong and discarding the weak.'

'My God, now you sound like Hitler,' she snapped, knowing it was the worst insult she could throw at him.

She saw his face darken with anger, but she hadn't finished yet.

'And what if I *had* faltered, as you put it? What of the risk to me? Did this test have to be done in such a public place? If the Germans hadn't thrown me in jail, the French would certainly have punished me. I would be a traitor to somebody, no matter what I said. Do you think so little of me?'

His handsome face darkened. 'You know I think very highly of you, but we are not playing a game of cops and robbers, Lisette, and much of what we ask you to do will seem tedious. But if you no longer think you can deal with it, then I will have no option but to send my irritating little cousin out of harm's way.'

'Why not just shoot me and be done with it?' she muttered, hardly caring what she said to him any more as the prospect of being sent home as a failure loomed frighteningly near.

'I would never do that, because it would be such a terrible waste of your talents,' he said coolly.

Wounded by what she saw as sarcasm, she

made to flounce out of the room, just as Claudine had done at the officers' club, and he caught at her hand.

'When these terrible days are behind us, *chérie*, there will be time to think of other things. Until then we must all put personal feelings aside.'

She pulled away from him and went upstairs to her bedroom. He may have been speaking generally, or there may have been a more subtle meaning behind his words. She took the smallest amount of comfort in hoping it might be the latter, and that he did have feelings for her that went beyond the use of her talents. Until then they must put all personal emotions aside and hope that this war ended soon, and that the Germans would be hounded out of France as quickly as they had invaded it.

Such thoughts were far too noble for Lisa's frame of mind. Just as quickly, she was incensed by them. Did no one ever fall in love during a war? Were there no births and marriages as well as deaths? Life didn't hang suspended for ever while nations battled against each other.

But she was certainly not going to beg for any favours from a man who was clearly so adept at putting his feelings into separate compartments.

The next time she went to the officers' club,

she realized that Claudine wasn't there. She mentioned it casually to Kurt, since he had been aware of the friction between the girls. He shrugged.

'She has been dealt with and is best forgotten. Now, shall we dance?'

The chilling way he spoke, disposing of any mention of Claudine in the same way Lisa suspected the girl herself had been disposed of, sent a new thrill of fear running through her. He might be polite, a perfect gentleman, a loving husband and father, but when it came to dealing with spies in their midst there would be no mercy. She would do well to remember that.

The ruthlessness wasn't all one sided, either. Reporting the information to Etienne later, he shrugged in the same way as Kurt had done.

'The man is right. From now on, we have no knowledge of her.'

They were two of a kind, she thought furiously. There was no difference between them at all. And then his voice softened slightly.

'Be warned, Lisette. Always be on your guard, and trust no one.'

Her eyes prickled with anger. 'But you must have told her to whisper in the officer's ear and persuade him to speak to me in English. It must have come from you – or someone like you. Whatever happened to her, you people are responsible.'

'That is the price we have to pay. She knew it, and so must you, and this conversation is at an end.'

In a flash, Lisa felt exactly as she had done all those years ago in her junior school, when she questioned too much and was ordered to keep quiet and told that all discussion was at an end.

'Then I'm sorry to have troubled you,' she said stiffly.

That night, stirred up by the memory, her thoughts kept drifting back to those days that would never come again. Simple, uncomplicated days, with family and friends who loved her, far away from here, and not in a country that was ravaged and uniformly grey with enemy gunfire and overlords with their goose-stepping and their hobnailed boots that struck dread into innocent people.

She thought of Wally, and wondered where he was now, and even if he was still alive. How would she know? These bastards would never tell her, even if they knew. She swallowed the sob in her throat. She thought about Renee and her eagerness to marry the oafish Eddie Bray, and then her need to get away from him. Where was she now? And Renee's flighty mother and her Austrian husband. Had they survived the taunts and suspicions of the village?

What in God's name was she doing here? It was the last thought on her mind as she finally fell into a troubled sleep. An hour later she was woken by someone tapping on her door and a voice urgently calling her name. She slipped a dressing gown around her shoulders before she opened the door to see Helene, similarly clad.

'You are needed, Lisette.'

Without further ado, Lisa tied her dressing gown around her more securely and followed the housekeeper along the passage and up to a part of the house that was normally kept private. They went into a room that was clearly a storage room, full of lumber and knick-knacks. Helene tapped on the wall, and a door that simply looked like another panel opened to reveal an inner room. A quick glance told Lisa there were several chairs and beds and a washbasin. There was also a large wooden crate at the side of the room, which she guessed held wireless and other secret equipment. She did not care to think what was behind a curtained alcove for the use of any who were briefly incarcerated here.

There were five people in the room, including Etienne and two of his estate workers. The others wore ragged RAF uniforms, and one of them was bleeding profusely from a shoulder wound.

'What do you want me to do?' she said at

316

once, aware that she was being allowed into the holy of holies for the first time.

'You may use English,' Etienne said. 'We are all trusted here, and it will reassure them to hear a Frenchwoman speaking so fluently in their language.' He emphasized the words, just in case she was about to declare her true identity.

'You will apply pressure to the cold compress on the officer's shoulder,' he went on. 'We must stop this bleeding, and they must be moved tonight.'

She moved over to the man on the bed. She tried to smile, but all she could think of at that moment was that this could have been Wally, and she prayed with all her heart that some kind soul was doing the same for him.

'Have I died and gone to heaven?' the officer said weakly.

'That's the corniest remark I've ever heard,' she replied in English, and his eyes widened in relief.

'Thank God you speak English, mademoiselle. We don't get on with this froggy language, do we, John?'

She laughed shakily, knowing that Etienne would have understood every word, and was childishly glad that he wouldn't have been too pleased. But this wasn't the time for egos, and she did as she was instructed, changing the cold compresses on the officer's shoulder as Helene gave fresh ones to her. She kept up a bit of banter with the officer all the time she worked, knowing that the wound must be horribly painful, even though he never complained.

As she had suspected, Etienne moved to the wooden crate to activate the wireless receiver and transmitter inside, and spoke rapidly. She could follow most of it, as he confirmed that the airmen were to be flown out that night.

The wounded one didn't look in any condition to be transported to an unspecified field somewhere in the country, let alone be flown in a rickety, unmarked plane back to England, with the risk of being shot down, either by enemy or Allied fire. The risks she took seemed to pale by comparison.

'Can't it wait another day?' she asked Etienne in French now, when he had finished his transmission. He shook his head.

'No. In less than a hour we must be ready to leave. You and Helene will clean up everything here and then go back to bed.'

'Oh, but can't I do more to help?'

She should have known better than to argue. A brief exchange told her that Henri would be waiting for the plane to arrive at the field, and the signal for landing would be given at a precise time. They did not dare to be late, nor fail to deliver the men, who would be carrying coded information of help to the Allies. It was all so slickly done that she would never again doubt the efficiency of the secret army.

But she had no objection to the swift kiss on her cheek from the two airmen when the time came for them to be helped down the stairs and out into the night, while she and Helene restored the hidden room to its previous condition, stripping the beds and burning the soiled compresses in an incinerator. Only then, in the early hours of the morning, did they retire. By that time Lisa was so tired she fell asleep immediately, and when morning came no reference was made to the night-time activities, and she discovered that this was the strict pattern that was followed.

From then on she was invited into the inner sanctuary whenever necessary, to assist and soothe and talk softly to the victims in their own language.

The war showed no signs of abatement, and the Germans seemed to be relentlessly gaining ground over months and into years, Lisa still couldn't believe there was nothing very significant in what she was doing. She was officially Etienne Arnaud's cousin, and a mere shop assistant with an access to the German officers' social life that was kept as discreet as possible. But despite its involvement in small, local pockets of sabotage, it took a very long time before the French Resistance movement became properly organized.

Etienne continued his efforts to get British airmen back to Britain, so all went on as before in the household, but to Lisa's dismay Albert Lamont suffered a heart attack and decided to sell his shop and retire. It was bought almost immediately by a firm of accountants who wanted nothing to do with a bakery nor a female assistant who knew nothing of the work. So Lisa was unemployed.

'What now?' she burst out to Etienne. 'Am I to return with the next British airman who needs to be transported back to England? Shall I pick up the reins of my old teaching job? I truly feel that I have no place here, Etienne.'

'You will always have a place here, *chérie*,' he said gravely. 'In my home, and in my heart.'

They were fine words, but they meant nothing more than that she was useful to him and his cause. And, truly, there was much to do at the farm that she could help with. Helene was getting on in years, and Lisa could do her bit, even if it was far less than she wanted or expected to do.

She couldn't deny, though, a secret thrill of intoxication when she was sent to the vineyard or the wine cellars with cheese and wine for the workers. It was true intoxication, she thought, her senses always bemused on first entering the dark, musty interiors, and she wondered how anyone could work there without becoming drunk with the strong, sweet smells of fermentation.

But she also learnt that Etienne had always chosen his workers with care. Few of the cellar workers had any idea of the extent to which he was involved in the secret organization. The attic room in the house remained a closely guarded secret except to those most trusted and involved.

The horror of the Japanese bombing of Pearl Harbor brought the United States into the war. Now, with their mighty strength, perhaps it would end ... But peace seemed as far away as ever on all sides as the Nazi regime became more entrenched in France, and the war looked no closer to being won by either side. Some said that for all Adolf Hitler's bluster perhaps even the occupiers were losing faith that they could triumph.

Being so far out of the city, the residents of Etienne's home had been free from the intervention from the military in Paris that he had once feared. During the last two years, by stealth and cunning – and a miraculous amount of luck – they had managed to avoid the fate of many of the other Resistance cells around the country, and continue their work unhindered. But the day came when this was no longer the case.

Lisa was helping Helene to hang the bulky sheets on the washing line when they heard the unmistakable rumble of army vehicles. Her first instinct was to run, to warn Etienne, wherever he was ... and then she felt the firm grip of Helene's hand on her arm.

'Keep still. Say nothing. Do nothing. We are simple countrywomen who have nothing to do with Germans.'

'But how do I stop my heart from pounding?' Lisa muttered.

'That is natural. Mine is pounding too. If we are approached, we are merely doing women's work, Lisette. Do you understand?'

'Of course I do.' The momentary fright fizzled away.

'You! You women!' they heard the guttural voice shout to them in laboured French. 'Where is the owner of the house?'

'If you mean M. Arnaud, he is in the wine cellars,' Helene said stiffly. 'I will fetch him for you—'

Almost at once, it seemed as if they were surrounded by a bristling of guns as the soldiers with him leapt out of their vehicles, awaiting orders.

'Stay where you are,' the officer shouted. 'We have reason to believe that this place has been harbouring the enemy. If this is true, you will all be shot. Is anyone else in the house beside you and the girl?'

'There is no one,' Helene said.

He motioned to several of the men. 'Two of you go and search the house. Two more watch the women while we search the cellars. Don't let them give any signals. The cellars will be where we'll find the bastards. I doubt they would have used the house with such a network of hiding places.'

Lisa understood everything perfectly, and she stood passively beside Helene. In her kitchen apron and with her red hair hidden under a kerchief she was thankful that she merely resembled a servant girl. She knew the Germans would find nothing, and she appreciated why Etienne had been so determined not to involve any more of his cellar workers than necessary in the subterfuge that went on whenever there were British airmen to be smuggled out of France. What they didn't know, they couldn't tell.

The two women were subjected to an hour of standing in the hot sun while the German soldiers presided over them, making comments now and then that would have made Lisa blush had she let on that she understood any of their snide remarks. Helene had begun to rock from side to side, and finally Lisa indicated that she needed to sit down on a garden bench. She helped her across, fussing over her all the while as the Germans followed.

'Let them think we are simple souls,' Helene whispered again. 'Wring your hands and show your agitation.'

Lisa didn't know what good it would do, but the soldiers soon got tired of watching these two women who seemed incapable of anything but flapping over one another, and they wandered away, bored by such in-activity. If Helene had been a man Lisa was sure she would have spat at them.

Finally the group emerged from the cellars, angry that they had found nothing. Etienne accompanied them, speaking loudly and gesticulating wildly in the manner of a businessman frustrated at having his day interrupted, and clearly furious that they had taken away a crate of his best wines as compensation for their trouble. But they were moving towards their vehicles now, and Lisa breathed a sigh of relief. All those close encounters in the officers' club had been nowhere near as unnerving as this, and she had been as fearful for Etienne as for herself. She couldn't bear it if he was taken away and interrogated.

'One of them is coming back,' Helene mur-mured.

Lisa jerked up her head to see a young officer heading their way, a frown between his eyes. He stopped right in front of Lisa. Her head was bowed when suddenly he thrust out his hand and lifted her chin so that she had no option but to look into his face. Her thoughts spun. She was sure she didn't know him, and yet there was something familiar about him. And instantly she remembered.

When she had worked in the Paris office all those years ago, this young man had visited one of her German colleagues. Lisa had only seen him once but his face was now etched in her memory. She prayed that hers wasn't etched in his.

'Do I know you, mademoiselle?' he spoke in German. She looked at him blankly, spreading her hands and shrugging her shoulders.

'Let me say again,' he said in broken English. *'Do I know you?'*

She shook his hand from her chin, reverting to a stream of blasphemy and abuse in French.

Helene put her hand to her mouth as if in shock, and the young man backed away slightly. Lisa wasn't sure if he was totally convinced, but the military vehicles were starting up, and the shouts from his colleagues told him to hurry up if he wasn't to be left behind. Helene added her voice to Lisa's, raising her fist at the soldier, and putting a protective arm around Lisa's shoulders, and he finally shrugged and turned to go as the convoy prepared to leave.

'That was too close for comfort,' Lisa gasped when the dust had settled and they were finally back in the house with generous nips of brandy to settle their nerves. Etienne's face was grave.

'Did he recognize you?'

'He thought so, but he could only have seen me briefly and it was years ago.'

'All the same, we can't afford to jeopardize our position.'

Her heart jumped. He surely couldn't mean he was sending her back to England? It would be so ignominious – besides which, she couldn't bear to be parted from him.

Nineteen

Fighting raged on in various parts of the world now, but the war seemed to be at a stalemate. The Germans in occupied France caused untold misery, despite the news filtering through on many a clandestine wireless set that the RAF was successfully bombing German cities. By the end of 1943 the last great battleship in the German navy, the *Scharnhorst*, was sunk, and as the days lurched into 1944 the news came that the Allies had rained thousands of tons of bombs on Berlin. Yet despite the combined efforts of the Allies the conflict showed no sign of ending.

All this was momentarily as nothing for Lisa, on that day when she felt sure Etienne was about to send her home. And she didn't want to go. She felt more passionately than ever that her place was here in the country that she loved. In the home of the man she loved. The stark realization that the two were so closely connected made her numb as Etienne took her hand, and she felt as if all her heart was in her eyes. She was thankful Helene had left them alone so she would not be aware of it. Women always sensed these things.

'Lisette, we are not abandoning you,' he said gently.

'No? It felt like it. It sounded like it! So what are your plans for me?' Childish though it was, she couldn't help the harsh disappointment.

'You are to go to Vertsable—'

'So you *are* sending me away!'

He continued as if she hadn't spoken. 'Vertsable is a remote woodland village about twelve miles from here. You will be companion to an elderly gentleman, and you will receive instructions from a contact who will visit weekly.'

At her disapproving look and pursed lips, he gave a slight smile.

'I will be your contact, *chérie*. Do not think you will be rid of me that easily, but it is no longer safe for you here. If anyone should ask, you were called away to care for your sick mother.'

'And the elderly gentleman?' she managed to say, even while she smarted at the un-intentional slight.

It couldn't be Henri Dubois, who certainly wouldn't appreciate being described in that way, and she truly didn't want to be among strangers in a remote woodland village miles from anywhere.

'I do not think you will be disappointed,'

was all he would say. 'We leave tomorrow, Lisette, so I suggest you help Helene to pack your things.'

She was numb with misery. No matter what Etienne said, she still felt as though she was being hounded out because she could put them all in danger if she stayed. The only consolation was that he would be her weekly contact, though for what she had no idea.

'Before you go, I have some news for you. This business with the search of the cellars sent it out of my mind, but I think it will please you.'

She eyed him warily. What news could he possibly have to please her?

'Your brother was in France until recently.'

Lisa gave a little cry, but before she could say anything, he went on.

'He was quite badly wounded, although not as seriously as at first thought, but it was enough for him to be repatriated. I can only tell you that he is alive and back in England working on the newspaper once more.'

One minute she was staring at him dumbly. The next she was weeping in his arms as enormous relief washed over her. And then, as it all sank in, she found herself beating on his chest in a fury. How dare he keep this from her until now! And if he had got news of her brother now, why not before? The raging thoughts milled around in her head.

'Hold on, *ma petite*,' she heard him say as

his arms gripped her tightly. Far from being an endearment, the phrase enraged her more.

'Why have you never given me news of Wally before this? I hope he has been told that I am safe and well too. You obviously have your sources but you didn't think you could trust me enough. You know he is the only one left of my family, and you must have known how much he is loved.'

'As you are loved, *chérie*,' he said, oh so calmly in contrast to her tirade.

His mouth was close to her cheek and she could feel his breath on her skin, warm and seductive and enticing. In an instant the fury was replaced by a heady cocktail of relief, exhilaration, love. Almost against her will, the whispered words were on her lips.

'And you.'

She raised her face to his, and before she knew what was happening, she was clinging to him desperately, and the kisses between them were urgent and primitive, revealing a shared need that had been resisted for too long.

When the kisses finally ended she still leant against him, reluctant to let him go, and his hands fondled her hair and the nape of her neck as if he, too, couldn't bear for this intimacy to end.

'You are very much loved, Lisette,' he said softly again. 'No matter how we are separ-

330

ated, never doubt that.'

How could she? She knew that separation didn't mean the end of love. She loved Wally, and Renee, and now, after all the celibate years, she knew she loved this man with a passion she had never known before.

But with the realization came a new embarrassment. Where did they go from here? Did they speak of tomorrows and happy-ever-afters? The only tomorrow in her mind was the immediate one, when she would be taken away from him. As if he was reading her mind, he tipped up her chin, in a way that was infinitely different from and more tender than the way the German soldier had done it. That had all happened such a short time ago, and yet she felt as though they had travelled a great distance in time.

'There is more news from London, although I doubt that we shall hear the full extent of it for some time.'

As his voice changed, she was instantly alert. There were wider things to be considered than the dawning love of two people.

'Tell me.'

She knew she was being privileged now. News from London had never been fully imparted to her before, and in her mind this also marked a change in their relationship. She could be fully trusted as well as loved.

'There's to be a big push forward by the

Allies sometime in an attempt to liberate France, bigger than anything seen so far, but more than that I cannot say.'

She was tempted to ask if he could not, or would not, but she knew instinctively that whatever information had come from London would be sketchy at present. The less they knew, the less they could tell. It was the way of things. But it gave them hope that one day all this would be ended. She shuddered suddenly, and his arms closed around her protectively again.

'Then I think I should go and attend to my packing,' she said quietly, the mundane words telling him that she understood.

'And tonight we shall have a special dinner and a bottle of my best wine before we say our farewells,' he replied. 'Our very special farewells, Lisette.'

She shivered again, but this time with a sense of anticipation and excitement coursing through her veins. It was all there in his voice, the question he wouldn't ask, and the answer was all there in her eyes. Tonight would be a very special night indeed, and the lonely nights would be over. Strictly speaking they would be only just beginning, but this one last night at the farm would be spent together. Lisa knew it as surely as she breathed.

When dinner was over, replete with good

food and a splendid meal that Helene had managed to concoct, and her spirits already intoxicated on Arnaud's finest wine, she put down her napkin and waited while Etienne came to stand behind her as she rose from the table. She felt his lips nuzzle the back of her neck, and his whispered words were like a warm caress.

'I will be with you in half an hour, *chérie*, unless you tell me otherwise.'

It was her last chance to remain chaste, unfulfilled, virginal, as an unmarried girl should be. She knew he was asking her to give him her greatest gift, and that he would honour whatever she said. She stood up and twisted around into his arms.

'Half an hour,' she repeated, and left him on limbs that were not quite steady.

There was time enough to bathe and don her prettiest nightgown and await her lover. She tasted the word again. Tonight Etienne would become her lover. Tonight, for a little while, they could put all thoughts of war behind them. Tonight belonged to them.

She was already beneath the bedcovers when he came into her room, her eyes opening the merest fraction as he clicked the door shut behind him. Within a few strides he had covered the distance between them, shedding his robe as he went, and moments later she felt the bed dip as he slid in beside her, and she felt the warmth of him reaching out for her.

'Etienne,' she whispered, and his fingers over her mouth shushed her.

'You don't need to say anything, *chérie*, nor to be afraid. We have all night to learn one another.'

Her heart swelled at such a sweet and unalarming way of telling he knew very well that this would be her first time. And it was so right that it would be with him, the man who was going to be hers for the rest of her life.

For one brief moment of selfishness, she prayed that there would be no interruptions to their joining, no shouts or stealthy whispers in the night, no necessity to hustle weary strangers into the attic rooms above. But the gods were on the side of two lovers who had needed each other for so long. The night was soft and mellow, a million stars twinkling above and a crescent moon throwing the merest light into the room where love was the only thing that mattered.

Lisa awoke to the sound of the birds' morning chorus, still wrapped in his arms. She listened to the steady sound of his breathing, her hands against his chest, and marvelled that this man, who could be so ruthless when it came to the purpose he had outlined for himself, could be so gentle and so tender in her initiation, and, ultimately, the lover of her dreams.

'What are you thinking?' she heard him say lazily, though since his eyes were still closed she had been unaware that he was awake.

She felt the heat in her cheeks.

'Only that I shall miss you so much – so much more – after this,' she said, knowing that nothing would be changed because of that one magical night.

As he moved slightly away from her, she knew their time was over. He gave her one last lingering kiss and then leapt out of bed, unashamedly and magnificently naked before wrapping his robe around him. He was brisk and practical now.

'Come, *ma chérie*, we must rouse ourselves. After breakfast we will go to Vertsable and you will get to know your new surroundings. You will like the village. It's small, but very quaint. And I shall see you often.'

But not like this. She knew without his saying it that this one night had to last them for the foreseeable future, and at that moment she hated Hitler with a vengeance for separating families and lovers. Etienne turned at the door of her room and smiled, and then he was gone, and she didn't see him again until he came down to breakfast after her, businesslike as usual, with Helene fussing around them both.

She knew, Lisa thought at once. She knew, and approved, even if nothing would ever be said about such a delicate matter. But she hugged the older woman with genuine affection as Etienne put her belongings into his car for the drive to Vertsable. Someone would follow them later on Lisa's bicycle, leaving it at the cottage for her use and going back with Etienne. Everything was arranged with the usual efficiency, and if she had learnt one more thing about Etienne it was his ability to adapt. It was an admirable trait in the present circumstances.

They left the farm without fuss, and drove through the verdant countryside to the dense woodland areas to the south and west. There was always something to surprise her about this vast country, Lisa thought with a rush of genuine affection, and nothing more so than the small village that finally came into view in a hollow in the woods. It would pass completely unnoticed from the main roads unless anyone knew it was there. Or some astute German patrol became curious...

'Oh, this is so beautiful,' she breathed involuntarily.

Typically, the old stone church dominated the village square, around which were the necessary shops to serve the small community: a patisserie, charcuterie, a general store and several others. There were no people about that morning, and the whole place seemed to have been frozen in time. The scattering of cottages appeared to melt into the surrounding woodland, and it was at one of these that Etienne finally stopped the car.

'Come and meet your new companion,' he said without expression.

In fact, *she* was to be the companion, she thought, half resentfully, not too sure how she was going to like caring for a stranger. And then the cottage door opened, and she gave an incredulous smile.

'M. Lamont – Albert!' she exclaimed, and was immediately clasped in her old employer's embrace. 'Oh, why didn't you tell me!' she gasped to Etienne, who was laughing openly now.

'I thought you had had enough shocks yesterday, so this was to be just a pleasant surprise,' he said.

'And so it is,' she said, knowing that if she had to leave Arnaud's farm she couldn't have wished for anything better. She knew very well that Albert Lamont had been involved in the resistance work, and that therefore, although she may not be close to Etienne, the work would go on. Whatever she had to do, she was not entirely abandoned. As the word slid into her mind she couldn't help thinking of it in another context. Abandoned she had certainly been last night...

She felt her face go hot, but they would surely attribute it to the joy she was feeling at not having to live among strangers after all. And M. Lamont looked so well now. For one moment she wondered if the heart attack had been a ploy to get him out of Paris and into a safer environment, but she wouldn't believe that. As if sensing where her thoughts were going, Etienne told her jocularly that one of her duties was to see that he remembered to take his medication regularly.

'And what else am I to do here?' she asked later, when she had been shown over the tiny cottage, and they were comfortably replete with delicious coffee and croissants.

The atmosphere changed at once, and as she listened, again she couldn't doubt the efficiency with which everything was organized.

'I will bring regular communications from London,' Etienne said. 'It is no longer safe to use the telephones and nor is Albert up to taking messages any further afield. This is where you come in, Lisette. From Vertsable you will cycle to your uncle's house in the country to visit him with any messages, and you will inform him when there is a need for pigeons. I am afraid that the use of Arnaud's in that respect must come to an abrupt end and your uncle will make alternative arrangements.'

She knew by now that the need for pigeons was the code for transporting British airmen back to England. Even between them they kept to the coded words.

'And who is this uncle?'

'His name is Henri Dubois,' Etienne said, his face breaking into a smile at last, 'and, before you say his home is nowhere near this place, he is no longer living there for the present, but at a safe house ten miles from here.'

It was a huge relief to know that she was among friends, but she was astute enough to know that they wouldn't have needed this elaborate change of plan if the German soldier hadn't thought he recognized her in the garden of Arnaud's farm. She thanked God she had resembled a peasant worker in her apron and kerchief, and not the sophisticated Parisienne from the office all those years ago.

'You are happy to do this, Lisette?' Albert Lamont said, seeing her frown.

'Of course,' she answered swiftly. 'I would do anything for France.'

If it sounded a little pretentious, she didn't care. It was the way she felt right then, knowing she could be a danger as well as an asset to them, and that trust had to be on both sides. She felt Etienne's hand cover hers, but the sweet moment didn't last as someone arrived from the farm with her bicycle. It was time to part.

There had been so many partings in her life,

Lisa reflected. So many people she had loved and lost touch with, whether through her own choice or necessity. But this was the hardest. Now, when she knew she loved Etienne Arnaud with a passion that went far beyond anything she had known before, fate had driven them apart.

But she couldn't let her own circumstances blind her to the work that was to be done. She was now Albert Lamont's companion, the daughter of one of his old friends, and she discovered that news of her arrival had already slipped into village gossip as smoothly as the tendrils of Etienne's grapevines. Albert took a daily walk, and now she went with him, ostensibly to keep an eye on him, but also to establish her position in Vertsable.

As the village burst into flower in the spring, it became clear that something was definitely afoot among the Allies. The messages from London were still unclear, save that they must be ready. Such tantalizing messages were madly frustrating with no clear signals as to what or when the great surge forward would be.

General Charles de Gaulle became commander-in-chief of the Free French forces in April. His plans to organize and arm the Resistance movement properly was greeted with a mixture of pleasure and suspicion. There were communist factions in the movement, which some saw as less desirable than helpful, and there was always the danger of clashes of purpose. Armed, these clashes could result in unnecessary bloodshed between people supposedly working towards the same end.

'We do better without arms,' Etienne said disapprovingly, on one of his weekly visits to Vertsable. 'It has not been necessary so far.'

'Why do you say that?' Lisa asked. 'Would you rather risk being shot and not being able to retaliate?'

'Of course not, *chérie*, but while we are seen to be unarmed we cannot be accused of resisting the Nazis.'

She noted his careful use of the words 'seen to be unarmed'. It told her more than he was actually saying. De Gaulle would make it official, and the Nazis would have no excuse – if they ever needed one – for gunning down anyone who posed a threat to them. She shivered, knowing by now that Albert had an ancient firearm in his attic. If it were found would there be reprisals on an old man for keeping such a thing? And on her, for being his companion? She was also sure that there were guns at Arnaud's farm. She had never seen them, but she hadn't doubted their existence for a minute.

'You will visit your uncle this evening, Lisette,' Etienne said now.

She was always glad to see Henri and

Gerard at the safe house in the country. Occasionally there was news of Monique and the children, although they would be young people now, she thought regretfully, and she would have known nothing of their growing up. But she recognized a different inflection in Etienne's voice, and she knew there was more to come.

'Pigeons will be needed in two days' time, and the arrangements will be made. You must see to it that Henri gets this message.'

'Of course,' she said, mystified as to why he seemed so insistent.

'Lisette, you must be extra vigilant,' he went on. 'The Germans are frustrated at still not claiming victory, and patrols are everywhere now. The farmhouse and cellars are being searched regularly, and thank God they found nothing, save helping themselves to my best wines. But they will be expanding their searches far and wide for proof of the Resistance, and when they find any evidence—'

'I know. Did anyone mention me again?' she asked fearfully, not needing him to finish the sentence. It was all too clear what happened to those who were caught.

'No, it was not the same patrol. I would gladly deliver messages to Henri myself, but my absence from the farm at night is unwise. Here, I am merely delivering wine to local customers, but I strongly suspect that the farm is being watched for any night-time activities. Just be careful, that's all I ask.'

She realized that Albert had discreetly left them alone now, and Etienne came to sit beside her on the old sofa and pulled her into his arms.

'This is as hard for me as for you, *chérie*,' he said softly, 'but it will not last for ever. Once it is over we can think of the future. Until then we must be patient.'

'I know, but it doesn't make it any easier,' she said with a sigh, finding no embarrassment in expressing her feelings to the man she loved, 'and, charming though he is, Albert is not my choice of life's companion.'

Etienne laughed. 'I should think not, indeed. You deserve a far more virile companion, but I fear that, too, must wait,' he added, and as they heard the footsteps of the older man returning they broke apart reluctantly.

For now, it had to be enough to know that he desired her as much as she desired him. But those thoughts were the furthest from her mind as she set out that evening on her bicycle through the dark country lanes. She didn't dare to turn on her headlight, and the only sound was the rustle of tyres on the carpet of undergrowth.

She had ridden about halfway to Henri's, glad of the moonless night and the cloud cover that hid her movements, when she became brutally aware of the silence of the night being suddenly disrupted. From somewhere ahead of her she heard guttural shouting in voices she recognized instantly as German. At the same time the darkness was split by bright lights and the noise of a motorcycle patrol. Her heart thudded so fast it felt as if it was about to burst in her chest, and with one instinctive movement she flung herself and her bicycle into the deep ditch than ran alongside the lane.

The cold, dank water made her gasp with shock, but she immediately immersed herself beneath it, pulling the machine on top of her and wondering just how long she could hold her breath. She crawled to the edge of the ditch, literally grasping at straws, and trying not to think what might lurk in these filthy stagnant waters that were far deeper than she had imagined after the winter rains. She briefly lifted her head to take deep breaths of air before plunging downwards again, and in those few seconds she heard the roar of the motorcycles coming nearer, their lights illuminating the whole area, and she prayed that she wouldn't betray her position by the merest ripple in the water.

They were almost past her when her heart stopped as the engines died and the shouting began again. From the crunch of his boots she sensed that one of the soldiers had got off his motorcycle and was nearing the ditch.

She heard him call to the others that there was something there.

The next minute his boot entered the water, followed by a burst of foul language as he realized its depth, and his fellow soldiers jeered and laughed at him. For one agonizing moment Lisa prayed that they were leaving. She couldn't hold her breath much longer. She felt dizzy and sick and she was sure she was going to die ... and then she had to let go of her bicycle as she felt it being hauled up out of the ditch. She chose that moment of confusion to turn her face away and gasp some air before plunging down into the depths again.

The jeering became louder as the soldiers taunted the one who was so suspicious, and seconds later they tossed the machine to the far side of the lane and rode off.

Lisa waited as long as possible until she was sure they had really gone before cautiously rising from the ditch, the pain in her chest so intense by then that she couldn't have remained there a moment longer. Almost sobbing with terror and relief that they hadn't found her, she crawled across the lane until she felt the familiar handlebars, only to discover that they were twisted completely around, the wheels had buckled and the machine was useless.

Almost weeping with rage and frustration she had to think what to do. She had to get to Henri and she had to continue on foot, despite her sodden clothes and the chill that was filling her whole body. God only knew what she might have swallowed in the filthy ditch, but she couldn't think about that now. She had to deliver the message, and she didn't dare move her bicycle, even though Gerard might have had the means to repair it. If the German patrol returned and remembered where it had been, their suspicions would be aroused.

She tottered in the direction of the safe house, appallingly light headed, with only sheer will power driving her on. Several times she fell and dragged herself back to her feet again, and there were times she imagined she heard the sound of engines approaching, and again flung herself into the ditch.

Finally, after what seemed like hours, with no moon to guide her and near to collapse, she saw the outline of the house ahead of her. She banged on the door, sobbing wildly. When it was opened she fell inside and into Henri's arms, gasping out the message that pigeons were needed in two days' time.

And then she knew no more as her bones seemed to turn to water and she slithered in a heap at Henri's feet.

Twenty

Lisa felt as though she floated in a water-colour world as vague shapes she couldn't recognize wavered in and out of her vision and then disappeared. Murmured voices said words she couldn't understand before they, too, receded. Occasionally she was aware of liquid trickling down her throat and of someone gently pushing pappy food into her mouth, urging her to swallow in order to keep up her strength. But she had no strength. She was as limp as a spent balloon, all the substance gone from her body. She was sure she was either dead and in some kind of transition period between earth and heaven, or about to go there. Everything was meaningless and hallucinatory.

Then came a moment when she awoke as if from a nightmare to find that her brain was beginning to unravel all the cotton wool of which it seemed to consist. She discovered she was in a large bed, cocooned in bedclothes, and it was dark. Through the small square of window in the room she could just make out a glimmering of stars. A frisson of logic told her that if she could see the stars from such a distance she was not yet in heaven. Hearing a small noise she turned her head the merest fraction and saw she was not alone in the room. A woman was sitting in a rocking-chair, snoring gently, her head nodding.

'Who are you?' Lisa croaked.

Her voice sounded thin and unnatural. It didn't belong to her. But who was she, anyway? For a panic-stricken moment she realized she could not remember her own name, nor imagine where she was.

The woman awoke with a start and gave a little cry. She immediately rang a bell, alarming Lisa even more. She was completely disorientated in a different way now, wondering if she had been abducted and if she would ever see home again. The word drummed in her mind while she tried to think where home was. She knew she must be French, because she had asked the question in that language, and she felt a brief and absurd sense of triumph at recognizing the fact.

The next moment the door opened and someone holding a lantern came into the room and strode across to the bed.

'Thank God you have come back to us, Lisette,' he said huskily. 'You have been away for a very long time.'

'Henri?' she whispered, not understanding, but with thankfulness flooding through her that at least here was someone she knew.

The full extent of how ill she had been took time to assimilate. The fact that she had been here in the safe house for more than a month and had known none of it was even more alarming. But as her senses gradually began to return, so did the images of staggering here half dead with wet and cold to deliver her message before she collapsed with a raging fever. She learnt that she had swallowed so much filth from the ditch that the infection had nearly killed her.

Only the constant attentions of Henri and Gerard and their housekeeper, together with a local doctor who had administered whatever drugs he could get hold of, had pulled her through. But it distressed her more than she would have believed to know that she had virtually lost all those weeks of her life and could remember none of them.

'The pigeons,' she murmured, trying to regain some sort of normality. 'Did the pigeons arrive safely?'

'Those and more,' Henri said.

'And Etienne?'

His name brimmed on her lips, wanting him near, longing for him to hold her, and wondering if it was now safe to return to Arnaud's farm where she could feel truly cherished. Not that she wasn't hugely grateful to Henri for all he had done, but it wasn't the same ... She saw his lips purse and her heart stopped for a moment.

'Calm yourself, Lisette,' he said, seeing her blanch. 'Etienne is well, but several weeks ago he was taken to Nazi head-quarters and interrogated. Naturally he told them nothing, and they had no option but to release him. The farm is now under constant surveillance, though, with the Germans confiscating whatever wines they choose. All rescue activities there have ceased, so I regret that for the foreseeable future you must remain here.'

She couldn't contain her dismay. 'Why can I not return to M. Lamont's or to the farm? Won't people think it strange that I disap-peared?'

'People disappear in wartime. It is of no consequence to the Germans or the villagers at Vertsable, and your absence will not have been unduly noticed.'

His complacency infuriated her as much as the fact that she was clearly of little importance now. She had been useful, and now she was not. She felt anger and humil-iation in equal measure. She had truly be-lieved Etienne loved her, but if that were so he would surely have wanted her with him.

'Etienne has been here to visit you many times, of course, and no doubt will do so again, but there is other news to cheer you,'

Henri continued.

'Wally?' she said eagerly, putting the news of Etienne's gracious visits to the back of her mind for the moment, and not really knowing why her brother's name leapt to her lips. Then, with memory rushing back now, she remembered that Wally had been wounded but was now safely back in England, his war over.

'Wally is safe, and hopefully we shall all be soon,' Henri said. 'We know that the Allied liberation of France is imminent.'

It was said so calmly, but the magnitude of his words made her gasp. She made to sit up too quickly in bed, but the faintness came again, and she sank back against the pillows, knowing she was not fully recovered.

'How do you know this?'

He became faintly arrogant. 'It is our business to know, *chérie*. If all goes to plan, and it will, the Germans will be fooled about when and where it will happen.'

He would tell her no more, but it was enough to fill her with hope, and did more for her well-being than anything else, except a visit from Etienne. He arrived two days later, by which time she had moved cautiously downstairs, but was under the elderly housekeeper's orders to return to bed for an hour each afternoon, where Etienne found her.

'She's a harridan, and she treats me like a

child,' she raged, once he had clasped her to him and reassured her that he really was there in the flesh.

'Simone is a mother-hen looking after her chick, although she is frail enough to need looking after herself,' he said, 'and you've become so thin, *chérie*.'

She looked down at her body. She had never been thin, but now she saw that she was almost emaciated. How could any man love such a skeleton? Misery threatened to overwhelm her, until she saw that he was smiling at her.

'Lisette, there's no need to dwell on such trivialities. Simone will soon fatten you up with her soups and bread.'

'Now you make me sound like a prize pig,' she said, but a smile hovered on her lips, too, because the way he was looking at her was anything but horrified. There was love and longing in his eyes, and she swallowed deeply, because there had surely been a time when he would have wondered if any of this would ever happen again.

'And what is happening outside these four walls? Henri told me you had been interrogated. Oh, Etienne, was it very bad?'

He shrugged, much as Henri had done. 'Nothing I couldn't deal with. The Germans are so stupid. They don't see what is right beneath their noses, and a few bottles of wine soon deflected their questions. Unfortunately, the bastards think they have a right to take whatever they wish from my cellars now. It doesn't affect production, but it offends my pride.'

Lisa hid a smile this time. He was being so very French at that moment, and she loved him for it. But there were other things she needed to know.

'And what of the imminent liberation Henri spoke of? He would tell me nothing of any significance, and it's *so* frustrating.'

'You know the way we work, *chérie*. The less you know—'

'Oh yes, I know all that, but who am I going to say anything to, stuck here miles from anywhere?' She folded her arms belligerently, and he laughed out loud.

'I'm glad you're not on your feet or I swear you'd be stamping around the room by now. Do the children you teach know that you behave this way?'

Their images flashed into her mind. The small eager faces; the tears and tantrums and cuddles of the refugee children learning English; Henri's small children who were no longer children...

'Have I touched a nerve?' she heard Etienne say.

'It all seems like another life, yet I can recall every moment so vividly.'

Just as she always could, of course. Remembering words and phrases, recalling images of people she once knew and cared about, her parents, her darling brother, Renee and her feckless mother, the lovely Tweedy...

'I think,' she said slowly, when he didn't speak, 'that when the time comes, I will be ready to go home. At least for a while. I need...' She took a deep breath and spread her hands helplessly. 'I need home. Just for a while.'

She hardly knew where the words came from, but once said they formed a small barrier between them. She could almost feel him retreat from her a little, but she couldn't help a sudden primitive urge to be back among her roots, like an animal seeking a warm dark place to lick its wounds and recuperate.

But it couldn't happen yet. There were more important things to be done here than run the risk of transporting a homesick woman back to England.

'I'm sorry, Etienne. I don't mean to be ungrateful,' she said quickly. 'I owe you all so much—'

'Don't be ridiculous. We are the ones who are indebted to you,' he said almost angrily. 'And of course you feel the need to be back with your own people as soon as possible. We all need to feel normality again.'

She was mute at his words. Did he mean that there was no future for them after all, and had she put the idea so firmly and wrongly into his mind? But she wouldn't beg, and she was again very tired as all the energy seemed to be sapped from her. Even the thought of liberation couldn't lift her spirits. Who knew when, or if, it would really come?

Henri brought news that the Allies had surged into Rome on June 4th, which was a welcome sign that the German defences were crumbling at last. There were rumours that Hitler had ordered his troops to blow up the Tiber bridges, but, for whatever miraculous reason, these orders were ignored, and Rome's magnificent historical sites remained intact.

'It's not our liberation, though,' he said quietly. 'That day is yet to come.'

The waiting wasn't very long. D-Day arrived two days after the fall of Rome as General Eisenhower's HQ informed the world that the invasion of Europe had begun. The Allied preparations had been infinitely well planned, even to the extent of fooling the Germans as to when and where the invasion would begin, just as Henri had hinted.

Throughout the night the German defences along the French coast were pounded by RAF bombers, supported by American bomber fighter escorts. The sky was dense with thousands of Allied troops being para-chuted from the air between midnight and the dawn of June 6th. Under cover of dark-ness, an armada of ships brought thousands of land troops, tanks and artillery, while minesweepers cleared the way for them to disembark safely.

'The Allies have got them on the run at last,' Henri said jubilantly as the coded wireless reports came in constantly, hailing the victory as the biggest combined air, land and sea operation of all time.

'It's not a victory yet, though, is it?' Lisa replied. She knew she should be rejoicing, but for the life of her she couldn't find any enthusiasm in her heart. All she could see in her mind's eye were the casualties that would emerge on both sides from this slaughter. War took no account of nationali-ties.

Henri glanced at her, seeing her pallor and the almost gaunt hollows in her cheeks. She was fragile to the point of breaking, and he hadn't really noticed it until this minute when the whole of France would be ecstatic with hope for the future.

'Do you often think of England, Lisette?' he asked, taking her by surprise. She almost betrayed herself, but she had been steeped in caution for too long.

'Of course. But please don't suggest that I am to be somehow transported back there on a magic carpet. There's still work to be done, Henri.'

'But not for you, *ma chérie*. I would not ask it.'

'You don't need to ask! You and Etienne brought me here for a purpose. Are you telling me now that I'm no further use to you?'

She felt his comforting arms go around her, and the brief anger fizzled away as she leant against him, accepting her weakness. Even such a little burst of temper had made her dizzy, and she had a sudden anxiety for her own health. Had she been so very ill, far worse than they had told her?

'Lisette, it takes time to recover from any illness,' he said, confirming what she suspected. 'And now that we are on the brink of victory I would prefer that, when you are up to it, you merely help Simone with some of the household duties here, if you don't feel it would be too demeaning.'

She could hardly say that it would, or that being a housekeeper was such a lowly task compared with the risky business of the resistance. She knew that Simone was old and unsteady on her feet, so she merely nodded, hiding her disappointment as best she could.

But, as she had surmised, victory was not going to be achieved in a day. Far from it. Now that the Allies had breached the French

357

coast so successfully, the fighting was bitter and ruthless on both sides, and it was inevitable that there would be huge casualties. Lisa could only be thankful that Wally would not be one of them. There was a time to be brave, as she was sure he would have been, and a time to know that you have done your best and gone home.

As the days went by, with ever more gruesome and distressing news from all sides, she knew how much she wanted that for herself. To long for home in the tranquillity of the English countryside was becoming a guilty secret that she would never tell Henri nor Etienne on the days when he came to see her. She was no longer told of their activities, and she did not ask. She also knew she was dreaming of an idyllic England that probably no longer existed. Towns and cities that had been ravaged by bombs could never be the same, even though it didn't apply to her own small corner of Somerset. But war touched everyone in some way, and four days after D-Day the Nazis took brutal reprisals on a small French village near Limoges.

Moving into the village in the middle of the day they ordered the whole population to assemble on the fairground. Systematically, the men were shot, the women and children ordered into the church, and then the entire area was drenched with petrol and set alight, quickly becoming a sheet of flames, leaving it a charred ruin with almost all of the inhabitants burnt to death.

The cold-blooded event unnerved Lisa more than anything else so far. Despite the horror of what had happened, she couldn't seem to rouse herself out of the apathy of her illness, and it shamed her, knowing that at least she was fortunate to be alive. Etienne had brought the dreadful news to the safe house, and she had wept in his arms.

'When will it ever end? Will there ever be a time to be normal again? To be able to laugh and love, and to live without fear?'

He folded her in his arms, and she knew how troubled he was by her response. She knew that in ordinary times he would shelter her from it all if he could, but these were not ordinary times.

'Our day will come, *ma petite*,' he said, breathing in the soft scent of her hair. 'Have faith in God and the Allies, and in all our brave countrymen.'

She shuddered against him. He knew exactly how she was wavering between loyalty to France, her chosen country, and the desperate longing to be away from here and back where she belonged.

'I do have faith, Etienne,' she whispered. 'I know it will not last for ever. The tide must turn, and when it is all over you and Henri, and so many others, will be rewarded for what you have done for France.'

'Perhaps,' he said, his voice a shade harder. 'But we do not do any of it for reward. We do it for love of France.'

'And so do I,' she said, more steadily.

If there was less physical connection between them now, partly due to Lisa's frailty, the emotional connection was as powerful as ever. She knew it as surely as the sun rose every morning on the verdant French countryside, and, for now, it had to be enough.

Inevitably, by now the sheer strength and efficiency of the Allied invasion had begun to take effect. By the end of July the Germans had been driven from Normandy; at the beginning of August they were leaving the Channel Islands, and at long last, on August 25th, French tanks led the Allied victors into Paris. The hated swastika disappeared from buildings, even though there was still fierce fighting before the Germans finally retreated. By then, organized Resistance forces were adding weight to the street fighting, and Paris was celebrating, even while known collaborators were being unceremoniously dragged through the streets and beaten.

Throughout the next few months the enemy was overcome in every field of action. And then came news from England that the Germans had launched a terrible new weapon on London and the south-east. The so-called flying bombs were replaced by a more sophisticated airborne weapon, the V-2 rocket, which gave no warning before it hurtled silently towards its target with devastating effect.

But in Europe nothing could halt the march of the Allies now. Not only were towns and cities in France being liberated, but those in other countries, too: Antwerp in Belgium, Athens and Salonika in Greece, Flushing in Holland and Tallin in Estonia. Far too late to be of any real use, Hitler formed a People's Guard in Germany, while in England the Home Guard was disbanded. Victory was tantalizingly near, yet never quite realized as another Christmas came and went.

By then Etienne Arnaud had reclaimed his vineyard and his dignity. There were no more German patrols taking whatever they wanted from his cellars, and the day finally came when he agreed to take Lisa back to the farm. She had wanted to return for so long now. Henri was her friend as well as her old employer, but she didn't belong here, and she longed to be within cycling distance of Paris – even though she no longer had her old bicycle, she remembered. She had no doubt that there would be another one she could use, though.

She was aware that people still had to be on their guard. There were pockets of resistance from the Germans, even now, when the majority had been driven out of the city. There was still the occasional sniper, ready to claim his own reward in heaven for killing one of his enemies.

'A reward in hell is more likely,' Etienne said, frowning, when she made the facetious remark as they were driving away from the safe house at last. 'I think you forgive too easily, Lisette.'

She was strong enough now to answer indignantly, 'I do not, but nor do I think people should bear a grudge for ever. We should be magnanimous in victory.'

'The war isn't over yet, and tell your fine ideals to the poor devils who have lost limbs or sight, and those who have paid the price for ever with their lives.'

She was silent, feeling that somehow they had lost something very precious between them. Maybe it had never really existed at all, except for those few brief hours when he had been so exquisitely hers.

All these weeks when they had been apart had made him remote and hard, and he still treated her as though she were a fragile bird, when all the passion of which she knew she was capable was returning with an avalanche of feeling. She ached for his love, but pride wouldn't let her beg for favours, and right now he seemed more like a stranger than a lover. She didn't know him any more.

But she was welcomed back at Arnaud's

farm with warmth from Helene and the estate workers. It hardly made up for the lack of warmth from Etienne himself, but there was little she could do about it. She bolted her bedroom door at night, and if she imagined she heard someone tapping softly on her door on more than one occasion, she merely turned over in bed, denying herself as well as him.

An old bicycle had been resurrected for her, just as she had expected. She was still a bit wobbly on it, and the fearful memory of what had happened the last time she rode was still vivid, so the first few times she went into Paris Etienne went with her. She was glad of his company, especially when she was confronted with the tragedy of so many flattened buildings in the city, and the ruined bridges over the Seine.

In February, news filtered through that the beautiful German city of Dresden had virtually been destroyed by a devastating night and day of relentless RAF bombing, and Lisa could only imagine that, if it looked worse than Paris, it must be agonizing. There were reports of thousands being killed and wounded, and it was all such a tragic waste. Seeing their own city like this only made their imagination of what was happening elsewhere more acute.

Despite the throng of cheerful people in

the Paris streets, she found it hard to raise her spirits, even now. Physically she was still weaker than she had expected to be, but once spring arrived she preferred to cycle into the city alone to merge into the crowds. She was always vigilant about the danger of German snipers still at work, even though they risked being strung up by the locals. But she was heartened by the numbers of British and American servicemen and vehicles in the city, cheered and fêted by local girls. There were Red Cross and other ambulances. And there was Renee...

Lisa gave a cry that was almost a howl, wondering if she was hallucinating again as she saw the flash of bright hair and a laughing face disappear into the back of an ambulance. As if she could pick out the sound amid the general chaos and excitement all around, some kind of sixth sense made Renee pause and turn around. Her mouth dropped open at the sight of Lisa, so much thinner, yet still so elegant, so very much the Parisienne. In seconds she had crossed the street and Lisa was being hugged half to death.

'My God, I can't believe it's you! I thought I was seeing a ghost!' Renee stuttered, as both of them began laughing and crying at the same time.

'You're not the only one!' Lisa almost sobbed. 'I was beginning to think I'd never see you again!'

'Well, you're a fine one to talk! You know where we live!' Renee said, taking refuge in anger. 'Why haven't you come home?'

The sudden change from tears to sparkiness was almost ludicrous ... and so like Renee that Lisa found herself weeping again, and simply hugged her.

'You don't know the half of it,' she gasped.

'Well, there's nothing stopping you now, is there?' came Renee's muffled voice in her shoulder. 'The war's going to be over soon, thank God, and your Wally's practically engaged, so it's time you thought about him for a change.'

'Wally's practically engaged?' she echoed, parrot fashion. Images of her brother flashed through her mind. Small and snivelling and scared after her father died; still clinging to her for support when Jess died; welcoming Tweedy into their home; joining up with fierce patriotism before he needed to; following his dream of becoming a newspaper reporter. She swallowed thickly. He was no longer a boy, and she had missed all those years of his growing up.

'Who is he nearly engaged to?' she said huskily, when she could think of nothing else to say.

'Barbara Woods from school – I don't have to describe her, do I?'

Renee gave a grin, knowing that the

memories would shoot straight into Lisa's receptive mind. Barbara Woods ... wiry dark hair that sprang into curls no matter how she tried to straighten it; white socks always at half-mast; gymslip frequently tucked into her knickers without her knowing it. But Barbara Woods would be a young lady now. Lisa swallowed again.

'And what about you?' Renee said impatiently. 'I've still got the letter with our pledges. I keep it with me like a sort of talisman, and I mean to claim my tanner if you've got married on the sly before you said you would!'

'Oh, Renee!' Lisa said, choked. 'No, I'm not married, but fancy you keeping that envelope all this time.'

'I don't need to ask if you kept yours. You'll remember every detail, of course. But I bet you've had a high old time with some French bloke, even if you do look as if you've been living on skeleton rations, same as we have in England.'

'We were rationed here, too, you know. It hasn't been all fun and games! Anyway, you didn't get invaded and occupied like we did.'

Oh God, Lisa thought. Here they were, so soon after meeting again after all these years, still playing tit-for-tat as if they were children. As if Renee realized at the same moment that they were glaring at each other, they were both laughing and hugging again, ignoring the amused stares of the crowds milling about them. Then Renee scowled as someone shouted her name.

'Damn and blast, I'll have to go. That's Joe, my driver. We're collecting some of the walking wounded to take back to England. If you had any sense, you'd hitch a lift and come with us. Why don't you, Lisa?'

It was so very tempting, and what did she have to stay for any more? While she was still thinking about this, the rat-tat-tat of machine-gun fire shattered the moment. Screaming crowds scattered, and there was utter chaos in the square as men rushed to the upstairs window in the house where the firing came from.

Everything seemed to happen at once. One minute people were mingling, rejoicing, chatting, finding friends, getting their lives back to some kind of normality, and in the next came the cruel reminder that there were still snipers at large, and that the war wasn't over yet. People were hurt, the ambulancemen were shouting for help and volunteers, and Joe was shouting for Renee.

The two friends were hugging more tightly now, as if in an instinctive movement to protect one another. And it took no more than a heartbeat for Lisa to realize that Renee wasn't moving in response to Joe's call. She wasn't moving except to slide more deeply into Lisa's embrace, as limp as a rag

367

doll. And Lisa became horrifically aware of the hot stickiness of blood on her hands as she supported her best friend.

'Over here,' she found herself shrieking. 'Joe – come quickly!'

She didn't dare move in case she did more damage. Or in case she discovered what she most dreaded. That Renee had been shot dead in her arms.

Twenty-One

'Is she dead?' Lisa sobbed, as Joe and his assistant took Renee out of her arms.

She couldn't bear it. She just couldn't bear to know...

'She's breathing, but only just, poor lass,' Joe said harshly. 'We don't have the equipment to deal with these injuries. We'll get her to St Germaine's hospital on the northern outskirts of the city. The nuns will care for her there.'

'I'm coming with her,' Lisa said at once.

'We don't have room for hangers-on, miss.'

'I'm her oldest friend, and she'd want me with her,' Lisa shouted, almost beside herself. 'I'm not leaving her now!'

They didn't even question that she spoke in English, nor how she knew Renee. Nothing else mattered. The fact that Renee was still alive – just – was the most important thing in Lisa's world right now. She could think of no one and nothing else, and, seeing the aggressive look on her face, Joe shrugged and nodded. The glance that passed between him and his assistant said it hardly mattered either way. The girl was going to die anyway.

They were callous ... but Lisa knew that in their job they sometimes had to be, or go mad.

Lisa held Renee's hand tightly as she sat beside the stretcher in the back of the ambulance, feeling every bump in the road as it made its way out of the city. Other ambulances would take care of the walking wounded, as Renee had called them. This was their girl, and they would do the best that they could for her.

At last the gaunt, grey-stone building of St Germaine's hospital came into sight, and several orderlies emerged at the sight of the British ambulance. Joe gesticulated to Renee and tried to explain what had happened.

Seeing the language difficulty, Lisa took over at once, and spoke agitatedly in French. She ignored her compatriots' amazement at her fluency. She was simply desperate for Renee to be taken in, and for a surgeon to look at her injuries. Her friend was already as white as death, and she hadn't opened her eyes nor spoken a word since the shooting, and, however hopeless it seemed, Lisa found herself praying desperately that it wasn't too late.

'We don't want to leave Renee, but we have to get back, miss,' Joe was saying awkwardly now. 'There are others who need us.'

Lisa hardly heard them. 'I'll stay with her – whatever happens.'

To her surprise, Joe leant down and kissed Renee's cold forehead before she was wheeled off on a trolley to the operating theatre.

'Goodbye, old girl,' he said gruffly. 'Keep your pecker up, and if you get to the pearly gates after all this, say one for me.'

He turned before he could see the astonishment in Lisa's eyes, briefly saying that he'd report what had happened to the necessary authorities. And then she forgot him as she hurried after the trolley, to be restrained by a determined nun.

'The doctors will take good care of her, mademoiselle. Please come with me, and I will show you where to wait. You would like some coffee, perhaps.'

She was being spoken to as a Frenchwoman now, and Lisa did nothing to disillusion the nun as she followed her to a waiting room. She hardly knew who she was any more, anyway. All her energy was focused on what might be happening in that operating theatre to the girl who had been her closest friend all her life. She got through several cups of strong coffee before she saw a grim-faced doctor and nun in conversation, and as they glanced at her her heart froze.

'I'm very sorry, mademoiselle,' the doctor said in a voice of controlled compassion. 'We did all that we could. The young lady is still alive, but I fear she will not survive more

371

than a few days, maybe even hours. The bullets struck her spinal cord, and it has proved fatal.'

Lisa licked her dry lips. 'Is she conscious?' she whispered.

'No. She may come round for a short while, but of course she is heavily drugged, and it is only a matter of time. I'm sorry.'

'Thank you.'

It was such a futile, meaningless and totally absurd thing to say. Why should she thank this man who was giving her the worst news of all, when she felt like screaming and railing at him ... ?

To her absolute horror, she realized she was doing exactly that.

Someone was holding her. No, more than that. Someone was dragging her away from the doctor, and she was appalled as she realized she was turning her venom on the nun who was trying to calm her. Then, just as quickly, all the fight went out of her, and she was sobbing in the nun's arms.

A short while later she was sitting in the waiting room and the aroma of hot sweet tea penetrated her senses. She held the cup in both shaking hands and sipped the liquid gratefully, sure there was a hint of brandy in it.

'Are you feeling better, mademoiselle?' the nun said quietly. 'It's always a shock to come to terms with death, especially in one so young, though I fear we have done so many times in these last years.'

'Renee's not dead yet,' Lisa snapped, and then her shoulders sagged at her ungraciousness. For, as the doctor had said, and as she had known in her heart, it was only a matter of time. 'I want to see her. Please,' she added.

Ten minutes later she was staring down at the girl she had once known as well as herself, but who looked nothing like the Renee she knew. Her skin was already waxen, her breathing laboured. As she bent to kiss the cold forehead, Lisa knew she was already saying goodbye. She turned away, blinded by tears, and knew no more until she awoke on a small bed in a clinically white room. The nun sat beside her.

'You collapsed, my dear,' she said, responding to the blank look on Lisa's face. 'Have you been ill recently?'

Lisa nodded weakly, too spent to say anything. Let them take care of her. All she wanted was to stay here, to be safe, to think of nothing ... except...

Renee's name burst into her consciousness, and she struggled to sit up, to be pushed gently back on to the bed.

'Your friend feels no pain. She will slip peacefully into the next world,' the nun said, crossing herself.

Peacefully? Renee never did anything

peacefully! Renee was vibrant and alive, living every moment. Renee couldn't die.

The following day she was told that Renee had passed away during the night without ever regaining consciousness. While Lisa was still numbed by the words, the mechanics of death took over. Were there any relatives to be informed? Did Lisa wish to arrange burial? She was overwhelmed by all the questions that had to be answered.

They assumed that Lisa was French, and that therefore Renee was also French. Lisa had been given the few belongings she had with her, and when the nuns said they could take care of everything she agreed with pathetic gratitude. She was a leaf in the wind that had no substance. It no longer mattered.

Two days later the burial went ahead with quiet dignity, and Renee remained for ever in France, one among thousands, since it was impossible for Lisa to arrange to get her home to England. The words burnt in her mind. Renee couldn't go home, but Lisa could, and she must. Renee's mother needed to know what had happened to her daughter, and there was no one else in the world who could tell her.

She left a note and a small amount of money for the hospital on her bed, thanking the nuns for all they had done. She had written another note, too. At least, it had begun as a note and ended up as a rambling, impassioned letter. She had written to Henri, knowing that even if she had disappeared from Etienne's life she couldn't leave the man who had been almost a father figure to her for all these years without some kind of explanation. But, in the end, it had been the hardest letter of all to write.

'My dear Henri,' she had begun, finding no embarrassment in addressing him so, and knowing he wouldn't misinterpret the endearment.

You, of all people, know how dearly I love France and everyone here. But I can no longer stay and remain sane. After everything that has happened, the war is over and yet I am in torment. My dearest friend Renee has been killed in Paris, after we had had a brief and unexpected reunion. It seems to make everything so pointless, and my heart is so full that all I want to do is go home. I don't yet know how I am going to get there, but I have a duty to Renee's mother to let her know what happened. And I need my family. I long to see my brother again, just to touch him and know that he survived. You will know what I mean, dear Henri, for I feel that you know and understand my heart, and in time I hope and pray that you and I will meet again.

So this is not goodbye, just *au revoir*, my dear friend.

With her eyes clouded by tears, she signed it 'Lisa'.

And then she slipped out of the building unobserved. She hardly knew where she was going, only that northwards was the road to the coast, and from there to England, and that was the route she must follow. Her thoughts flew briefly to Etienne, and she knew that she must try to forget him. He was part of her past, another life. For now she refused to accept that she would never forget for a moment all that he had been to her.

By now the whole of France was simmering with excitement that the end of the war was so close. The Resistance movement would be disbanded, people would resume ordinary lives and the terrible days would be gone for ever. In God's scheme of things, the war would be but a moment that had moved on...

These noble thoughts were abruptly interrupted as Lisa stumbled in the dusty road. An American army vehicle almost ran her down, and the servicemen were bawling at her for her carelessness. The next moment the vehicle had stopped and a GI jumped out and came back to were she stood swaying.

'Are you hurt, mademoiselle? You nearly got yourself killed,' he said loudly, in the way the English and Americans addressed foreigners.

She stammered back in English. 'I'm sorry. I'm trying to get to a ship to take me home. To England.'

'Say, are you British? You can hitch a ride with us if you like.'

He came more sharply into focus, and a few minutes later she was squeezed in between the bulky bodies of the Americans. No lack of food rations there then, she thought fleetingly. But all such trivia was forgotten as they offered her chocolate that she hadn't seen in months, and assured her that they would see her safely on to a ship, provided she had proper identity papers.

She did, of course, since nobody travelled anywhere without them these days. The GIs were breezy and efficient, and the formalities eventually went through, and she could have wept at their kindness. God bless our allies, she thought silently, thinking that if she wasn't careful she would soon be weeping an ocean of tears. And if she didn't get rid of these flowery thoughts, came a spark of her old spirit, she'd soon be drowning in self-pity.

Several weeks later she got off the bus in Mallory in the early evening. As usual at this time of day, there were few people about, and none that recognized the thin, weary woman with her red hair pinned up into a knot on her head, carrying so little baggage. It was just growing dusk, and the dew was sweetly scenting the grass and foliage. Lisa stood perfectly still for a moment, wallowing in the aura of a village that was typically English. Birds that hadn't yet gone to roost were lazily singing, and daffodils and crocuses were still in full bloom in village gardens.

It was years since she had breathed good clean English air, and she could hardly believe she was really here. Her eyes swam with weak tears, and she felt so unlike the strong person she had always thought herself to be that she forced herself to grit her teeth and walk through the streets towards home.

Memories surged through her as she came at last to the house where she had been born. Her dad with his bombastic union ways; her gentle mum who always wanted her to do well with her special skills despite her unease at letting her go to France; Gran Cissy and her waspish warnings about keeping their clever, blossoming girl on the straight and narrow; her darling Wally.

She deliberately kept her eyes averted from the house right across the street, where she had run so many times in excitement or despair to share her innermost secrets with her best friend.

Lisa pushed open the door of her house. Nobody locked their doors in Mallory, and why would she knock at her own front door, anyway? The smell of stew wafted through from the kitchen, making her mouth water. Someone was humming tunelessly. Her heart jumped. It was so heartbreakingly familiar, even though she knew it couldn't be her mother. It would never be her mother again.

She tried to speak, and the word came out in a husk of sound.

'Tweedy.'

Startled, the buxom woman at the stove turned around sharply. For a moment the two of them simply looked at one another, unable to speak, as if suspended in time, and then Tweedy held out her arms, and Lisa was stumbling into them.

There were a lot more tears before they were finally able to sit down sensibly with a pot of tea and try to believe that Lisa was really home. There were too many explanations to give immediately, and some that she never would. It was enough, for now, that she was here.

'I have some news,' she said painfully at last. 'I have to go and see Renee's mother tomorrow.'

Lisa heard Tweedy sniff, and for a second it was the ghost of her mother passing on her disapproval of the flashy woman with so many 'uncles' for Renee, and eventually the Austrian husband.

'Renee died a few weeks ago, Tweedy,' she said, making herself say the words. 'That's why I'm home. I have to tell her mother – and Eddie Bray, too, I suppose. She is still married to him, after all.'

'Much he'll care,' Tweedy said. 'But I'm truly sorry for the poor girl, Lisa. So near to the end of the war, too. She'd have loved the celebrations the village is planning. We're all getting out the flags and bunting in readiness.'

Lisa looked blank for a moment. She could hardly be unaware that victory was imminent. The GIs on the American ship had been full of it, and of their part in it. If they bragged about it rather a lot she didn't blame them, but too much had been happening in her personal life recently for her to take much notice. And she immediately knew how selfish and insular that was. The whole world would be holding its breath for the end of this terrible war, and one village girl's death was only important to those who had loved her.

She took a deep breath, drawing on the reserves of strength that she knew must be buried somewhere deep inside her, and gave Tweedy another hug.

'Oh, it's so good to be home, and I'm

longing to see Wally and hear all his news,' she said unsteadily.

'My goodness, yes, you don't know, do you?' the woman said.

'If you mean do I know that he was injured and discharged, and that he's practically engaged to Barbara Woods, I do know, as a matter of fact.'

She almost laughed out loud at the look of astonishment on Tweedy's face.

'Well, I always knew there was something special about you, Lisa, but I didn't know you had a sixth sense, nor that you could see into the past as well!'

'I'm not that clever! Renee filled me in with all the news, before ... well, *before*.' She swallowed. 'Where is he, anyway? I thought he'd be home by now.'

'He'll be here in about half an hour. Why don't you have a wash and change your clothes, my love? You look as if you've been sleeping in those for days.'

She spoke delicately, and Lisa looked down at herself. The elegant Frenchwoman was replaced by someone looking decidedly grubby and careworn, and all of her nearly twenty-nine years. The thought gave her a little shock. All those years ago she had gone to France as an eager girl, with a spirit full of adventure, and now she was nearly thirty years old, and no longer a girl.

'I think I'll do as you say,' she said.

'Everything's still as you left it, Lisa,' Tweedy said, before she could ask.

Lisa nodded and went upstairs to her old bedroom, strange and familiar at the same time. She wept over old photographs and knick-knacks, her threadbare old teddy bear, gaped at the clothes in her wardrobe, which seemed oddly old fashioned now, and which hung loosely on her spare frame once Tweedy had brought a jug of hot water for her to wash herself. She was refreshed and calmer by the time she heard a familiar whistling downstairs, and she rushed down to greet her brother.

'Wally. Oh, *Wally*,' she said joyously. 'My God, haven't you grown!'

She clung to him while he tried to get used to the fact that this wraith was really his beautiful sister whom he had honestly thought he was never going to see again.

'Is that any way to speak to a hero?' he said, his voice hoarse with emotion.

And then Tweedy took over, telling them sternly to sit at the table and fill their bellies with good, wholesome stew before it got cold, and that there would be time for talking afterwards.

It was so homely, so ordinary, so *normal* that they both obeyed without question, even though the two of them could hardly keep their eyes off one another. Wally looked well, apart from his slight limp, but Lisa knew how dreadful she must look compared with the way she had been when she had left so mysteriously in the night all those years ago. She was no longer the same person.

But, later, explanations were made, or as many as Lisa would allow. She still had a duty to Henri and Etienne, and until the armistice was officially signed her loyalties were still somewhere in France. Wally would understand that without even asking, but she wasn't the only one with a sixth sense, and with his newspaperman's nose, he knew there was far more to tell than she was ready to give.

She told him of the circumstances of Renee's death, and there was finally some release in the telling. Tomorrow it would be different, when she had to face Renee's mother and Eddie Bray, but by tomorrow she would have had a good night's sleep in her own bed.

The village was coming to life the next morning when she set out for the fish and chip shop. People recognized her and said hello, and she tried to ignore their astonishment at her changed appearance. It was all too soon to think about doing any kind of work, and she wasn't sure she could cope with classes of noisy schoolchildren. Perhaps a job like Renee had once had, caring for one or two children in someone's house, would suit her better – the way she had cared for Monique and Henri Dubois' children. The thought caught on a sob, and she pressed on until she saw the shop sign ahead of her.

It wasn't open yet, and she knocked at the side door, ready to face Renee's mother's shock when she saw her.

'Good God, is that you, Lisa? Where have you sprung from?' she exclaimed instantly. 'Wherever it is, you look as if a good meal wouldn't hurt you, my duck! Come on in and have a cuppa and an oat cake.'

The ritual had to be gone through, however much she hated doing it. Lisa went inside, thankful that there was no sign of the Austrian husband. Lisa wasn't inclined to ask after him; this was personal, between two people who had loved Renee. By the end of the telling, she found herself clutching the older woman's hands, both of them tearful and choking.

'I've brought you the things she had with her,' Lisa said. 'It wasn't much, and I'm sure the authorities will be in touch with you eventually.'

She didn't know any details, and didn't want to. She wanted to get out of this cloying little house with its lingering aroma of frying fat, and the fact that, from the expanding size of her, Renee's mother didn't seem to have gone short in the war. She still had a good heart for all that, thought Lisa, and she succumbed to the woman's kiss when she finally left.

The one thing she hadn't passed on to her was the letter Renee had had in her bag that was so very personal to them both. Her friend had done what she'd wanted and got married as early as she could, and now Lisa had to go and inform Eddie Bray that his wife was dead.

She walked to Bray's farm, willing the calm of the countryside and the fresh morning air to filter into her, but it was still an ordeal telling Eddie. She hadn't thought he'd care, but he was surprisingly moved as he leant on the rail of the cowshed. He expressed himself in his usual graphic way.

'Bloody murdering bastards, those Jerries. Me and Renee went back a long way, and it's a real bugger that she had to go like that. Renee was my first girl, and you never forget the first love in your life, do you?'

Nor the last...

'I knew you'd want to know what happened, Eddie, and I'm sorry to bring you such news,' she said quietly.

'Oh well, there's no use crying over spilt milk, is there? I've got me a new lady friend now, and life goes on, doesn't it?'

Lisa left the farm quickly, before her sympathy with him turned to fury. But the fury was healthier than sinking into morbid regrets, and by the time she returned home she was exhausted but also thinking more clearly. She was in no fit state to return to full-time work, and nor did she need to, as both Tweedy and Wally had assured her last night. In any case, there was money accumulating in her bank account to pay her way, and if she thought they were treating her more like a middle-aged invalid than a relatively healthy young woman, she let it pass.

The house was empty that afternoon. Wally was at work, and Tweedy was at one of her village meetings. Lisa relished the fact that she had the place to herself to reminisce over old times and renew her acquaintance with every corner of the house. She drew in her breath briefly as she gazed across the road towards Renee's old window, where they had shouted to one another so often. And then she turned away, to get on with the task she had promised herself she would undertake that morning.

It wasn't easy. What did you say in a letter to someone you loved with all your heart when you had disappeared from his life with no explanation? For the first time, she allowed herself to think how frantic he must have been when she didn't arrive back from Paris that day. He would undoubtedly have heard of the shooting in the square, but, unfortunately, such things were not unknown, and there was no reason for him to have connected it with Lisa.

But even if she had no idea when or how her letter would ever arrive at its destination, Etienne deserved to know what had happened. At least he would have known through Henri that she was safe, but, since it was impossible for her to return to France right now, she had to explain the rest in writing as best she could. She was thankful to be sitting alone at the kitchen table, able to transport herself in imagination to her lover's side.

'My dear Etienne,' she began, and immediately came to a complete stop, hardly knowing how to continue.

'Stop being so feeble,' she told herself. 'You want to tell him, so *tell* him.'

But tell him *what*? That she loved and missed him so much that it wrenched her heart to be so far away from him? That she ached for the sound of his voice and the touch of his hand, and his sweet caresses?

She blinked back the tears, knowing that those were things she couldn't put in a letter. Far better to simply tell him what had happened, and that one day she hoped to return. He hadn't been exactly amorous towards her of late, and perhaps after the war his feelings for the English girl would no longer be the same. She swallowed hard, refusing to let herself sink into self-pity, and began to write.

You would have wondered why I didn't come home that day, Etienne, and, even though I know Henri will have explained, I wanted to tell you the whole story. I once told you of my old friend Renee, and how close we were as children. Well, by the sheerest chance I met Renee in a square in Paris that day.

Her mouth trembling, she went on to relate exactly what had happened, keeping it brief, because if she didn't she knew she would fall apart in the telling. Then she let him know how she had come to be on a ship for England with the help of the US forces, and that she was now back where she belonged.

She hesitated over those last words. This was home, but it wasn't where Etienne was. It wasn't where her heart was.

She said quickly that she hoped one day they would meet again, and after a moment's thought she signed it 'Lisette'.

If he read anything into the fact that she had signed the letter with the name he had given her, it was up to him. She wasn't even sure what she was trying to tell him by it. She walked to the local post office with the letter, astounding the postmistress both by her appearance and the request to send a letter to France.

'I don't know if it'll get there, Lisa love,' she said doubtfully, 'nor how long it'll take. It might get censored, too.'

'That doesn't matter. There's no official secrets in it,' she said, trying to make a joke of it. 'Just see that it goes on its way, will you, Mrs Chard?'

'That I will. And how are you these days? We haven't seen much of you recently. Been away, have you?'

At the words, Lisa was so very tempted to say she had just been doing a bit of frivolous shopping in Bristol ... or risking her life every day by working with the Resistance in occupied France...

'That's right,' she mumbled instead, and hurried out of the post office.

Wally wasn't going to let her moulder away, as he called it. He and his girlfriend, the very pleasant Barbara Woods, invited her out with them to the pictures and to Barbara's home for tea, and never made her feel she was in the way, which she certainly began to feel she was. She was just marking time.

In early May the war was officially declared over at last, the joyous church bells rang everywhere, schools were closed and the village sprang to life, filled with celebration and plans for street parties. Tweedy and Lisa made jellies and cakes with whatever rations they had, to go with the rest of the supplies the village women magically found. Children too young to understand what it all meant wore paper hats and joined in patriotic songs, just glad to see happy and smiling faces around them again.

'I've invited a friend to our street party, Lisa, and to supper afterwards. I hope you don't mind,' said Tweedy.

'Of course I don't. Do I know her?'

The woman's face went pink. 'It's not a her. It's a him. His name's John Wright, and he's a baker.'

After a moment Lisa said, 'And is John Wright your "Mr Right", Tweedy?'

She laughed self-consciously. 'Well, I rather think he might be, if you don't think I'm being a silly old fool for saying so.'

They hugged one another, and Lisa didn't think that at all. It was sweet and charming, and with Wally preparing to get officially engaged now the war was over, that just left her.

A few weeks later, when the initial post-war euphoria had died down a little, and summer was already on its way, Wally approached her warily. Lisa had known he had something on his mind ever since her return.

'I've a suggestion for you, Lisa,' he said finally. 'I have a shrewd idea what you've been up to all these years, and it would make very good copy, and if you were willing I'd be thrilled to handle it for you.'

She looked at him with a frown, and he went on more urgently.

'Sorry. That's newspaper talk, and a bit clumsy. What I mean is that you must have an intriguing story to tell about your experience looking after the French children, and then remaining in France against all advice during the war years. We could run it as a series of articles in the newspaper – or we could even write it together as a book. You couldn't have been in hiding all those years, so where were you – and, more importantly, what were you doing?'

He could no longer keep the excited edge out of his voice at the idea of being the one to disclose such a personal story. She could see the youthful enthusiasm in his face – and she could imagine Etienne's rage if she ever contemplated such a thing without his knowledge – if at all.

She shook her head vehemently. 'What I was doing is something you'll probably never know,' she snapped.

'But *probably* might mean *possibly*, yes?'

He was at once her engaging, pleading small brother, twisting her words and aiming to wrap her around his little finger as he'd managed to do so often as a child, and against her will she found her mouth twitching.

'Go and think about something else, Wally. Interview some of our returning heroes. They're far more important than I am!'

Besides, without Etienne's approval, she

would never betray her involvement in the French Resistance, however small it had seemed to her. And she had never had a reply to her letter, nor even known if he had received it. He had abandoned her just as surely as she had abandoned him.

'I'm going for a walk,' she said abruptly, sensing Tweedy's interest in their conversation and aware that the small house was suddenly stifling her.

The early June day was warm, the sun climbing steadily in a blue sky, and she needed to breathe and assess what she was going to do with her life. She had been home for weeks now, and she had done nothing about finding a job. She thought again that she was just marking time, and it was no way for a healthy woman to behave. And she was healthy now, with Tweedy's insistence on fattening her up, as she called it. She would never be fat, but she had lost the gaunt look she had had when she returned to Mallory.

She walked away from the village and down to the river, and inevitably her thoughts were all of Etienne now. Wally had stirred up everything she had known it would be impossible to forget, not least Etienne's beloved face. She sat on the soft grass of the riverbank for a long time, remembering everything so minutely, and not pushing it all to the back of her mind as she had foolishly tried to do. How could she have thought for a moment that she could forget the love of her life, her heart-beat?

She gazed unseeingly into the river, and became aware of a vague shadowy reflection in the water that wasn't her own. She frown-ed, not wanting any intruders into her dreams, and then the shadow became sub-stance, and as she turned around she thought she must be hallucinating again as she scrambled to her feet.

'What are you doing here?' she stammered. She made an involuntary step backwards, and Etienne quickly stepped forward to catch her in his arms.

'What do you think? I've come to take you home to France, if that's what you want, though I'm not sure that you do, and I need to hear it from your own lips,' he said rough-ly, and then his voice changed to anger. 'How could you have simply disappeared without a word, Lisette? For all I knew, you never got back to England. For all I knew you were dead.'

She stared at him, her heart beating wildly. She had no idea how he came to be here, but knowing Etienne such matters were a small trifle. He did whatever he wanted to do, and finding her would have been a simple matter compared with his covert wartime activities. Besides, he knew where she lived ... And he would never have done anything so mundane as telephoning first. Not for something so important. He would always be the hunter...

As her thoughts spun, she knew Tweedy would have had no hesitation in telling the handsome stranger she had seen once before where to find Lisa. Tweedy would have thought it the most romantic thing that he had come looking for her.

She was still stammering, finding it hard to speak coherently considering the way her heart was still thudding in her chest. 'I wrote to you, explaining everything. It wasn't me who died. It was my best friend, Renee. Didn't you get my letter?'

He brushed her words aside with an expressive French gesture.

'Letters have a habit of going astray. What did this so-called letter say?'

Her nerves were too fragile to ignore the implication. 'Are you suggesting that I didn't send it? Do you think so little of me?'

They stared at one another for a timeless moment, still locked in one another's arms, still locked in frustration. And then Etienne gave an expressive oath.

'You must know I think the world of you. But you came back, so I need to know if this place means more to you than I do. I love you with all my heart, and all I want is for us to be together for always. More than anything I want you to be my wife, Lisa.'

The fact that he used her real name at that moment made her spirit soar in a way she couldn't explain. But this wasn't the time to analyse it.

'Do you know how often I've dreamt of this moment?' she whispered, all her reservations slipping away, her love for him so evident in her eyes that he couldn't ever misinterpret it.

He stopped any more words with a deep and passionate kiss that took away every moment of the pain and heartache of the time they had been apart.

'Then do I take it that your answer is yes?' he said, reverting at once to being the demanding, dynamic Frenchman. 'I'm too impatient to wait any longer, and I'm not leaving here until you accept my proposal, Lisa, my beautiful girl.'

As she clung to him, the answering word he ached to hear was a sweet breath on her lips, and she registered at once why his use of her real name had meant so much to her. It seemed to tell her more than words that she was far more to him than the English girl who had been so useful to the French cause. It told her that she was indisputably *his* girl, now and for always.

In a weird and wonderful way she also knew why, all those years ago, she had vowed never to marry until she was at least twenty-five years old. Not until the right man came along, whom she could love with all her heart. The man in whose arms she was so tightly clasped and cherished.